ROGUE MAGIC

KIT BRISBY

Riptide Publishing
PO Box 1537
Burnsville, NC 28714
www.riptidepublishing.com

Cover art: L.C. Chase, lcchase.com/design.htm
Editor: Carole-ann Galloway
Layout: L.C. Chase, lcchase.com/design.htm

ISBN: 978-1-62649-528-9

First edition
January, 2017

Also available in ebook:
ISBN: 978-1-62649-527-2

ROGUE MAGIC

KIT BRISBY

For my grandmother, who showed me magic. And dirty books.

TABLE OF CONTENTS

CHAPTER 1
SOME SIGN OF LIFE

Byron Cole was well into his personal best score at Trivia Dash. His phone blinked with the next question, bright against the darkness around him. Another distant explosion shook the subway car, and the little boy across the aisle began to cry.

The trivia timer was already winding down. Byron clenched his jaw and skimmed the question and answers.

What year did Charlotte's Law pass? It was ninety-eight or ninety-nine. A girl in his second-grade class had been sent to foster care that year, when magic users were first forbidden to raise their own children.

He went with ninety-eight, and his run of correct answers ended. Sighing, he tucked his phone back into his messenger bag and rehearsed his speech silently.

Thanks to our nation's vigilance and dedication, the United States has incarcerated those mages who pose a threat to our freedoms. And now Cole Industries has developed a system to relieve the tax burden of these rogue mages by using them to generate electricity to sell back to the power companies. Magic is an untapped resource and can produce the kind of clean energy America needs.

He ran through it again, wishing he'd emailed himself a copy. He'd written the speech himself, so he shouldn't have been nervous about messing up, but this was his first assignment in front of a microphone. And he wasn't prepared for follow-up questions he couldn't answer.

No one had explained to him how exactly mages were going to generate electricity.

At the moment he was picturing thousands of stationary bikes. That was better than tuning in to the restless chatter around him. If his uncle hadn't advised him to take the subway instead of a town car, he would have been at the press conference by now. But he agreed with the reasoning: He needed to humanize Cole Industries, give people someone to relate to. Someone who took public transportation.

And got stuck on public transportation.

"The police will be here soon," the young woman sitting beside the sniffling boy was saying. She wore cut-off shorts and sparkling tennis shoes. An older sister or a nanny, maybe.

"How do you know?" he asked between shuddering breaths.

Byron felt a pang of remorse for ignoring the boy until now. Adults had a way of doing that to kids when terrible things happened. "The sirens. Hear them? They're close," he said, hoping no one else realized that didn't mean a thing.

The dim emergency lights were still working, and the car wasn't on fire, so the likelihood of being rescued any time soon was slim. Judging by the number of explosions that had gone off like thunder, nearby first responders had too much on their hands to deal with a stalled subway train. Thankfully, the boy gave a shaky nod and wiped his nose against his sleeve, apparently satisfied with Byron's answer.

"Do you think it's the terrorists?" an older woman asked. She sounded more hopeful than afraid, as if a terrorist attack was the best possible reason for the subway to have lost power in the middle of a pitch-black tunnel. It took Byron a long moment to realize she was addressing him, and by then others were watching him questioningly. They obviously didn't realize he was only twenty-two.

He shifted in his seat, and his name badge for the press conference he was now incredibly late to caught on his sleeve. The Cole Industries logo gleamed. No wonder they expected him to know something. He plucked it off and shoved it into his pocket.

The woman's voice went shrill. "Well?"

"I wouldn't be surprised if our delay is related to an act of terrorism." Byron kept his tone low and even. "The alert level is pretty high right now."

"Animals." She made the sign of the cross hastily.

"I'm sure we're safe. If they wanted to hurt us, they would have already." A small part of him enjoyed the brief thrill of authority. At work, his colleagues—seasoned bioengineers and the pioneers of occult nanoscience—were more likely to ask him for a cup of coffee than his opinion. "All we have to do is wait for first responders."

The woman sank back in her plastic seat, shoulders sagging with relief, but he had no real basis for reassuring her. Cole Industries was about to make a massive announcement regarding the next generation of their patented suppression technology, CALM. If anything was going to rile up the local cells of mage-rights extremists, it was a bigger and better way to control magic. For all he knew, they were about to die.

"Maybe it's only construction," a guy said softly. He'd been in the corner, seemingly asleep. But now he crouched by the boy, offering him a small package of crayons—the cheap, waxy sets of four they distributed at restaurants. He wore a white T-shirt and black slacks. A server, probably. Not at an upscale place, judging by the swirling edges of a tattoo peeking out from beneath one short sleeve.

"What do you say?" the nanny prompted, patting the boy's shoulder.

The boy tore the package open with his teeth. "Thank you."

The server smiled. "We're safer down here than up there."

"But my daddy's up there," the boy said. The tears returned, silent and fat.

"Um." He sank back on his heels and looked up at Byron helplessly, as if he'd reached the extent of his ability to soothe children.

"I'm sure your father is fine," Byron said absently, his gaze stuck on the guy's shaggy mess of brown hair. He'd never considered himself the type to have a type, but after today, he wasn't going to rule out pale boys with pretty curls as a front-runner.

The young man met his eyes in a bemused way that highlighted the charm of his thick eyebrows and dark-brown eyes. Byron turned away, his chest warming with a jitter of attraction.

"Late to work?"

Byron glanced back at him and yep—he was still incredibly attractive. He wanted to say something to that end, but he was out of practice when it came to flirting. "Sort of. I have a thing to go to." This was why he preferred engaging in public relations from the safety of his own computer rather than having to act professional in public.

His words had a way of jumbling up and making him sound young and foolish when he needed to seem anything but.

A soft smile didn't make the server any less appealing. He gave Byron a look that held enough significance to make Byron's pulse quicken. The plain, shameless interest didn't calm Byron's nerves. Nearly an hour trapped underground in a broken-down subway had been boring. Being flirted with by an adorable guy? Kind of terrifying.

He didn't have to worry about his predicament for long though; the police abruptly pried open the door and shouted for everyone to stay calm and follow evacuation orders.

Byron gathered his messenger bag and waited for the little kid and the nanny to walk out first. Seven years at a high-profile boarding school had given him plenty of practice with evacuation drills, and it was second nature to fall in line and follow the light. This was a lot easier than trying to carry on small talk with a flirty, tattooed boy.

The burning smell from what should have been fresh October air above them made it hard to focus though.

The group quietly ascended the emergency stairs from the subway tunnel to the next level. Then it only took a few minutes of walking through a damp, narrow hallway to get to a ladder leading to the surface. Byron lined up behind the child, so he could catch him if the boy lost his grip. The kid climbed twice as fast though, clearly more accustomed to ladders than he was.

When he'd surfaced and picked himself up, Byron reached back for the evacuee behind him and found his hand clasped in the warm grip of the server with curls. Despite the thrum of helicopters overhead and the air thick with sirens, it occurred to Byron that this might be his only chance to ask the guy out. What harm would it do to break the grinding routine of entry-level PR work and catching up on baking shows on Netflix?

He should probably evaluate his coping mechanisms. Police in riot gear were dodging around abandoned taxis a few blocks away. A fire raged in the distance, smoking and steaming under the ministrations of several fire rigs. All signs pointed to an act of terror, and he was focusing on a server's ass hugged by inexpensive slacks.

"Thanks." Their hands remained entwined a moment too long. The man blurted, "Levi," just before Byron could manage an introduction.

"Who's Levi?" Byron asked.

"Me."

"Oh, right." He shook his head, flustered. "Of course. I'm—"

The storefront beside them exploded.

I'm going to die.

Would it be like the plane crashes and car wrecks that haunted his nightmares? But this time he wouldn't wake up in a sweat. This was it.

Nothing happened.

"Shit." That was Levi beside him, crouching with both hands raised as if to ward off the explosion.

"Oh God," Byron whispered.

"I'm sorry." Levi's eyes were huge and scared. "I didn't . . . It was an accident. Shit!"

Levi *had* warded off the explosion. With his hands—with magic. A shimmery barrier encircled all of them: The men and women from the subway car. The little boy. The police officers who already had their guns trained on Levi's trembling form. The first responders who had been jogging toward them and now stood still and stunned.

"Lower your hands, mage," one of the officers barked out.

"Dude." Levi's voice broke and his shoulders hunched in on himself. He flinched at the sound of boots scuffling closer. "If I stop, we'll burn. We have to move away from the fire first. Can't you see the flames?"

Most of the officers remained stalwart, advancing slowly—but a few looked up and around. Levi wasn't exaggerating. Angry licks of fire were dancing along the perimeter he'd created.

Byron wasn't about to wait on the decision-making skills of a group of rookie officers who'd been given evacuation duty. He began ushering the others to the far end of the bubble, away from the fire. He only had to gesture. Everyone shuffled with the wooden movements of people in shock. Levi remained still, clearly stricken with fear too raw to be fake.

Hadn't it occurred to him that he could probably stop bullets with the same magic that shielded them from the explosion's shrapnel and heat?

If he was really that clueless, he couldn't be dangerous.

"I'm going to take a few steps back," Levi said, swaying. "Okay? We're all stepping back."

When the entire group was out of the reach of the flames, the shield disappeared with no fanfare. It was simply there one moment and gone the next.

The others from the subway took off running down the street, toward the riot squad and the ambulances. But Byron couldn't move. A sharp chill ran through him despite the pressing heat from the burning building across the road.

Levi's shoulders sank like he wanted to curl in on himself and disappear too. Byron was startled to find himself wishing he would.

The punishment for unsanctioned use of magic was life in prison at best. For the powerful mages, it was execution.

Levi had to be strong. He'd stopped the raw force of an explosion. There were rumors that powerful mages could transform into small animals or bugs. Surely he had enough magic left to escape with his own life?

Byron clearly wasn't the only one wondering if Levi could flee. One of the approaching officers hit Levi with a baton, driving him to his knees. Byron flinched and reached out as if he had the authority to stop them.

"Please. I didn't mean to." Levi made soft, pained sounds on each ragged breath. "It was an accident."

They began to beat him, batons thudding against his back. He fell forward, bracing himself with his palms on the pavement and crying out.

He'd performed powerful magic by lifting his hands, but now he did nothing to defend himself from the blows that accompanied each demand that he keep his hands down on the ground.

"Mr. Cole." One of the officers took Byron by the elbow. "Are you hurt?"

Levi's pained expression gave way to betrayal that sent a lance of unreasonable guilt through Byron's middle.

"Yes. I'm fine," he said. *Thanks to Levi.*

"I recognize you from the Police Foundation gala. The magic containment unit is en route. Cole Industries vehicles. Let me escort you to an ambulance." Fresh-faced and eager, the officer couldn't be much older than Byron. It was a wonder none of them had put a bullet or ten through Levi's skull yet. No one would fault an officer for killing a mage in self-defense—and that's what it would be called if Levi so much as twitched his fingers in the wrong direction.

"I'll stay," Byron said, noting the officer's name badge. *Madison.*

He didn't need to stay. But he could explain his presence away easily enough: he'd never witnessed Cole Industries' equipment in the field firsthand, and his curiosity had gotten the best of him. Even his uncle would believe that.

"Are the terror suspects in custody?" he asked, gesturing at the blaze. Half a dozen ladder trucks idled a few blocks over, likely waiting on an all-clear after Levi's display of magic.

"Only this one." Madison jerked a thumb toward Levi. His hand trembled.

Anger flashed across Levi's face. He tossed his hair out of his eyes. Blood ran down the side of his face. "Seriously? If I wanted to kill people I could have let them die. In the giant explosion."

The air seemed to stir.

"You said yourself saving them was an accident," one of the officers near Levi said, gun trained on his back. "You didn't really mean to protect anyone else but yourself."

"So I rigged an explosion and then saved people from it? Super logical. I'm a criminal fucking mastermind."

Christ, Levi. Stop talking. All of this was on tape thanks to the officers' body cams. Angry sarcasm or not, that would hold water as a confession. The best Levi could hope for now was a quick death, and he wasn't even going to get that if the public thought they had a terrorist to burn.

A special unit vehicle hurtled down the street like a tank on steroids. Byron had seen plenty of videos of test runs, but surround sound didn't compare to the angry roar of the engine. It was the size of a monster truck. Embarrassingly bulky.

Levi was so small in comparison.

The vehicle skidded to a stop, and half a dozen men and women in hazard armor poured out. One of them hit Levi with a long-range stun gun without a word of warning.

Levi fell onto his side and convulsed, eyes blank with pain as the current ran through his body. The regular police officers shuffled back, unabashedly staring.

Madison rubbed his jaw and frowned. "I've only seen magic, you know, on TV."

Every season some new show featured a villain using special-effects magic to rob banks or go on a killing spree. "Magic on TV isn't real," Byron said, voice tight.

Levi gasped on the hot concrete. That was real.

"Think they can stop him?"

"Stop him from what?" Byron snapped. It wasn't like Levi was threatening anyone. And in a moment, he wouldn't be able to use magic at all, thanks to Cole Industries.

A woman from the containment team nimbly clasped CALM bands around Levi's wrists while he lay on the dusty concrete struggling to breathe, tears streaking down his face.

Byron tried to shake the feeling that all of this was wrong. He'd spent his entire life listening to his uncle justify magic control. Thanks to a minor in ethics with a concentration in occult theory, he understood better than most the reasoning behind keeping magic heavily regulated. CALM bands gave mages the opportunity to live normal lives, and they protected the general public inexpensively—a fact that tax payers loved.

"Stop him from doing magic." Madison shuddered. "The Devil's work."

Byron's teeth clicked together as he swallowed back a sharp reply. He wasn't one of the uneducated bigots who hated all mages—even bound mages—because magic was "Satanic."

"Yes," he managed, watching a containment unit officer reach for the button that would activate Levi's CALM bands. "I think they can stop him from doing magic."

Garbled orders sounded from the radio at the officer's hip. She pressed the button.

Levi began screaming.

It was awful—like nothing Byron had ever heard in his life. He knew in an instant that he would never forget the mindless, raw sound.

Madison turned to Byron, eyes wide. "Is that normal?"

"No. We don't manufacture torture devices."

Do we?

Levi's screams died down, and then choked off.

He stopped convulsing.

He stopped moving at all.

Byron held his breath in turn, waiting for a twitch. A gasp. Some sign of life. But nothing happened. Levi lay there pale and contorted, with rivulets of bright-red blood streaking from his nose and ears.

The woman who had activated the bands crouched and touched Levi's chest, hand inching out like she was reaching into a basket of snakes. "He's not breathing."

"Perform CPR!" Byron shouted. No one moved. "Listen to me, there's a project. It's part of the announcement today. We're searching for mages like this man, untapped potential. If my uncle finds out we lost a prime candidate . . ." He let the empty threat hang.

After a long pause, two of the containment unit techs began resuscitating Levi. Byron sat down hard on the curb, his legs numb. Helicopters circled above. He could already see the headlines. *Billionaire's heir narrowly escapes death at the hands of a rogue mage.*

When Levi's chest began to rise and fall again, Byron didn't feel any relief. Dread, thicker than smoke, caught in his throat—and he remained at the curb long after they had carried Levi's limp form into the special unit vehicle and driven him away.

He didn't even know Levi's last name.

But he would soon.

CHAPTER 2
A MINOR MORAL CRISIS

Cole Industries canceled the press conference.

After being checked out by the paramedics and giving a statement, Byron had been allowed to head home. He'd ridden in silence in the backseat of a town car for two hours in the horrendous traffic clogging up the city in the wake of the terrorist attack. All the Trivia Dash had left him with a dead cell phone.

Now Byron sat on his couch watching the news replay an overhead shot of Levi being loaded into the containment unit. He'd called his supervisors at the office under the guise of letting them know he was all right, and they'd confirmed what he'd hoped for—and dreaded.

Cole Industries had already requested custody of Levi. It was essentially a stay of execution. Cole Industries had access to all incarcerated magic users, and carte blanche to use them however the organization saw fit. It was part of the intricate, unprecedented contract Cole Industries had with the United States government to develop magic-containment technology.

"This isn't how I pictured seeing you on TV today," Eleanor said.

His roommate—and best friend—taught high school downtown, and the school was close enough to the explosions that it had been closed for the rest of the week.

"You wouldn't have seen me on TV today anyway." Byron sank back against the cushions and rubbed his eyes.

"Actually, my tenth graders were supposed to watch the press conference in ethics class. Several of them are writing their term papers on Cole Industries' role in the private prison system and suppression devices."

"I'm surprised the superintendent is letting that fly." Even top universities struggled to fill seats in classes that debated magic control. Students trying to attend those classes had to run a gauntlet of antimagic protestors and smaller groups of students protesting mage registration.

"We have the highest percentage of registered, bound-mage students in the district. These issues are relevant to my kids."

"Still ballsy, E." Byron had seen enough drama on Eleanor's Facebook wall to know that parents were looking for blood, furious with kids having the freedom to discuss radical ideas.

It was only lunchtime, but Byron felt like he'd been awake for days. He slipped his tie off and draped it over the side of the couch. Eleanor leaned against him, as if she instinctively knew he craved the contact.

"Obviously I have big balls." Her breath huffed with a silent laugh as she nursed the dregs of a lukewarm cup of coffee. The power flickered briefly, but not enough to turn the TV off.

"The biggest." It had been a running joke since they were little. She'd been the cooler, older kid on weekends at the shore—their parents slinging back cocktails at sunset while Eleanor dared Byron to sneak mini-bottles of vodka out of the cooler.

He'd always refused.

"The CALM kids are just as afraid of terrorists as the rest of us." She sobered. "They didn't ask to be born with magic. It isn't fair to lump them in with terrorists taking innocent lives."

"Careful," he said halfheartedly. "Your reputation will go from liberal to radical before you know it."

"I don't give a rat's ass about my reputation. It can't get any worse than how pissed my parents are about me teaching." Her words had no force behind them though. They both knew she couldn't afford to lose her job.

"I've seen how rabid those parents are on your Facebook wall. People are looking for blood. You could get fired for standing up for CALM kids."

"They need someone to stand up for them. It isn't safe at school anymore. Two more kids in my homeroom got beat up this week. Their parents are going to homeschool them now."

"They're probably better off at home." Byron ignored her gasp. "They won't get into college anyway. Most employers won't hire them."

"Oh, okay." Her coffee sloshed around in her Nyan Cat mug. "We just give up on them, then. Lost causes."

Any other day, Byron would have been up for a debate with Eleanor. But the argument didn't entertain him the way it used to. The argument now had kind brown eyes and a warm, solid hand. And a name. *Levi Camden.*

"They're harmless," he said absently.

Eleanor sighed and turned the volume on the TV down. She pushed her chin-length hair behind her ear. This month it was a reddish brown. Last month it'd been dirty blond. She referred to her color indecision as a midlife crisis, though she was only twenty-six. "Seriously. What is going on with you?"

"That man . . ." Byron blinked away the memory of Levi's brown eyes.

"The terrorist they caught?"

"I'm not sure he was a terrorist. I met him on the subway, and he used magic to stop the explosion from killing over a dozen of us."

"Did you hit your head?" Eleanor caught his gaze. "I don't want to be a dick here, but generally you toe the line pretty hard. Terrorists use magic and mages are terrorists and Cole Industries has 'Murica's best interests at heart, and all that."

Byron pressed his fingers against his eyes.

"Well?" she prompted. "Wasn't that going to be the gist of the press conference today?"

"He didn't strike me as the type of person who'd destroy things and kill people."

"Ignoring the fact that you're making a really random judgment call there, can't rogue mages warp perception?"

"You know how Warren is. I've been wearing an antiglamour device since I was ten. Even if Levi had been using perception-based magic, it wouldn't have worked on me." Byron glanced up at the TV. "Hold on. Turn it up."

A middle-aged anchor was speaking gravely beside a graphic with a photo of Levi that looked like it had been pulled from Facebook. Levi smiled broadly from a booth in a bar, his arm around a black man with his face blurred out. Two half-empty beers in glasses sat on the table in front of them.

"Authorities say twenty-one-year-old Levi Camden of Brooklyn has been arrested for unsanctioned use of magic. The suspected rogue mage is not registered with the Department of Occult Supervision and was not outfitted with CALM devices at the time of the incident. Investigators are contacting Camden's immediate family, coworkers, and friends to determine whether or not there were prior indications of magic capabilities. Under the Homeland Security Act, any individual knowingly harboring a rogue mage may be sentenced with up to five years in federal prison.

"The Keep CALM Alliance published a release distancing the activism group from any and all known terrorists, reiterating that KCA's focus remains on facilitating peaceful relations between bound mages and the general public."

"They shouldn't have to say that," Eleanor muttered. "Of course that's their focus."

"The manager at Café Ciccone, where Camden was a member of the wait staff, has released a statement condemning magic use. According to investigators, there is strong reason to believe that Camden is a member of the terrorist cell that triggered explosives killing eighteen people in New York City early this morning."

"Levi should have kept his mouth shut," Byron said.

Eleanor glanced at him, her blue eyes questioning beneath her delicately arched brow.

"Camden's mother, fifty-one-year-old Cynthia Camden of Taunton, Massachusetts, did not respond to our calls. According to a public social media profile, Camden was active in the local arts and LGBT communities. He had no known ties with magic rights organizations."

"He's cute," Eleanor said.

"I didn't notice. I was busy almost dying in a horrific explosion," Byron said, turning the TV off.

Eleanor nudged him. "You thought he was cute, admit it. Is that what this weirdness is about? Don't feel guilty. You had no way of knowing he was a mass murderer."

"He's not— I didn't— Damn it. No. I didn't flirt with him. And I'm not being weird."

"You're *definitely* being weird. You never watch the news unless Warren's bloviating about saving the universe."

Byron ran his fingers through his hair. They caught in the tackiness of the styling cream he'd used to keep the stick-straight black mess in some semblance of the eighty-dollar haircut only his stylist could tame. It was all so absurd. Hair cream and a suit worth a month's salary and Eleanor jabbing him about flirting.

Everything was trivial in the face of Levi going into cardiac arrest in the middle of the street because the CALM bands had done something very bad to him they'd never done to anyone else.

Or maybe Byron had never been made aware of CALM bands doing that to anyone else.

"I'm teasing you," Eleanor said quietly, interrupting his thoughts. "I know you didn't flirt with that guy. He *is* cute, though."

Byron sighed. "He saved my life. And not only me—all those people. And he seemed surprised by his own magic. Do you think he really was? Is it possible to live for twenty-one years without knowing you're a mage?"

"That's a question for your coworkers, not for me." When Byron remained silent, eyeing the high ceiling of their apartment, she went on, "But I think it's interesting you're entertaining the notion that he didn't know he had magic."

"Why is that interesting?"

"Because you seem determined to defend this guy."

A traitorous flush heated his neck. "Think about it though. He was scared. Genuinely scared."

"Jesus, Byron. You're obsessed."

"I guess I'm having a minor moral crisis. Maybe I'll help you grade those ethics term papers. Learn something from your students." He let out a weak laugh, trying to lighten the mood.

Eleanor gave him a long, unamused look and stood up, taking her coffee cup and his. She headed into the kitchen with her phone in her other hand, thumb already unlocking the screen.

Left in the silent living room with the blank TV in front of him, Byron wondered what else the news was saying about Levi. He couldn't bring himself to turn it back on and face it.

One thought played in his head over and over, a little more treacherous every time: If he had the ability to stop destruction and death with the wave of his hand, he'd risk his life to keep that power. He wouldn't give it up. Not for the law. Not for anyone.

If he'd had magic—some way to predict the future or see in the dark or travel great distances in a blink of an eye—he could have saved his parents. He would have.

He would have used magic without hesitation.

It was easily the most treasonous notion that had ever crossed his mind. How did one server from Brooklyn have the ability to unravel the values Byron had wholeheartedly subscribed to his entire life?

It was giving him a headache, and even that gave him pangs of guilt. Yes, his head hurt, but he wasn't frightened or in agony. He wasn't all over the news being called a mass murderer. He wasn't in danger of being put to death for using an innate gift.

The practice of magic had always been abstract to Byron. Sure, he'd been around bound mages, but they couldn't pull off a party trick, let alone legitimate magic. Not with CALM bands on. And the rare rogue mages who got caught using magic were only characters in the newspaper. A lawyer in Scottsdale. A stripper in Reno. A truck driver in Alaska. Distant threats immediately neutralized by the most foolproof method available—execution.

Levi wasn't abstract. His hand had been warm and human, and he'd been so frightened, not of the deadly shrapnel and fire, but of the men and women he'd saved.

Byron needed a beer, not another cup of coffee. "Shit."

CHAPTER 3
OFF THE RAILS

"Did you knowingly and willingly use magic on the morning of Thursday, October second, at 9:16 a.m.?"

Levi wondered how many days had stretched between the beginning of October and now. A week? A lifetime? At least several days judging by the scruff on his jaw.

An investigator sat across from Levi, flanked by a man and woman dressed like cops from a bad sci-fi movie. They held menacing batons and wore black bodysuits with armor sleeker than any bulletproof vests Levi had ever seen. Not that he'd ever seen a bulletproof vest outside of TV shows.

The investigator was a tall guy, with the sallow complexion of a lifelong smoker and the tight expression of someone clenching their butt with fear.

"I didn't check the time on my phone before everything blew up," Levi said.

"Unlawful magic use is punishable by death." The investigator squinted until the protruding bags under his eyes obscured his gaze. "Do you think this is funny?"

"No. I think it's funny that you think I have a magical time stamp."

"But you admit to using magic."

"Whatever happened is probably on fifteen security cameras. Why don't you review the footage and tell me?"

Talking about magic came surprisingly easy now that he had nothing to lose. After waking up on a gurney in a room too cold and sparse to be a real hospital, he'd tried to use his magic in a panic. A blistering flare of pain had immediately rendered him unconscious. The next time he'd risen out of the darkness, he'd had a breathing tube down his throat. That alone had been unpleasant enough to stop him from trying again.

Now his ribs throbbed with every breath, his head ached like he'd had three bottles of wine for breakfast, and his magic was all wrong.

It was still there. But his magic was a tightness inside of him, like a breath held too long. It *hurt*.

Whatever the CALM bands on his wrists were doing made his entire body sore like one big bruise. The bands weren't heavy, but they weighed him down every waking second.

"Believe me, the security footage will come into play during your trial," the investigator said.

"Will my trial take place in the town square? Right before the bonfire?" Levi waved his fingers like smoke and flames rising from his body.

The investigator flinched.

Levi sighed. Inspiring fear was a new, shitty experience. He hated killing spiders and felt marginally bad for killing cockroaches. He'd never been in a fight. He didn't even leave bad reviews on Yelp.

"What will make this quicker?" he asked. "Can't you tell me that much?"

"What do you mean?"

"What's the path of least resistance here? The fast track to execution."

"The Federal Bureau of Investigation and the Department of Occult Supervision want a thorough report on this incident and on any instances of magic use that may have occurred before the alleged unlawful use on October second," the investigator said. Levi had already forgotten his name. There were too many bad guys to keep track of.

"So no matter what, I have to deal with all this bullshit before they end up killing me anyway?"

"No, you have to deal with all this *bullshit* before we turn you over to Cole Industries' people." For the first time, the investigator smiled. "They have a use for you."

Levi folded his arms and shrank back in the cold, hard chair he'd been sitting in for three hours of interrogations. He'd always told himself that a violent death was inevitable—and pretended not to care. It was the risk he'd taken when he'd decided not to submit to registration and wear CALM bands. But that was an epic load of bravado. Execution wasn't the way he wanted to go out. It wasn't something he wanted his mother and friends to see.

And being poked and prodded by magic-hating scientists sounded even worse than being executed.

"They can't experiment on me." Levi's voice tripped in his sore throat. "I—I have rights. Human rights. It's torture."

"You forfeited those rights when you failed to identify yourself as a mage and submit yourself to the CALM program," the investigator said.

"That's fucked up," Levi said, glancing from him to the guards. They were people. People in scary outfits. Nothing more. "You know it is." Desperation thinned his voice. The room swayed.

The investigator closed his leather notebook with a snap that startled Levi's attention back from the panic whittling away at his composure. "I will repeat the question again. Until you give me a straightforward answer, we'll keep this up. I have all night."

"Can we order a pizza?" Levi shot back.

"Maybe you can conjure yourself something to eat." The investigator cleared his throat. "Did you knowingly and willingly use magic on the morning of Thursday, October second, at 9:16 a.m.?"

Blanketed with weariness, Levi couldn't come up with another deflection. He wanted to go back to the cell. He wanted to sleep. Sleep was his only escape, and he'd been up for longer than he could keep track of now. Maybe he'd be able to nod off despite the way his magic was beating at his rib cage like a frantic bird.

"I used magic that morning. It wasn't willingly or knowingly." Levi ducked his chin, feeling like a coward. "The explosion scared me, and I made a shield without thinking. I could have stopped myself after that, but it would have meant murdering all of them."

"When you say 'shield,' are you referring to an incantation?"

"I don't know any enchantments or spells or incantations." Levi didn't try to mask his bitterness. Magic existed within him, but he didn't know how to use it—how to control it. Until that morning, he'd been more likely to short out a toaster than create a life-saving bubble. "It happened on its own. It was an accident."

"Were you aware of being a mage prior to October second?"

Levi closed his eyes and pictured his mom in her little second-floor apartment. He saw her small hands wrapped around his wrists and the tears in her eyes as she'd made him promise to never, ever let his magic out. He'd been six years old and so angry at the bulldozers tearing down the complex across the street where his friends had lived. They'd had to move to make room for a big store. He'd wished so hard that the construction men would go away, and one of the bulldozers had tipped right over, like a toy. It had been easy.

So much easier than lying every single day of his life.

"No, I wasn't." Levi opened his eyes and met the investigator's beady gaze. "I'm sure you can imagine my surprise."

"I'm sure you can imagine my skepticism, Mr. Camden," the investigator said, parroting his tone. "I'm no expert on magic use, but what I saw on those tapes didn't resemble the work of an amateur."

"No one's an expert on magic use." Levi gave a soft, hysterical laugh. "Because it's outlawed. Because you shackle us and clip our wings. You take our children away. And burn us and torture us. No one knows what magic can do because you're all so fucking afraid."

"And you've developed those strong opinions this past week? In the six days since you suddenly and shockingly discovered you had magic on the morning of the terrorist attack?"

Levi scrubbed one hand down his face. "I read blogs," he said lamely.

"How long have you been involved with the terrorist group responsible for the attack?"

"I'm not a terrorist. If I had known about those explosions, I wouldn't have been anywhere near them."

"Really? You wouldn't have stopped the terrorists?" the female guard asked abruptly. The investigator made a big show of turning to glare at her, but she continued to watch Levi steadily. "If you'd known?"

The question stole Levi's breath. A long moment passed before he found his voice. "I don't know." When he blinked, the exhausted tears he'd been fighting for hours fell. They felt good against his face, and he didn't bother wiping them away. "I'm not a superhero. I don't owe anybody anything."

After a brief frown, she steeled her expression. "Pardon me," she said with a nod to the investigator. "It wasn't my place to question the suspect."

"Did people die?" Levi asked. "In the fires and explosions? I was stuck on the subway and we couldn't get any reception down there. What happened?"

"Do you want to make sure your attempts at terrorism were successful?" the investigator snarled.

"I told you I had nothing to do with it."

"Then why do you want to know?"

"Because I'm a human being?" Levi fought the urge to shout. "And she thinks I should have saved the world. Just wondering who else I was supposed to protect other than the people on that subway car who are probably already lining up to watch me get burned at the stake."

"That's not what I meant," she mumbled.

"This interrogation has officially gone off the rails." The investigator stood and made a big show of smoothing out the wrinkles in his suit. "And I'm late to dinner. Take the suspect back to his cell."

Without another word, he punched a few numbers into the keypad and left the interrogation room.

"Asshole," Levi muttered. He didn't resist when the guards took his arms and lifted him. To his surprise, his legs barely held his weight. Someone supplied a wheelchair, and they dumped him into it. He hunched over. Linoleum tiles glided beneath his bare feet. If he pretended hard enough, this could be a really awful hospital visit, not a trip back down the elevator to the small cell that contained nothing but a metal toilet.

The female guard kept her hand on his shoulder. It was warm. He wasn't sure if she was restraining him or supporting him, but he appreciated the touch. "I'm not one of those terrorists," he said quietly.

Her hand tightened on his shoulder. "It doesn't matter."

CHAPTER 4
A NORMAL MAN

It hadn't taken the tabloids long to find Levi's Twitter account and embed tweet after tweet in articles alleging Levi's sordid history as a rogue mage. But none of his tweets were substantially incriminating.

Byron knew because he'd spent hours reading back through years of tweets. Thousands of them. As Byron scrolled, Levi's number of followers grew with rubberneckers flocking to his pseudo-celebrity status.

None of Levi's tweets referenced magic or terrorism or anything that could be remotely construed as radical. His only political leanings seemed to be related to better bike lanes and affordable health care. As the news had reported, he appeared to have been involved in the local LGBT scene, but not as an activist. The most aggressive thing he'd posted was an angry message at his internet service provider for repeated outages.

Levi's social media presence painted the portrait of a very average, somewhat aimless young man.

Sitting in bed with a laptop, Byron found himself chuckling at Levi's rage over the spoilers from last season's big dramatic finale of a popular cable show about an alien FBI agent. He nodded in agreement with Levi's assertion that Hide-Chan Ramen had the best noodles in the city. He cringed when Levi lost job after job when new restaurants opened and subsequently closed.

Byron noted a nine-month series of tweets that indicated Levi had been in a relationship with a club owner named Sam two years before. Byron recognized the broad shoulders of the man whose face had been blurred out on the news report.

It didn't take much searching to figure out that Sam was Sam Johnson, a former attorney who had abruptly switched gears from social justice advocacy to the hospitality industry. His club, Summons—a hybrid between an art gallery and a dance club—had remained a steadfast hotspot in the gay community for several years. Levi's Twitter account didn't get into the details of their breakup, but they still tweeted at each other occasionally. Sam was Byron's best chance to learn more about Levi, but the cops were probably way ahead of him.

Levi's last tweet was dated September fifteenth, right before midnight. *Do you ever wonder what your purpose is? #navelgazing.*

It was the most oft-cited tweet used to characterize Levi as a radical willing to terrorize in the name of magic. It was a stretch at best, and slander at worst, to use such a vague statement as evidence. But Byron understood needing to blame someone, to put a face to terror. Specifics, inaccurate or not, were better than facing down the possibility that bad things happened for no reason.

It was a similar tug that pulled him deeper into Levi's timeline until it was clear he wouldn't learn enough there. He needed to know more than what any curious person could find online.

It was surprisingly easy to gain access to Levi Camden's apartment.

He told the police chief he was working on a public statement from Cole Industries—a deeply personal message from the perspective of a would-be victim of the terrorist attack. The chief gave him a spare key.

"We've already documented everything in his apartment, and the Bureau found nothing of note there," he said warmly, taking Byron's shoulder in a fatherly grip. "So don't worry about prints or moving anything. And honestly, I wouldn't be surprised if you took a dump on his living room floor after what he's done to this city."

"I assure you, that won't be on my agenda," Byron said, smiling through a wave of irritation.

It had never escaped Byron's awareness that being part of the Cole dynasty afforded him many privileges. Until the police chief bent the law for him, it had never occurred to him how easy it would be to take advantage of that.

Not that he was complaining. He needed to learn more, and there was no better place to get started than Levi Camden's studio on the third floor of a building in Bedford-Stuyvesant. The apartment was tiny, but bright-yellow walls warmed it. The scuffed floors bore the marks of decades of tenants. Byron locked the door behind him and realized he didn't have much of a game plan or any idea what to look for.

Fat flies buzzed around a sink full of dirty dishes. He turned on the hot water and began to wash them.

Levi's dish soap smelled like lemongrass. The dishes were mismatched—a deep-blue plate, a floral teacup, and a red cereal bowl. He smiled as he scrubbed at dried pasta sauce. Something about the bright colors made doing dishes suck less.

It didn't take long to wash and dry the dishes with a tea towel covered with foxes. The reality of what he was doing in the apartment crashed back into his mind as soon as he was done.

Not only was he spying on someone's life, but he was compromising his ability to do his job. He'd lied to the police chief, but the truth was he'd likely be tasked with writing something for Cole Industries, and the more he dug into Levi's life, the more biased he'd become. What could he possibly come up with to villainize Levi?

This didn't look like the apartment of a terrorist—though what *did* a terrorist's apartment look like? Surely not covered in propaganda posters and machine guns and bombs.

While terrorist behavior was inhumane, those who killed for their beliefs—however misguided and cruel—were still people. They weren't robots. Maybe they all had colorful dishes and bright-yellow walls in sunny little studios in Brooklyn.

"You shouldn't be here," Byron said to himself, uncomfortably filling the silence. He opened a window to let the sound of the street in so the apartment felt alive—and not like a mausoleum.

Levi's single bed was unmade. Above it, a mismatched gallery wall displayed drawings and small photos with saturated Instagram filters. Byron climbed onto the bed for a closer look. He took his shoes off first.

It was impossible to ignore the faint smell of another person. It wasn't a bad smell—skin and citrusy soap. Byron exhaled heavily and turned his attention to the gallery: a scrawled drawing of a cat, a photo of Levi and a middle-aged woman with shockingly white hair, a photograph of the NYC skyline from the Brooklyn Bridge, a grinning selfie of Levi in the woods, and a picture of him in a green feather boa with his arms around two beautiful drag queens.

Byron grinned automatically, charmed by Levi's candid expressions. His hair was mussed and curly in each picture, as if he'd never met a brush in his life. His dark-brown eyes squinted and deep laugh lines formed around his bright smile.

The final frame held an elaborate abstract drawing that seemed to have been done with ballpoint pen on a cocktail napkin. The intricate, swirling lines were familiar, but he couldn't quite place them.

He left the bed unmade.

Nothing in the room screamed magic and intrigue. The desk beside the bed held two computer speakers and a mouse, but no computer—the cops must have taken it. The bookshelf contained a few graphic novels, gourmet cookbooks, and photo books; it didn't seem like Levi spent much time reading. He didn't own a television. Three framed posters hung on the wall above Levi's desk. Byron squinted at them for a few minutes until he figured out they were modern art renderings of popular film posters.

Byron opened the fridge and found a mix of takeout boxes, craft beer, and jars of vegetables with hand-drawn labels. He recognized the brand from the farmers' market at Union Square. No eyes of newt or lizard tails to be found. Magnets on the fridge door held a list of phone numbers and names, a well-worn transit map, a business card for an acupuncturist in Williamsburg, and another photo of the woman with white hair. In this picture, she smiled with the same unguarded grin Levi had.

"Cynthia Camden," Byron said out loud. What would happen if he called her? How would he introduce himself? As the man who had stood idly by while Levi was punished for saving lives? As the nephew of the face of mage persecution?

"Containment," he corrected himself. Persecution? That sounded like something the radical mage-supporters said on websites run on overseas servers where the United States couldn't shut them down quickly enough. Byron had to read those sites for work to understand what kinds of social conversations involved the Cole Industries brand. Public relations was nothing more than influencing the narrative—burying the bad and amplifying the good. Maybe all the radical things he'd read were starting to get to him. Maybe he was losing his mind.

Byron sat down at the little bistro table between the kitchen and the bed, and studied the circular rug. It was covered with gray cat hair. He spotted a litter box and bowls for food and water, but the box contained no litter and the bowls were empty.

"All right, Nancy Drew," Byron said with a sigh. "This is getting you nowhere."

What had he expected to learn in the first place?

Restless, Byron stood back up and peeked into the tiny bathroom. He knew why he was here. It wasn't to find signs of magic. No one living in a city on high terror alert was going to be stupid enough to leave evidence in plain view. At least, not someone with the unmistakable cleverness Byron had seen in Levi's eyes.

He'd come here to prove the point that stung like a sore: Levi was a normal man—a Brooklyn waiter with a tattoo and expensive beer with unpronounceable names in his refrigerator. He was a twentysomething who kept pictures of his mom around and stayed on good terms with exes. He liked art and colors, and he wasn't an animal.

Levi would be better off as an animal than a rogue mage. The thought struck Byron like a blow, stole his breath.

At least people supported animal rights.

They walked dogs in strollers. They picketed against leather at fashion shows and rallied against hunters. They sank whaling ships.

Suddenly weary, Byron sat on the edge of Levi's bed. He knew how things were going to go, because he was part of it. No one was going to stand up for Levi.

Anyone who spoke up for Levi would be labeled an extremist, no matter how bad things got for him. Too many people saw mages as subhuman whether they realized it or not—and legislation reflected it. Mages had already lost the right to vote. The right to raise their own children. It would seem absurd to advocate for Levi. After all, what was one more mage incarcerated—and a terrorist no less?

Byron had grown up with the privilege of ignoring mage rights. He'd never had anything at stake. Beyond losing his parents, he'd never known a moment's real struggle. His entire life had been a preordained path of success.

Until now, he'd never considered that success might leave him on the wrong side of history.

He ran his hands across Levi's sheets, smoothing the wrinkles he'd made. His fingers twitched, and he couldn't shake the sticky thought of the press conference he'd been commuting to the morning Levi saved his life.

"What am I doing?"

The Harvest Initiative press conference—the speech he'd written—all of that had been theoretical. He didn't know what the project's machines *really* did. He hadn't pressed, choosing instead to embrace his family's legacy. A legacy of national security and innovation.

Witnessing the crime of magic in person had broken Byron's resolve. He couldn't muster the unwavering beliefs that made CALM a household name and the grim reality of anyone born with the scourge of magic.

For Byron, magic was no longer something that happened to other people. It was something that had saved him from certain, horrific death. Magic flourished inside a man Byron had touched—and been undeniably attracted to.

"Talk about navel-gazing," Byron said with a sigh, recalling Levi's tweet. He touched the outline of the metal pendant he wore beneath his shirt—the antiglamour device his uncle's security detail had given him over a decade ago. If it wasn't for the protection it gave him, he'd wonder if Levi had enchanted him.

He couldn't stop thinking of Levi's smile and the fall of hair that almost obscured his playful eyes.

"You're not evil," Byron said to the square photo on the fridge. It was another group photo—several men and women crowded close to get into the shot. They were laughing and smiling. Levi had his head on a woman's shoulder and his gaze on the camera.

It was safe to bet that Levi posed no danger to anyone—that he didn't deserve to be tortured and executed.

Dread settled in his gut. It was one thing to have an opinion. It was another thing entirely to do something about it.

Was he willing to bet his life?

CHAPTER 5
AMID CERTAINTIES

One week after the bombing, Byron invited Victoria Alvarez to coffee. Five minutes before they were scheduled to meet up, she slipped into the booth at the back of the coffee shop near her facility.

"Is this about Eleanor?" she asked as she set a mug of tea down on the table.

"What?" Byron had a lot of things on his mind, but none of them were his roommate.

"Listen, neither of us wanted this to be awkward for you." She narrowed dark-brown eyes framed by impeccable liner. "And frankly, it's none of your business that she and I are having sex. If it escalates into a serious relationship, I can assure you that we'll spend time at my place, not yours."

Byron pressed his fingers against his eyes until he saw sparks. "Vic. I had no idea you were . . . what?"

"Great." Victoria slapped the table with her palm like a judge hitting a gavel. "In that case, I'm having sex with Eleanor. I'm glad it's not awkward."

"It's awkward now, because it's barely 8 a.m. and you're talking about sex with my best friend. How did that even happen? You hate teachers."

"I hate my ex-girlfriend, who happens to be an educator. I do not hate all educators. And it happened after the AMID gala."

Byron sputtered. "You slept with my date."

"She was your plus one. There's a huge distinction there."

"You slept with my *plus one*." He shook his head. "This is why I don't bring normal people to work events."

Victoria laughed.

They'd met a year back when she'd approached Byron looking for insight into research in magic defense—a field that dovetailed nicely with Cole Industries' binding technology. Still an intern at the time, he'd been the only person at Cole Industries inexperienced enough to answer emails from strangers and agree to meet them for a business lunch. Her passion and intelligence had been infectious, and he'd done some proposals during his capstone project, so he'd given her a hand unofficially. They'd had a standing brunch date ever since.

She was ten years his senior and one of the most brilliant scientists he'd ever met, but she didn't talk down to him—despite his frequent inability to comprehend her work.

Now her dark eyes flashed wickedly. "It's cute that you think she's normal. If you knew what she was like in—"

"Oh God, let's stop there. Listen." Byron pushed his coffee to one side and leaned close. "This is serious."

"If you're here to tell me we've lost funding, I'm going to need something stronger than this tea." Victoria's fingers tightened on her mug.

"It's nothing like that." What he'd helped her put together had prompted Cole Industries to pour astronomical amounts of money into her work—taking it from research to prototype. "Warren wants AMID weapons in the Ukraine by next summer. People love a big flashy product that blows up radicals."

"You're lucky that I know you're smarter than that, Byron," she said, mouth tight and unamused.

"It doesn't matter if I'm smarter than that. Warren needs investors to cheer for you. And nothing gets people cheering like blowing up terrorists."

"Our technology is meant to save lives, not escalate conflict." Victoria stirred her tea with delicately irritated fervor. "What is this about, Byron?"

"Have you heard of the Harvest Initiative?"

Victoria's gaze snapped up. Her fingers fluttered to her tight black bun. "Of course I've heard of it. Cole Industries is developing a sustainable source of power to combat the energy crisis," she said. "And I'd have heard more if the press conference hadn't been . . . interrupted."

"Listen, Miss-I-graduated-from-MIT-at-fifteen. I'm not talking about *public* knowledge."

Victoria glanced around the near-empty coffee shop before narrowing her gaze. "I've heard rumors. Warren is trying to convert magic into clean energy."

"In so many words, yes."

"He'd literally have you killed for discussing classified information at a coffee shop, Byron. Did you hit your head in that explosion?"

"That's what Eleanor asked," Byron said, trying to shake off the fact that she sounded completely sincere.

Victoria's lips pursed, as red as strawberries.

"I didn't hit my head. But I think a great deal of this is . . . problematic. The Harvest. Recent legislation. The magic registry." Byron cringed. "CALM bands."

"Now I'm *sure* you're suffering from a head injury."

"Eleanor said that too."

"Byron. These are dangerous things you're saying." She leaned closer. "Dangerous things you're thinking. We don't live in a world where you can discuss whether or not it's right to do what Cole Industries is doing. And if you question their actions, you're questioning the future of my life's work."

"I know."

"So where are you going with this?"

"I need to have Levi Camden transferred to AMID."

Victoria sat back and exhaled noisily. "I don't need America's most hated terrorist in my laboratory. You're supposed to be getting me good press, not a media circus."

"This isn't about PR. It won't be public knowledge. Hell, it can't be public knowledge."

"I told you we're moving away from running tests on unwilling participants," she said. "We're waiting on approval from the French embassy to have their military mages participate in the next trial. I don't need any more test subjects."

"That's exactly why I need your help."

"You need to explain yourself quickly, Byron." She stirred her tea so hard it made a little vortex in the amber liquid. "You know I adore you. You got me this break. But you're not making sense right now, and to be frank, it's extremely concerning."

"Warren's going to transfer Levi Camden to the Harvest facilities."

"That's to be expected. I heard the kid short-circuited his CALM bands. He's a problem."

"The bands are completely safe." Byron caught himself parroting the disclaimer he'd heard a million times, and flushed, lowering his voice. "He short-circuited himself."

The official stance on Levi's reaction to the bands was that he'd attempted violent magic that had backfired on him. Whatever had really happened, Levi hadn't tried it again. He was still in CALM bands in custody.

"Again." Victoria gave him a long look. "The kid's a problem. And I fail to see what this has to do with my lab."

"I don't think he deserves to die."

"Byron." Victoria smoothed back a nonexistent stray hair with trembling fingers. "Are you testing my loyalty? You can have your uncle's people visit AMID immediately. You'll find us up to code. We're fully above board and more than committed to Cole Industries' vision and the Department of Occult Supervision."

"It's my loyalty in question," Byron said quietly, trying not to take her distrust personally. "I need to learn more about him. About the Harvest. The only place he'll be safe is at AMID. And if he can help you—willingly—all the better. I know this is . . . You don't owe me this, Vic. I'm asking you to help me."

"You're out of your mind."

"I might be. He saved my life."

"Is that what this is about? Payback?"

"No." Byron rubbed his forehead. "A little. I don't know. I can't stand back and know he's going to die because he saved our lives."

"If your uncle finds out about this, *we're* going to die. How could you ask me this?"

"I'm asking you this because you're the only scientist working in the occult field who's spoken up against testing on prisoners. You've drawn that line in the sand when literally no one else has had the balls—the courage to."

"I *suggested* a line in the sand," she said quickly.

"Still. That man saved dozens of lives. I don't think he's a terrorist. I don't think he's an enemy."

"Magic is the enemy," Victoria said softly.

"What if it's only the enemy when it's used with intention to do harm?"

"That very question could put you on a watch list. It would certainly cost you your job."

"I don't have time to keep debating this." Byron reached across the table and rested his hand over hers. "I'm asking you to put in a request to have Levi Camden transferred to your lab. I'll handle things from there."

"Oh, you'll use the power of pretty words to get me out of a career-destroying, potentially life-ending accusation of treason against the United States?"

"I haven't figured the whole plan out yet. And I know transferring Levi sounds crazy. But if you'd seen what I saw, you'd feel it too."

"I'd feel crazy?" She reversed their hands to grip his, her fingers strong at his wrist.

He stared at their hands. "You'd feel certain."

"How are you recovering from the unpleasant incident the other morning?" Warren Cole asked. His mirrored glasses warped Byron's reflection.

Warren had lost his sight at six years old after contracting a rare, severe virus. According to the many biographies written about his early life, he'd never let the sudden disability slow his pace. As a young entrepreneur and computer engineer, he had famously pioneered software that helped those without eyesight navigate the first computer operating systems. But it was his role in harnessing magic that made him a household name.

Despite being short for a man, he commanded a room with his firm posture and stern expression. For as long as Byron could remember, his uncle Warren had intimidated him—even now.

Byron folded his arms to steady himself. "I'm fine. It shook me up a little that day, that's all."

"Nothing a stiff drink couldn't remedy, I'm sure," Warren said, offering a thin smile.

"Of course, sir." He'd tried downing several beers the night after the attack, but it hadn't remedied a damn thing.

Warren propped his elbows on his massive desk and continued to smile, face turned toward Byron, as if he could see him. "What is it you've come to discuss, Byron? All is well at work, I trust."

Byron cringed internally. Truth be told, the past week at work had been a total waste of time. With his concentration shot, he was going through the motions, and if he wasn't careful, he'd make a stupid mistake soon.

"Yes. Work is fantastic."

"You needn't oversell it, son."

Byron laughed awkwardly, a staccato sound. "It's fine, though."

"My time is limited this morning. There's no sense in beating around the bush. What's on your mind?"

"It's about Levi Camden." Byron tried to keep the words from tumbling out in a nervous rush.

Warren tilted his head. "The terrorist mage?"

"Yes. From the attack the other day."

"I was told you recommended him for the Harvest Initiative. Quick thinking, and good instincts. As soon as we're ready for phase two, I'll have him transferred to our facilities. You were spot on. He's an excellent candidate."

"Thank you, sir." Byron kept his expression neutral. Although his uncle could not see, he seemed to have the ability to read moods, and the last thing Byron needed was for his uncle to know how he really felt about Levi ending up in the hands of Cole Industries. "As you're aware, I've been working on a publicity campaign for the defense startup we funded last quarter."

"Yes, for that female engineer. Her antimagic weaponry is promising."

"Antimagic integrated defense, sir. AMID."

"There are brilliant young minds involved in that project, though it's a shame they're not developing offensive tactics. We can't win wars by tucking tail, am I right?"

But Warren hadn't gotten rich winning wars. He'd gotten rich meting out what the public saw as mercy—the chance for mages to remain part of society, to stay alive during a time when fear of magic had hit a frenzy and mages had been murdered by the dozens, every day.

Guilt tightened Byron's throat. Cole Industries was a symbol of peace and innovation. His family's legacy. And he was working against it. "Of course, sir."

Warren clasped his hands together and rested them on his desk. "What does this have to do with Camden?"

"AMID recently put in a request for an active mage to test projection neutralization against," Byron said, hoping Warren was too busy to have read the actual request. It had specifically been for a volunteer—not a prisoner. "As long as you don't need Camden until phase two, we could have him transferred to the AMID facility. If I'm able to document their efforts, I can craft a compelling narrative around the project. Something highly investor-friendly."

"I like the way you think, son. That shouldn't be a problem." Warren shifted his posture as if scrutinizing Byron. "Why Camden in particular? We have plenty of mages in detainment, not to mention overseas detainees that could easily be transferred to AMID."

"Well . . ." Byron feigned hesitation. It wasn't too hard to sound unsure. "To be honest, I feel a personal connection."

"Oh?"

Until this moment, Byron had never told so much as a white lie to his uncle, but the words rolled off his tongue with surprising ease. "I came so close to getting killed by him. I'd find it satisfying to see AMID's equipment tested on him."

Warren chuckled. "That's hardly a reasonable motivation. But it's understandable. Just remember—these are animals we're dealing with. Abominations. We do ourselves a great disservice to sink to their level."

"Yes, sir. Is there someone else you recommend?" Byron tried not to hold his breath.

"No, no. Camden will do. Be sure not to cause him any permanent damage, though. He may prove to be a crucial element to the Harvest Initiative. I believe Dr. Crane is evaluating his classification this Friday, so when he's finished, I'll have Camden transferred to AMID. I assume they're prepared to handle a prisoner?"

"They've worked with detained mages in the past. I'll touch base with Dr. Alvarez, but I don't foresee any problems. He's already equipped with CALM bands."

"And you'll be spending time at the facility?"

Byron swallowed. "Well. I'd like to write a thorough press release. It would help to watch the proceedings firsthand."

"We're talking about a criminal, son—a terrorist. Aren't you concerned for your safety?"

"Not when your technology is involved." Byron smiled, grateful for the opportunity to lay it on thick. "I wouldn't be much of a Cole if I didn't trust CALM bands to keep me safe."

"Well, keep in mind that magic isn't the only way to hurt people." Warren reached for a slim, silver pen in a wooden stand and tapped it against the plain white notepad in front of him. All of it was for show. He never wrote by hand, instead relying on a laptop equipped for the visually impaired. "If I recall, you don't have the best track record when it comes to hand-to-hand combat."

Warren was apparently never going to let go of the fact that Byron had been beaten silly in a sixth-grade martial arts tournament.

Byron managed a small, dry laugh. "Do you think additional security measures would be wise?"

"That shouldn't be necessary." Warren hummed. "But I'm sure Dr. Crane will want thorough updates. You know how he gets with his pet projects."

Byron didn't know. But something about Warren's tone made his hands clench until he willed them to relax. "I'm sure Dr. Alvarez would welcome visits if he'd like to keep tabs."

"Excellent. Keep me updated, and be sure to send me your documentation. I'll include a report at the all-hands in January. Our investors love seeing our technology in action."

"Absolutely. Thank you, as always, for the opportunity to serve Cole Industries."

"Mr. Cole?" Warren's secretary's voice crackled from the phone on his desk. "Your ten o'clock is here."

"Send her in." Warren turned a blank gaze toward Byron. "Duty calls, son. I'll have transfer paperwork sent over for a Saturday arrival at AMID."

"Perfect, sir." Byron took his leave on trembling legs.

Warren's assistant rolled his eyes at him, and he managed an awkward wave before hurrying into the elevator. Even there, he remained very still, as if the security cameras in the elevator might be able to detect his relief.

He tried to pretend that nothing was happening, that he'd only made a social call to Warren's office near the top of Freedom Tower. It was impossible. As he dropped floor after floor, his spirits rose, and a reckless grin tickled at his lips until he couldn't hold it back anymore.

CHAPTER 6
CORRUPTED

The lights in Levi's cell blared down at him relentlessly, and every meal was the same. With no way to track the time, days blurred into one ugly stretch.

Levi had never gotten so much as a parking ticket before, and he'd only seen a few prison movies. Prison life was utterly foreign to him. He couldn't keep his mind occupied beyond doing sun salutations with trembling arms. Mostly he stayed curled up against the cold wall and gave in to the terrifying idea that he might be here forever—might feel like this forever.

The tender hum of magic in his soul was gone, replaced with emptiness and dread. It left him untethered from the world he'd never fully realized he'd had. At first, the sensation had been irritating, like an itch, but the longer he remained in the bands, the more the absence of his magic consumed him with grief and dull, relentless pain.

Though he slept fitfully, restless in the oppressive silence, he preferred it to being awake. That left him trapped in his own head, panicked by his inability to mark the passing hours. Fear left him nauseated, but skipping meals made him even sicker. Sometimes he wondered if he'd die like this, if the panic that raged through him would choke his breath away until he died on the concrete floor, saving the government the trouble of putting him to death.

That wasn't how he wanted to go. Not trapped and forgotten in a prison cell.

It was during one of his bouts of restless, unhappy wakefulness that the cell door opened all the way—the real door, not the tiny hatch that sometimes opened for a plastic food tray.

Levi wiped his eyes and crammed himself back into the far corner, beyond caring that they'd think he was a coward. Everyone who interacted with him here wanted to hurt him, and he wanted nothing to do with any of them.

"Levi Camden?" a short man asked warmly, smiling. He had a doughy face and graying comb-over, and wore wrinkled slacks and a white lab coat. "I'm Kurt Crane. I'm a scientist."

"Hi," Levi said automatically. His shoulder blades ached against the hard wall at his back.

"I need to work with you for a bit this morning, to evaluate your magic levels."

Levi inhaled sharply, his whole body going tense. This wasn't another interrogation. *Evaluate* was a fancy way to describe experimenting on him.

Crane winced sympathetically and showed his palms in what was probably supposed to be a calming gesture. "We classify mages based on several criteria for research purposes."

"We?" Levi barely croaked the sound out.

"Cole Industries."

Everything Crane said was terrifying, but it was more than anyone had said to Levi since his last interrogation. It was almost as if this man respected him as a human being. "Why are you telling me all this?" He cleared his throat against the hoarseness of disuse.

"I'm a man of science. I believe in being straightforward." Crane's words sounded rehearsed, but before Levi could make up his mind about that, Crane reached out. "Do you think you can walk with me?"

Levi wobbled to his feet. Struggling to walk on his own beat being dragged around or strapped to a gurney. He leaned against the wall for support. "I reek," he said, too tired and wary to be embarrassed by it.

"Yes, you do. I'll see about getting you cleaned up before we begin."

Crane offered his arm, and Levi took it out of necessity. He kept his head down as they walked and shuddered when Crane patted his hand soothingly.

It was slow going.

True to his word, Crane and two guards escorted Levi to a nearby shower room that reminded Levi of high school. Shower heads ran along one tiled wall, with no separators between them or privacy curtains of any kind. Levi didn't mind. Not when he had the chance to wash layers of sweat and fear away.

Crane let him go, and the guards helped him all the way onto the cold tiles and pulled off the thin uniform he'd been wearing since he woke up. One of them balled up the discarded clothing, and the other turned on the tap. It made a high-pitched squeaking sound before a cold spray hit him. Levi hissed involuntarily and crossed his arms at his middle.

The guard holding his clothes gestured at a liquid soap dispenser on the wall and stepped back. Both guards kept an indifferent eye on him, but Crane watched him keenly, studying him. Levi turned his face away and pretended he wasn't there.

The water quickly became hot, easing the tension in Levi's shoulders. He couldn't rinse away the metal around his wrists—or heal the raw sores he'd gotten from compulsively scratching at the bands—but he could blast away the grimy slickness of fear and panic.

Levi spent longer than necessary washing his hair. When he closed his eyes and let the water beat against his head and run down his face, he almost felt normal—as if he wasn't standing in an open shower being watched by guards who were probably more concerned that he'd find a way to off himself than that he'd escape.

"Aren't you guys afraid of me?" he asked, trying to get out of his own head while he hurriedly scrubbed the slippery soap at his armpits and crotch.

"There's nothing to be afraid of," Crane said. "Your magic is under lock and key, so to speak."

"If there's nothing to be afraid of, why do people treat bound mages like shit?"

"Fear of the unknown. Media hype. Religious objection. Resentfulness. You name it. Your kind has a lot working against you."

"You sound like a magic sympathizer," Levi said, rinsing the soap out of his hair and from the scraggly, pathetic excuse for a beard that had formed at his jaw.

"Oh, I sympathize with the plight of mages. At the same time, I recognize a need for regulation. Strict regulation, not the irresponsible so-called regulations they're moving toward in Europe."

Levi tuned Crane out as he began to ramble about the latest conflict in the Ukraine and how rebel groups were beginning to enlist mages. Crane blamed overly liberal magic laws in parts of Europe and Eastern Europe. It was the same shit Levi was used to hearing pundits drone about on the TV above the bar back at Ciccone's.

He'd spent hours folding plastic forks and knives into tissue-thin napkins at the beginning of his shifts, considering leaving the country for one of the regions overseas that openly welcomed mages. But it had been getting harder and harder to travel in and out of the country, and if he'd have left, he would have been alone, unable to speak the language and at risk of being deported back to the United States if he made a false move.

He'd never worked up the courage to run away. His magic had remained under the surface—a comforting backbeat to his pulse.

A steady comfort he couldn't feel anymore.

"I have a headache," he said, interrupting Crane's rant.

"Really? I'd love more details when I'm at my computer." Crane tossed him a thin white towel, then watched with unabashed curiosity as Levi dried himself—trying to keep as much covered as possible. "I'm sure you're aware that you've suffered several irregular side effects to the CALM bands."

"No. I don't know what's normal." Levi couldn't verbalize what had felt like being turned inside out and set on fire. In a way, it was comforting to know it wasn't a typical reaction. Many children wore CALM bands, and it had pained him to think of them being tormented on top of the emptiness of being bound.

"I assure you, your reaction was quite unusual. Fascinating, even."

Despite Crane's words, his friendly tone drew Levi in. He knew better, but the parts of his mind that made rational observations had gone fuzzy with exhaustion. It was so nice to be talked to like a normal person. "'Fascinating' isn't the word I'd use."

Crane laughed like a barking seal. "I'd imagine not."

One of the guards handed Levi another gray jumpsuit and a pair of white boxers. He shimmied into them quickly, noting with disappointment that the guards still didn't have any socks or shoes for him. He hated the vulnerability of being barefoot. It was probably a deliberate psychological tactic, but knowing that didn't make it suck any less.

They left the shower room and walked in silence down a series of halls. He didn't feel any stronger, but at least he wasn't filthy. Being clean made it a little more bearable to shuffle weakly, struggling to put one foot in front of the other. Wherever they were seemed to be underground. The air was cold and too clean-smelling, and he hadn't seen a window since he woke up for the first time after they put the bands on him.

Crane left the guards in the hallway and led him through an unmarked door. It closed behind Levi with a pressurized *whoosh*.

The hair on Levi's arms stood up. "So," he said, widening his stance to keep from toppling over. He crossed his arms.

The lab was like a surgery room on TV—all sterile whites and stainless steel and huge, bright lights hanging from the ceiling.

"I assume you attempted magic before your shielding feat." Crane sat down at a console computer and began flipping switches that looked like they coordinated a rocket launch.

"No. Never." The lie came as instinctively as the shield had. He wasn't stupid enough to talk about magic with Crane. Especially not here. This fever dream of a dentist's office on steroids.

"What a shock it must have been for you, creating that shield." Crane spun his chair to study Levi.

Levi nodded. "Yeah. It was shocking."

"What did it feel like, knowing you had unbelievable power coursing through your veins?"

"Uh." He shrugged awkwardly. "It's all a blur."

The first time he'd consciously played with his magic, he'd been hiking the Appalachian Trail between high school and his failed attempt at college. At the bottom of a deep gorge, feeling for the first time in his life that no one would ever know, he'd exhaled and let the magic flow out of him. The leaves had stirred and swirled at his feet, but that was all that had happened.

"Deep in thought?" Crane asked.

"No. Sort of. I was thinking that if I'd been able to use magic before, I would have stopped bugs from biting me on a hike."

Crane gave a slow, curling smile that unsettled something in Levi's gut. "That's a slippery slope. One day it's pest control, and the next it's tricking your landlord into thinking you've paid your rent each month."

"I would never do that." Would Crane mind if he sat down? His legs ached as if he'd been running for miles.

"Anyone would say that. No one thinks they'll be corrupted by power. It's a disease that spreads slowly. A cancer," Crane said, his voice hardening.

Levi took an involuntary step back and tripped on the edge of a low platform in the middle of the room. He fell on his ass and winced. What little cushion he'd had there was long gone.

"If magic corrupts so absolutely, why hasn't a mage ever risen to power?"

"Because humanitarians like Warren Cole have made it possible for us to nip problems in the bud."

"Humanitarians." Levi rolled his eyes. "Right."

Crane was on him in an instant, moving shockingly fast for a man who appeared soft and weak. He shoved him back onto the platform, and Levi's head struck the polished concrete, the biting pain startling a cry out of him.

"Never insult Warren Cole in my presence. Do you understand me?" Crane leaned over him and hissed in his face, his breath thick with the smell of stale coffee. "And don't mistake my kindness for foolishness, Camden. I recognize you for the menace you are."

Levi held very still. He wasn't firing on all cylinders himself, but he recognized madness when he saw it—and Crane's eyes held a dark gleam of fanaticism. That, more than the machines that circled them, frightened Levi to the core.

"Okay. I'm sorry. I've heard . . . good stuff about your boss. I saved his kid's life, you know."

"Warren Cole is childless."

"That other guy, then. The other Cole guy."

"Byron." Crane hauled him up. "He is Warren Cole's nephew. His brother's only son."

"Same difference."

"Byron Cole is an embarrassment. He works in *PR*. Don't think your unintentional heroics will buy you special treatment here."

"Okay." Levi's knees shook, and his head was pounding from striking the floor. "So . . . that whole straightforward thing."

"Yes?" Crane showed his teeth.

"What are you going to do to me?"

Crane touched the side of Levi's face with a clammy hand. "I'm going to make your magic sing."

CHAPTER 7
SUMMONS

Byron was pacing at the back door of Summons at 10 a.m. A cleaning crew arrived, pushing by him with suspicious glances, as if he were a criminal and not an extremely out-of-place professional. Across the alley, a few men carried crates of vegetables from an idling delivery truck into a restaurant kitchen. The engine hummed, and the delivery workers chatted and sang along with a Spanish song playing on the radio. Summons wouldn't open for hours, and if pressed, Byron wouldn't be able to come up with a good excuse to be there waiting.

He sucked down the last bit of an iced latte. *Maybe I should go back to work.* This was a terrible idea.

"You must be lost."

The voice startled Byron, and he turned to find Sam Johnson standing in front of him. He carried himself with wary tension, as if Byron posed a threat.

Byron could immediately see what Levi had seen in him. Sam was gorgeous, with kind eyes. Tired eyes.

"No," Byron said. "I did get lost on the way, but I'm here to see you."

"If you're a reporter, you can reach out to my publicist. Her contact information is on our Facebook page."

"You have a publicist?" How many people had already come to talk to him?

"I'm sorry—who are you?"

"Byron Cole. I'm here about—"

However kind Sam appeared, he wasted no time dragging Byron through the back door of the club and into a poorly lit hallway with its walls painted black.

"You're the son of a bitch who was there. I saw you on TV. You stood there and let them try to kill him." Sam pinned Byron to the wall and held him there—several inches off the floor.

"I know," Byron wheezed, and grappled with him, trying to gain enough purchase to breathe. "Please hear me out."

Sam let go but bracketed him against the wall with his arms. He was dressed in a plain black T-shirt and tight jeans, and he had his ears stretched with white spacers that gleamed against his dark skin. Anger brightened his eyes, but sadness still dominated his features and his exhausted voice. "You have one minute. The clock is ticking, Cole."

Now that he was here, face-to-face, Byron wasn't sure what to say. He'd hoped to gather information, but what had he expected? Even if Sam had been angry that his ex-boyfriend was a mage, he probably wasn't going to give up information about him. Not to Byron, anyway.

"I'm trying to help Levi." Byron rubbed his throat and hoped he didn't have bruises to explain away.

"Is this a trick?" Sam's hands ran up Byron's sides and chest. "Are you wearing a wire?"

"Hey!" Byron batted at Sam's hands ineffectually. "No. Listen to me. Actually, pretend I didn't even say that. It could get both of us in a great deal of trouble."

"'Both of us,' says the heir of Cole Industries."

"Fair. But listen." Byron took a deep breath. "There wasn't anything I could have done that morning. I hadn't even decided to do something then, anyway."

"You're making no sense, and you have ten more seconds."

"I'm trying to save his life!"

"You might be hot shit because of your last name, but you're not above federal law. You can't save his life. No one can save him." Sam's voice grew hoarse and sorrowful. "Levi's dead."

"You still love him," Byron said.

Sam stared at him for a long beat. "You're out of time," he said gruffly, ushering Byron toward the alley door by his collar as if holding a puppy by the scruff of its neck.

"I don't want to make any more trouble for you." Byron's phone buzzed in his jacket pocket, signaling a text message.

"I'm not in any trouble." Sam pushed Byron and pinned him against the door that led out into the alley. "I'm not the one locked up waiting for a death sentence."

"I'm sorry," Byron said helplessly.

"That's one way of putting it."

"Take this at least." Byron tried to hand Sam a business card with his cell number scrawled on the back.

Sam closed his fist around the card and tossed it to the polished concrete at their feet. "Why?"

"So you can call me if you change your mind," Byron said, glancing down at the sad little crumple of card stock.

"About what?" Sam scrubbed his palm at his short hair. "What do you think I can do?"

"Help me figure out what to do. I don't care if you knew about his magic or not."

Sam gave Byron a shake that rattled his teeth. "Careful."

"Ow. He needs all the help he can get."

"And you think you're going to make that happen?" Sam said with a low growl to his voice. "You, a college kid—"

"I graduated last—"

Sam opened the door and gave him a shove.

Someone laughed in the distance as Byron stumbled out into the alley and caught himself against the broad side of the vegetable truck. He turned back toward Summons, but the door was already closed. The lock clicked.

His phone buzzed again. He pulled it out of his pocket and frowned at Victoria's name on the screen.

Meet me at AMID. There's something you need to see. And below that: *It's about the favor you asked me.*

Byron's pulse quickened. He jogged toward the nearest intersection, his free hand raised to hail a cab. A vibration ran through his fingers, and he looked at his phone again.

B. It's bad.

CHAPTER 8
OCCULT 101

Byron revisited his childhood habit of nail-biting on the drive to AMID. Any other day, his stomach would have lurched at the sight of his bleeding cuticles, but he had more pressing matters at hand. Like Victoria's ominous text.

The trip would have been faster on the train, but he hadn't been down on the subway since meeting Levi. He sat in a cab in a sea of yellow and brake lights, listening to an obnoxiously loud screen on the back of the driver's seat play advertisements for Broadway musicals. As they idled at a red light, he caught sight of a teen boy and girl holding signs on the corner.

Set us free, one sign read in scrawling black marker. The other said, *Magic is love*. A man walked by and spit at the kids' feet.

Normally, Byron would have turned away, avoiding the unease that struck him when young people put themselves in harm's way for their beliefs. Now he watched them, his hands curling into fists. They were huddled close together, bumped by foot traffic and aggressive shoulders. He couldn't hear what others were saying to them over the blare of the screen in the cab, but he could guess.

The light turned, and he lost sight of the kids.

When he arrived at AMID, he dropped his pendant in a basket with his wallet and phone and waited for Oscar, the security guard, to scan him. He tried not to shift from foot to foot like an impatient child.

"Sorry, Mr. Cole." Oscar was about eighty years old, and whenever Byron wasn't freaking out, which was any other time, he brought him bagels from the shop around the corner. "We've been ordered to double-check everyone."

"Of course. Trust me, I don't want to end up anywhere near an explosion again," Byron said, his voice too loud and enthusiastic. Oscar gave him a strange look, but waved him through. One long escalator ride and two separate elevator rides later, Byron found himself in the front office of the underground AMID facility.

Victoria appeared at his elbow like something out of a fun house.

"Vic! Jesus, you startled me."

"Come to my office." Her tone, quiet and tense, did nothing for his nerves. She led him down a winding series of halls to her secluded office where a huge LED screen on the wall projected a live view of the street above. She stood at her desk for a long moment before opening her laptop.

"This is from the briefing I received from Warren's office in anticipation of Camden's arrival," she said. "Your mage? He's beyond classification. He short-circuited Kurt Crane's machinery."

"I don't understand. Is that bad?"

"Yes. But not as bad as this." She spun her laptop to face Byron and clicked a button that brought up a grainy video. "There's no sound. Thankfully."

Byron started to ask her what he was supposed to be seeing when Levi entered the frame, stumbling and falling onto the middle of a circular platform like an altar. A baggy gray jumpsuit hung on his painfully thin frame. "What am I looking at?"

"Crane's lab. I don't know if you've met the guy, but he's sociopathic. Six years ago he conned your uncle into giving him a handful of incarcerated mages to run tests on. All of them died in that lab during his trials. One of my best people worked for him for about four months, but after that she put in her notice. He's . . . The man is unhinged. I realize he's doing his job, but his methods go far beyond what's necessary to evaluate magic levels."

Byron cut her off with a sharp gesture and squinted at the screen. "What the hell?"

A figure out of the frame was holding a long baton against Levi's middle. Twice, Levi tried to scramble up and away from the baton, but each time whatever it was doing to him seemed to intensify. He convulsed violently, and Byron didn't need sound to tell that Levi was screaming. When the baton was finally drawn away from his body, he made no attempt to escape. He only curled up slowly, his body still trembling, and hid his face in his arms.

Levi's shoulders shook. Byron imagined his muffled sobs, and his jaw tightened with anger.

"That's Crane?" he asked. "Hurting him?"

"That's not how he'd put it. He'd say 'evaluating' him." Disgust thickened her voice. "That staff he prodded him with? It's not CALM tech. Crane developed this equipment for Cole Industries. It's made from pressurized ash."

"Ash?"

"It's a type of tree. A naturally occurring magic conduit."

Byron rubbed his forehead. "Trees are magic?"

"Your stupid earnest face is making me question my commitment to this nation's security, Byron. Yes. Mankind's understanding of the magic in this world goes far beyond what you learned in Occult 101."

"That's not a real class."

"Ash focuses magic, calls it like a magnet. It essentially forces a mage to expel magic against his or her will, but the bands stop the magic from manifesting outside of the body. The standard classification level is determined by how hard the bands had to work to keep the magic in. In layman's terms, obviously."

Layman's terms weren't really helping. "Why have I never heard of this?"

Victoria's lips pressed tightly before she answered. "You never asked."

Byron's chest went hollow. "And all bound mages are tested like this?"

"No, no. Only the prisoners."

"Why was he screaming? Is the ash hurting him?"

"It's not the ash itself. It's his magic interacting with the bands, and it's not normal. Discomfort, maybe. But not this. The bands aren't torture devices. There are hundreds of thousands of Americans wearing them today, and only a handful of them have ever reported pain, let alone what this man was clearly experiencing."

"So the bands only hurt him when he's trying to use his magic?"

Victoria sighed heavily. "That would be my theory, but CALM has never been studied with a mage of his caliber. Hold on. This is the part I want you to see, if you can handle it."

"I can handle it," Byron said immediately. Whatever he was about to watch had already happened, and he felt obligated to keep his eyes on the screen—to be there with Levi. To bear witness.

"I'm not watching it again." Victoria sank heavily into her chair and rubbed her temples. "What bothers me the most is that they sent this to me with no explanation or warning. As if I would endorse treatment like this. Even if the kid's a terrorist—"

"He's not."

"—this is well outside any international standards of ethical treatment. It's sick."

As she spoke, Crane entered the frame—more disheveled than he appeared in his official photo on the Cole Industries website. He touched Levi with a tenderness that sent an icy chill down Byron's back, and slowly unzipped Levi's jumpsuit. For one sickening moment, Byron thought he was witnessing the beginning of a horrific sexual assault. Then Byron saw the electrodes in Crane's hands—saw that he was sticking them one by one to Levi's pale ribs.

"The ash staff is considered rudimentary magic-focusing technology," Victoria said quietly, staring at her lap. "If you can even call it technology. These machines . . . Crane's creations . . . they're similar. I've heard rumors that they don't enhance magic, they—"

"This must be the Harvest Initiative," Byron realized aloud.

Victoria's voice dropped to a whisper. "I hope you're wrong."

Levi didn't struggle as Crane taped electrode after electrode onto his torso. Crane rolled him over, and Levi's head rocked to the side limply. Byron felt a flare of hope. If Levi was unconscious, maybe he wouldn't wake for whatever came next—whatever had shaken Victoria so much.

That hope was dashed within seconds when Levi stirred and pushed weakly at Crane's hands. His eyes widened when he saw the wires attached to his skin. He grabbed a handful of them and tugged.

Crane slapped him in the mouth.

Byron hissed. "Shit."

Levi stilled for a moment, before pushing up on his elbows and going after Crane with uncoordinated desperation. He managed to graze a punch along the side of Crane's head, but that only earned him another slap. Blood stained his lips.

Crane pressed a button that opened a metal restraint. It snapped down around Levi's wrist, and Levi twisted with an animal motion, trying to free himself.

"Don't panic," Byron said. "Don't—"

But it was too late. As Levi struggled against the closed restraint, he failed to pay attention to the rest, and Crane quickly fastened three more. Bound by his wrists and ankles as if crucified, Levi had no way to escape.

Crane wiped the blood away from Levi's mouth with his bare hand. Byron could only see his profile, but he appeared to be speaking steadily, as if lecturing Levi. He bent and kissed Levi's forehead and ruffled his hair, then exited the frame.

Left alone, Levi continued to shout and struggle wildly against the restraints. Byron wasn't schooled in lipreading, but he could read a few choice insults. It warmed something in him despite the cold dread in his throat. Even after being tortured, Levi had plenty of fight left in him.

Then everything changed.

"Oh my God," Byron covered his mouth.

Levi's entire body had bowed in a rigid contraction. He didn't convulse—he remained horrifically contorted. His eyes squeezed shut, and his mouth twisted in a closed grimace. Pain distorted his features.

"Is Crane electrocuting him?" Byron asked, fighting a thick wave of nausea.

"No." Victoria rested her mouth against her palm and stared at the floor.

Seconds went by too slowly. Byron watched at the clock on Victoria's computer. An entire minute passed.

When it stopped as quickly as it had started, blood was trickling steadily from Levi's nose. His eyes remained open but unseeing, rolled back unnaturally. The screen went fuzzy, and Byron realized it wasn't a bad connection but smoke filling the room.

"Jesus Christ, Victoria. Please don't tell me he's dead."

"The tape ends soon. Crane and Camden were evacuated safely. Camden's in a medically induced coma, but his condition is stable. He didn't inhale much smoke before they got the fire under control."

"Levi caused it? The fire?"

"Indirectly. Crane bit off more than he could chew and fried his machinery. He's lucky he didn't blow up his entire lab. The good news is, this buys us time."

"What's the bad news?"

"It's only buying us time before Crane can figure out how to do that all over again in the new facility. After this embarrassment, he isn't going to let fire or destruction get in his way."

"Why did he let you see this?"

"Warren's office sent it over with the medical records. I'm guessing Crane isn't thrilled, but they probably wanted to make sure I didn't over tax our equipment testing on the kid."

Byron closed the laptop and sat on the edge of Victoria's desk, his heart pounding wildly and his stomach lurching. "When Warren introduced me to the Harvest plans, I pictured something like giving blood, you know? Painless."

"That's certainly not the reality we're dealing with here."

They sat in silence for several minutes. Byron stared at his hands. He had a single callus on his right palm below the finger where he wore his father's wedding band, and no other marks. He wasn't a fighter. Instead, he used words to bend reality—did more damage that way. If he went back to work and did his job, no one would ever have to know what happened deep underground. No one would ever ask.

If he didn't expose the truth, no one would.

"I can't let them know I object to what I just saw," Victoria finally said. "Do you understand that? We'll lose our contract. I'll lose everything."

Byron straightened, hope flickering weakly. "But you do? Object."

"I'm a scientist. I've made it my life's work to develop ways to save people. That . . . that was torture. It was inhumane."

"So you're with me?"

Victoria gave him a look. "Don't say that like you have any idea what you're doing."

That was fair. "Well, I can't do nothing."

She sighed. "Yes, Byron. I'm *with you*. I wouldn't have shown you this if I wasn't."

"Thank you." Byron pretended not to see her eyes roll.

"He'll be transferred as soon as he's given medical clearance." Victoria massaged her temples. "It could be tomorrow, it could be a week. Until I can evaluate him, I have no way of knowing the real damage Crane caused."

"And we can go from there?"

"Yes. So get your shit together. Figure out what we're supposed to do with a half-dead and extremely pissed-off mage with powers beyond our comprehension, and don't let your uncle catch wind of any of this. What you saw on that screen—it's bigger than me and you. They'll stop at nothing to keep the specifics under wraps."

"I don't think my uncle would . . ." Byron couldn't finish. Cole Industries had invested fifty million dollars into building the Harvest Initiative facility. Their future success hinged on it.

"Exactly."

CHAPTER 9
FOR GOODNESS' SAKE

Byron loved pho more than any other food, but that night, he only pushed the noodles around with his chopsticks as he tried to pay attention to Eleanor's small talk. The memory of Levi's face contorted with pain haunted him.

"Victoria said you stopped by," Eleanor said in a vaguely prying tone that meant she knew more than she was letting on or wanted to know a lot more in a hurry. She also said it impatiently, as if she'd already said it once or twice. Which was probably the case.

"So it wasn't a fling with you two?" Byron asked.

"Nope. Stop deflecting."

"Seriously though, you're already . . . talking?"

"Girls move fast. You know that."

He gave a noncommittal grunt.

"Come on," she said. "What was it all about? She wouldn't tell me anything."

Byron stirred his pho listlessly, watching one lonely jalapeño slice bob and sink in the pungent broth. "It's classified."

"Technically, so is every single thing you say when you gossip about work."

"This is *really* classified, E. Not who's-sleeping-with-who classified."

She took another huge bite of her bánh mì sandwich and watched him with her big blue eyes. "It's about that mage you have a crush on, isn't it?" she asked with her mouth full.

"I don't have a crush on him."

"Right."

"What did Vic tell you?"

"Nothing at all." The teasing left Eleanor's tone, replaced with hurt. "Only that you came by. I thought you already finished the gala write-up on AMID."

"It wasn't that. She needed to show me a video."

Eleanor studied him. "It's bad, isn't it? Whatever's happening. You look terrible."

"Good thing it's Friday, then," he said weakly. He was running out of near-death-experience sympathy at work, and they'd expect him back full-time soon. But he hadn't slept soundly since the explosion, and the idea of working on press materials for the Harvest Initiative sickened him.

"Are you coming down with something? I've never seen you pick at pho."

"No."

"Byron."

"I want to tell you everything. You know I do." It was truer than he wanted to admit. He had no idea what he was doing, and she had an uncanny way of untangling his problems.

Eleanor laughed halfheartedly. "But then you'd have to kill me?"

Byron's breath hitched. "That's the thing." He set his chopsticks down and reached for the bottle of sake between their plates. It was their long-standing Friday ritual to order Vietnamese takeout and down enough sake to wash the tension of the work week away. But no amount of booze was going to erase the tension that had been building in him since Levi's arrest two weeks before.

"Wait, are you being serious?" Eleanor asked.

"Yeah. I think lives are at stake."

"Your life? Victoria's?" Her voice thinned. "Byron, you can't tell me things like this and expect me to pretend like I'm not curious. Like I'm not worried."

"Then don't ask me questions. We can catch up on the DVR and sleep in until brunch." The words sounded empty to Byron. He wiped his mouth.

Eleanor was staring at him. "This is a lot bigger than a bad-idea crush, isn't it?"

"I don't want to burden you with it."

"Look at it this way: We're roommates. If you've fucked up, they'll still come after me. I'm already screwed, so you might as well tell me."

Byron downed a tiny cup of sake and poured another. He emptied that one, and one more, before he finally felt the warm edge of a buzz. "Victoria showed me a video from the facility where they're holding Levi Camden. He was tortured—almost killed."

"I don't want to sound cruel, but how could that possibly surprise you? Everyone in the country currently hates that kid."

"It's not like a guard roughed him up. This was . . ." Byron tipped the cup of sake back. It always tasted better the farther he got down the bottle. "It's the thing my uncle's been working on for years."

"The thing you were supposed to announce at the press conference?"

"Yeah, except the announcement wasn't— I didn't— We weren't going to go into any details. I don't think they'll ever share details, not after what I saw. They didn't even tell Victoria what they were doing. Not exactly. Not this."

"Byron. Slow down. What did you see?"

"One of the Cole Industries scientists hooked Levi up to a machine that siphoned his magic." The hair stood up on Byron's arms.

"What do you mean, 'siphon'? Like sucked it out?"

Byron nodded. "I don't know how to explain it, E. It was like watching someone having their soul pulled from their body. He was screaming. He screamed until he didn't move anymore."

"Where does the magic go after they suck it out?"

"That's what the Harvest . . ." Byron tapped his cup against the table. It slipped out of his fingers and rolled across the table. "That's what it means. They're developing a way to convert magic into energy. Electricity."

"Byron." Eleanor set her sandwich down. "What are you saying?"

"All those mages in prison. They'll use machines on them." Byron tried to remember his speech—nauseated by how much it had left out, how much he hadn't known. "Magic is a clean, renewable source of energy."

"You're telling me that Cole Industries is building a human power plant?" Eleanor grabbed the sake and took a long swig directly from the bottle. "That's pretty fucked up."

"People will love it. Free, safe electricity when we're in the middle of an energy crisis? Rogue mages made to work for the tax dollars used to incarcerate them? Warren will be a hero."

"No. Not everyone's a right-wing nutjob. Incarceration is one thing, but torture?"

"It's not going to be advertised as torture." The spinning was Byron's job—making the Harvest Initiative sound like a chance for the United States to take the lead in the global race for renewable energy sources. Only now he knew better.

"Holy shit, Byron. Please don't tell me you're thinking about whistle-blowing."

"I don't know. None of the technology is ready yet. Levi set the damn lab on fire when they tried it on him. We have time."

"Time to what?"

Byron frowned at the cup.

"You don't have a plan at all?" Eleanor asked.

"I don't know why you and Vic expect me to have a plan."

"Victoria is in on this?" She sat back in her chair. "No way."

"Stop asking me questions when I'm drunk." Byron squinted at her.

"You wouldn't be drunk if you'd eaten your pho instead of glaring at it for half an hour."

"I'm not hungry."

"You're dragging Victoria into your quarter-life crisis," Eleanor said, her voice thin.

Scared.

Guilt washed through Byron. "She's the only one who can help. We're going to have Levi transferred to AMID. He won't be tortured there."

"She's okay with this?"

"She saw the tape."

A soft, private smile crossed Eleanor's face—softening the tension around her eyes. "And she cares about justice."

"Justice isn't what most people would call saving him. The majority of people who say they want justice want vengeance. They want Levi burned in Times Square. And a celebratory parade afterward."

"Byron, can you really blame them? You know my thoughts on bound mages, but this isn't a high school kid being denied college admissions. That man's been accused of terrorism. The last attack was the deadliest yet. People want blood. They want to see him suffer."

"I know that's what they want." Byron shuddered. "And he's suffering, trust me."

"He's not the first rogue mage to get caught, and he won't be the last to be executed. Why do you care so much this time?"

"Don't tell me I have a crush again, E. That makes me sound like a teenager. This isn't funny."

"Fine." She brushed her foot against his under the table the way she had when they were kids and Warren had been lecturing Byron on his failings over Sunday dinner. "But help me understand. Is it because he saved your life?"

"I think that's part of it. I don't know. I touched him."

Her eyebrow quirked.

"Only for a second," Byron said impatiently. "But he's real. He's a person. I would bet my life on the fact that he's not evil."

"I think that's exactly what you're doing. Except worse, really. There's no way you can win this bet, because even if you're right and he's a good person getting the short end of the stick, your life is still on the line. You know that ethics paper I asked my students to write?"

"Yeah." Byron frowned, struggling to follow the rapid pace of her thoughts when his tired, sake-soaked mind wanted to wallow in hopelessness.

"A few kids complained to their parents, and they escalated it to the administration. I ended up on paid leave for three days."

"What?" How obsessed had he been that he hadn't even noticed his roommate not getting up for work at 5 a.m.? "Why didn't you tell me?"

"Because you've been distant and weird since the attack!"

"I'm sorry." Byron grabbed his sake cup and turned it over. It clinked softly against the table.

"Don't be. It makes sense now. You're obviously wrestling with serious shit. But if a few snobby parents almost got me fired for asking kids to write about bound-mage rights, think about how people would react if they knew you were sympathizing with a rogue mage tied to a horrific attack."

Byron squinted, trying to focus. "Why don't they make demands?"

"The parents?"

He shook his head. Something hovered at the edge of his awareness like a budding headache. "The terrorists. They make their ideology clear—freedom for all mages. But they don't make demands. It's weird."

"They're extremists, not politicians."

There was more; there had to be more. But Byron had a solid buzz on, and it wasn't doing him any favors. "Levi's not a murderer," he said morosely. Traitorous warmth tickled below his ribs every time he spoke Levi's name.

"You keep saying that."

But she was right. People could die because of this regardless of Levi's innocence. "I don't want to get Victoria killed."

"I'd love it if neither of you got killed. Think about it. Maybe there's another way you can help. Plant seeds of doubt. You're a writer—you could start a secret blog, write an editorial in the paper, I don't know."

"That won't save Levi."

"Is that what you think you can do?"

"Yes. No. I don't know."

"I love you, Byron. You're my brother."

"There's a 'but' coming, isn't there?"

Eleanor smiled ruefully. "Yes."

"Lay it on me."

"But you can't change decades of momentum because you have a gut feeling about one mage. He used magic flagrantly, on the same day a shitload of people died in an explosion no one's been able to pin on anyone else. Your uncle obviously has him earmarked for awful experiments—"

"Which might be my fault."

"—and you don't just work for Cole Industries, you're— I mean come on, Byron. You're not exactly flying under the radar."

"That's the only reason this might work!"

"You mean the plan you don't have?"

"Any of it," Byron said, feverishly. He sat up straight and nearly overturned his bowl of pho as he waved his hands around. "All of it.

No one's going to question what I'm doing. Who would suspect me of sympathizing with mages?"

"You may have half a point there." Eleanor moved the pho away from him. "I'm pretty sure everyone who knows you thinks you're fucked up from the explosion."

That sounded like an insult, but Byron was too excited to care. "Maybe it'll work."

"Maybe you can stall for a while by squirreling him away at Victoria's place, but it's not like they're going to let him stay over there forever. You can't actually save him, Byron. Do you really think Warren would let you get away with that?"

"Levi could help us . . ."

"Byron."

"If we got the bands off him."

Eleanor went still. "Byron, you're scaring me. What are you talking about? Letting him escape. *Helping* him escape?"

"Well, I told you not to ask me about it."

Her eyes brightened with unshed, angry tears. "We've never kept secrets from each other."

"I've never had a secret this big."

"That's for fucking sure." She reached for the bottle, finished it quickly, and set it down with a sigh. "You're right, though. You shouldn't tell me much more. I'm a teacher, you know? I'm not trained at lying."

"The way I am?" No wonder she'd gone into teaching. At least she could make a difference on a small scale. All Byron's future held was feeding the culture of fear that had led to the dehumanization of people born with magic.

"That's not what I meant," Eleanor said softly. She got out of her chair and came to Byron. He wrapped his arms around her middle and pressed his face against her. She wasn't skinny, and she was incredibly strong, and the combination made for satisfying embraces. The ache in his chest released a little when she held on to him and rubbed his back. "This is stupid and crazy," she said. "But I'm proud of you for taking a stand."

"Even if it doesn't work?"

She shuddered but didn't let go of him. "I don't want to think about that. Revolutions have to start somewhere, I guess."

When she said it like that, it didn't sound like trying to save one mage with kind eyes from torment and eventually death. It sounded like changing the whole damn world.

"Ah, fuck."

"Yeah," Eleanor said. "Pretty much."

CHAPTER 10
FAR AWAY

Sam knew exactly where Levi liked to have his stomach touched, and he didn't settle for touching it—he licked and nuzzled there until Levi squirmed halfway off the mattress on Sam's floor.

"Stop," Levi whined. "I can't come again. You're confusing my dick, and I hate you."

"You love me." Sam brushed his lips back and forth through Levi's happy trail before kissing the thoroughly-spent length of his dick. When Sam pushed up onto his arms, his eyes were warm, and Levi's heart ached because he did love Sam, but not the way Sam loved him.

So Levi said nothing.

Hurt flashed across Sam's face before he recovered with a crooked grin. "I wish you'd let me help you, at least."

Levi flipped over and buried his face in the pillow that smelled sweet and spicy from Sam's lotion. "Not that again." He wiggled his butt.

"Nice try." Sam kissed Levi's lower back and slapped his ass. He flopped down next to him in the bed, running his fingers along Levi's shoulder blade. "I'm not that easy to distract."

"You really are, most of the time."

"I'm still on topic, see? I'm very serious. There are people who can help you."

"Why are you obsessed? You don't have a dog in this fight."

Sam poked him in the ribs. "Since when?"

"You know what I mean." He batted Sam's hand away. "Why are you so obsessed with magic?"

"I don't know. Maybe I have sympathy for marginalized populations. Maybe I'm simply a decent human being."

"Those seem to be in shortage these days."

Sam draped a heavy arm across his back. Quiet music played from Levi's phone: a bluegrass melody that Sam hated. The mournful strings reminded Levi of how his magic—unused, unsatisfied—sang a solemn tune in his blood.

"People are more decent than they give themselves credit for," Sam said.

"I am too well fucked to make sense of that statement."

"If people gave mage rights thought—real thought, not cable-news thought—they'd see that you're all being wronged. Things will change in time. I believe that."

"In our lifetime?"

"Maybe not. But I have friends, Levi. They know things that would help keep you safe. Ways to conceal magic, ways to let you practice right under their noses. If you'd let me introduce you to them, you'd see."

"This was a lot more fun when we were banging." Levi rolled over to face Sam and kissed him once, savoring the taste, all sex-warm and soft.

Sam kissed him back, and then watched him and stroked his arm. "I worry about you, love."

"I know."

"Then why won't you let me help you?"

"Because I've been fine my whole life. I'm fine like I am, being a normal person. Your friends will get caught someday, and when they do, it'll be their asses on the line. My ass," Levi said with a smirk, wiggling it again, "will be safe and sound."

"You're mixing a lot of metaphors."

"Oh, but am I?"

They both laughed as Sam pounced on him, rolling his heavy body down against Levi. He was hard again, and Levi wanted him again, wanted the quiet simplicity of being fucked until he almost couldn't hear his magic pleading with him, begging to be set free.

Levi struggled, trying to get free. Something wrapped around his wrists. His eyes were gummy and his head hurt and he wanted to be awake, but it was so hard.

"Enough of that," a man said.

The voice wasn't familiar. Something touched Levi's face, and he flinched. Then a wet cloth moistened his eyes, and he could finally see. He was in a hospital room, and a man in mirrored glasses was standing at the foot of his bed, holding a white towel away from his body like it disgusted him.

"Are you finished with that whining?"

Levi tensed and gave a jerky nod, recognizing the man who stood before him. Warren Cole. He was the father of magic-neutralization technology. He'd made it easy for every mage on the planet to be controlled like a caged animal.

Warren smiled. "Was that a yes?"

"Yes," Levi whispered.

"You're being transferred to a facility I sponsor. They test antimagic weaponry. I trust you'll cooperate."

Levi swallowed against a sour taste, his throat raw and painful. Testing. Weapons. Hurting. When he blinked, tears ran down his face. "Yes."

"You're very important to me, Mr. Camden." Warren strolled to the head of the bed and idly tapped Levi's IV bag. "I trust you'll take care of yourself."

He didn't sound like that psycho Crane. But his quiet voice was even more frightening. Levi fought back jerky breaths and closed his eyes like a stupid little kid wishing the shadows in his bedroom away.

"Your presence there will help others. Perhaps you'll find that comforting." He flicked his hand with a dismissive wave. "My programs create jobs and security. Soon they'll have even greater benefits for the American people."

Levi swallowed against a wave of nausea. The silence was heavy with expectation, but he didn't know what Warren wanted from that—what he was supposed to say.

Fuck you. "Okay."

A soft chuckle from Warren made the hair on Levi's arms prickle up. "If you try to harm yourself, you'll be stopped. And you'll be punished." The word lingered, a promise.

Restrained and sick and hurting, Levi couldn't imagine further punishment. Didn't want to. His heart thundered in his ears. He could barely hear his voice over the rush. "I won't do anything."

"Good. I don't relish torture for the sake of torture. It's a waste of energy, and we live in a world where energy is precious, do we not?" He didn't wait for Levi to respond. "That being said, should the need arise, have no doubt you'll be disciplined by those with a keen interest in it."

Levi squeezed his eyes closed tighter against rising panic, fighting the prickle of more tears. He'd done nothing to deserve this. Maybe he should have.

He could have.

As if reading his thoughts, Warren let out a soft *tsk* that drove away the last of the anger left in Levi, replacing it with cold, dizzying fear.

When he opened his eyes, Warren was gone. Only fear-turned-panic remained, graying the edges of Levi's vision. Stealing his breath. The bed rocked back and forth like a little boat at sea, and the room went black.

CHAPTER 11
UNSTABLE

Modern furniture and hardwood floors warmed the private AMID lobby. But every piece was carefully bolted down, and the small space held nothing that could be thrown or used as a weapon. Every design touch had been orchestrated for security. Though the general public had not been made aware of it, the lab was one of the United States' premiere development facilities for antimagic weaponry.

An armed security guard pushed Levi's wheelchair. Levi wore hospital scrubs, and his curls had gone frizzy with bedhead. Livid circles under his eyes stood out like bruises. Warren Cole walked behind him, his cane clicking at the guard's heels.

Byron's hands went sweaty as he watched through a one-way mirror. Victoria signed papers on a Cole Industries tablet with her fingerprint and handed it back to the guard. It took Byron a moment to remember to hit the button to turn the sound on through the observation mirror.

"I'm sure you understand that my primary concern is my nephew's safety," Warren was saying.

"Absolutely, sir. If you'd rather he didn't observe our testing, I'd understand. We rarely allow observers, but given he's an employee and family . . ."

Warren smiled. "I appreciate you indulging him. Perhaps he'll write up an interesting report for our investors after this. And if not, Byron may find a sense of closure. I'm told he was rather rattled by the whole unpleasant incident."

"Of course."

Warren's hand clasped down on Levi's shoulder, and Levi flinched and ducked his head. "You've been sent the medical report. It's my understanding that our staff has kept Mr. Camden heavily sedated. You'll be doing the same?"

"Within reason." Victoria offered a tight smile. "Our methods do require a subject be conscious."

Warren gave a low chuckle. "Well, I'll leave you to that unpleasantness, then."

Byron turned his attention to Levi. His empty gaze was fixed between his lap and the floor. Nylon straps fastened his slender wrists to the arms of the wheelchair. His feet were bare and his ankles were strapped to the chair as well. He didn't struggle against the restraints—didn't move at all beyond shivering.

From where Byron stood, several feet away, he could make out bruises on the insides of Levi's elbows. Levi looked nothing like the bright-eyed boy he'd met on the subway. Even his shoulders, broad despite his narrow frame, hunched inward like crumpled paper.

The mirrored window between them felt like miles. A visceral need to touch Levi and check him over dizzied Byron. He didn't know the first thing about medicine, but he needed to know that Levi was still solid and breathing—that he'd get better.

"I'll reach out with any questions or issues," Victoria was saying.

"Ah yes, that reminds me. Kurt Crane will be coming by Wednesday afternoon at three o'clock to check on Mr. Camden's vitals and so forth. I'm sure you won't mind showing him around."

"I'd be honored to." Victoria's smiled carried through her voice. She had an uncanny ability to fake sincerity.

"Perfect." Warren offered his hand, and she shook it firmly.

She placed her palm on the biometric panel at the door and held it open for Warren and the guard. When the door shut behind them, she quickly crouched in front of Levi's wheelchair and ducked into his line of sight.

"Levi. I'm going to take you somewhere safe for you to rest."

Levi didn't move, and Victoria glanced at the mirror helplessly. Despite knowing she couldn't see him, Byron shrugged. What had they expected? Not a cheerful greeting. Levi had been conscious for several days, but his medical report stated he'd only responded minimally to even the most basic commands and questions.

Victoria wheeled Levi out of the room. Byron paced in the observation room, anxious, but not anxious enough to go after them. He'd talked this over with Victoria, and neither of them had been able to decide whether it would be a good idea for him to approach Levi—who would likely associate Byron with his tormentors.

Since Victoria would be introducing Levi to his temporary quarters, Byron simply waited. His phone didn't get reception down here, but he had a strong wi-fi signal, so he checked the headlines on his news feed, too stressed to click through and read anything.

Department of Occult Supervision Names Levi Camden as Prime Suspect

Dry Cleaner Gives Exclusive Interview About Terror Suspect Levi Camden

Expert on Occult Culture Chimes in on Levi Camden's Concealed Magic

10 Signs Your Neighbors Might Be Rogue Mages

Modern Dating: Why You Should Ask About CALM Status Before You Meet

6 Anti-Glamour Devices Worth Splurging On

The Top 20 Rogue Mages You Should Know About

NYC Bombings Beg the Question: What Do They Want From Us?

Did Levi Camden Act Alone?

He sighed and tucked his phone into his pocket. With the media gleefully frothing over Levi's capture, how could Byron ever expect to sway the public's feelings on magic?

That was getting ahead of himself. For now, he had exactly one person to win over. Though it had only been two and a half weeks, it felt like years since Byron had last been in the same place as Levi—years since he'd met him.

Byron grimaced. It hadn't been much of a meeting.

Levi knew nothing about him. He probably thought Byron was a spoiled brat who reveled in the persecution of mages. When Byron closed his eyes, he could picture the betrayal on Levi's face when he'd realized who Byron was—that he'd inadvertently saved the heir to the Cole Industries empire.

It was madness to think Levi would want to help him, but if they didn't work together, he had no chance of saving Levi from a lifetime—however brief—of torture.

Victoria rushed into the room, startling him. She crossed her arms briefly, and then put her hands in her pockets with uncharacteristic restlessness. "He became agitated when I moved him from the chair to his bed." Her gaze shifted to the floor. "I had to restrain him—I'm sorry. I can't give him freedom in that room until his behavior stabilizes."

"Did he fight you?"

"Not exactly." Victoria frowned and her hands fluttered around her bun. "I wish he had. He was clearly afraid."

"You have that effect on people," Byron said weakly.

"I gave him lorazepam, and that should help significantly. He'll likely sleep for a few hours."

"Thank you." Byron drew her into an abrupt hug. It wasn't something they did often—or ever, really—but she looked like she needed it.

"He's so frightened," she said softly, as her small arms snaked around his back and held on with surprising fierceness. "He has no idea how much power there is inside of him. We should be afraid of him, not the other way around."

"Not *afraid*. Just realistic. Prepared."

"I hope you are, Byron. And I hope you don't try anything rash with this boy. If your instincts are true, he had no idea what he was doing when he saved you all." She pulled away and smoothed a few stray hairs back into her bun. "In distress, he could easily lash out with violence and destruction without intending to."

"It's not like I'm going to go in there and tear his bands off."

Victoria gave him a knowing look. "You're thinking about it," she said. "Don't pretend you're not."

"Of course I am. Eventually. Not today."

Victoria led him out of the observation room and down a brightly lit hallway. They walked by a series of smaller offices and storage rooms into the cavernous weapons-testing room that made up the bulk of AMID's facilities.

"Maybe not this week," she said. "Maybe not ever. Not until you're sure he isn't going to destroy all of us with a flick of his finger. Got it?"

"That's the thing." Byron's gaze drifted toward the high ceiling. It reminded him of an airplane hangar or a mechanic's garage. "We'll never know for sure. If we set him free, it'll be a leap of faith."

"You've already put thought into this." Victoria's well-manicured brow knit into a frown.

Byron rubbed a twitching muscle in his neck. "I haven't had much to do besides think about all the ways this could go horribly wrong, while trying to figure out maybe one single way this could go right."

"I don't think this can go right."

Byron leaned against a polished metal workbench. "Did you know Warren was going to come here?"

"No. Security usually calls up to tell me." She exhaled heavily. "Is it like him to make a house call like that?"

"No," Byron said. "I mean, I've never heard of him interacting directly with a prisoner, that's for sure." He didn't socialize with his uncle, but he saw him enough professionally to have a general sense of how Warren did business.

"If his behavior was out of the ordinary, we should be concerned," Victoria said.

"Are you regretting bringing Levi here?"

"No." She rubbed her arms. "Not after seeing him. I feel protective of him."

"That must be weird," Byron said, smiling a little. Victoria's life's work consisted of finding ways to repel mages threatening United States troops—not nurturing rogue mages.

She offered him a thin smile in return. "Yes, Byron, I find it 'weird.' Honestly, sometimes I wonder how you write for a living."

"Short bursts of genius, usually under terrifying deadlines."

"Let's hope you find another burst of genius when it counts." Victoria stifled a tiny yawn. "All right. I've been up since 2 a.m. My people should be arriving for work in about an hour. I need to get caffeinated and keep my employees from figuring out that Levi got transferred over here. I'm the only one with access to the live security feeds. Nothing's recording now, and I need to reprogram them to loop the entirety of last week."

Admiration warmed Byron's chest. She adapted so easily, thought about the dangers that didn't occur to him. A prickle of worry chased the warmth away as he considered the others—the colleagues she couldn't control. The ones who could never know why Levi was really here. "Do you think someone will try to hurt him like Crane did?"

"No. My people are good people. If I have to tell anyone about our guest, they'll only know the official story—that he's here to help us test prototypes. But it's best kept under wraps."

"And we don't actually want to zap Levi with antimagic weapons."

"Exactly," Victoria said. "Being the driven, brilliant engineers they are, my people would be disappointed if they couldn't try out our more promising prototypes on him. But it's fine. I'll work it out. Trust me, I'm not keen on 'zapping' that young man."

"Would anyone be sympathetic to our—"

"Please don't say 'cause.'"

"You know what I mean."

"No." Victoria picked up a wrench and waved it around like she planned on thumping Byron in the crotch with it. "We're not recruiting any law-abiding, hard-working engineers for your crusade."

"Even if they'd be down for it?"

"Even if," she hissed, the wrench hovering.

Byron sobered. "We can't do this on our own."

"Get your own people. You can't have mine. I recruited these kids from the best occult-engineering programs in the world. They weren't easy to find."

"It's not like magic sympathizers are going to be easy to find either." Byron straightened with a sigh.

"Why don't you see if there's someone in Levi's family?"

"That doesn't seem safe." He snatched the wrench away from her and set it down. "His family will be under surveillance."

"Half-assed surveillance." Victoria glanced at the clock on the wall.

"What makes you say that?"

"We have a contract with the FBI. They came to pick up tech a few days ago, and I asked how the Camden investigation was going."

"And people just tell you things you're not supposed to know?"

"Sometimes." Victoria shot him a winning smile, instantly flirtatious. "They said Cole Industries called them off."

"Why?" That didn't sound right.

"I don't know. It was chitchat, not an interrogation. But you're safer than you think if you sniff around his people. Find someone who cares about him," she said, studying him in a way that clearly communicated *someone must care about him as much as you do.*

Byron thought about Sam—his bright smile and the way he held Levi in photos. He could go back to Summons. Find out how closely Sam was tied to the mage-rights community. "Maybe I'll check into that."

"Are you going to stick around?"

Byron shook his head. "I need to go in to work."

"On a Saturday?"

"If I don't catch up I'm going to get fired." He was only slightly joking. "I'll be here tonight after dinner."

"Tell Eleanor I said hi," Victoria said, her voice soft with not-quite-guarded fondness. It took Byron aback. Despite all that they were taking on—the life or death circumstances—she clearly had his best friend on her mind.

It must be serious.

"I will."

Victoria escorted him to the public area of the building. There, they parted wordlessly and he hurried up the escalators, his heart only then racing.

He hoped Levi would sleep all day and find a small measure of peace.

The city air enveloped Byron as he reached street level. It was a few minutes before sunrise, and the night was heavy and warm. Unlike down in the antiseptic depths of AMID, it smelled like gasoline and street meat and the dusty-vibrant-acrid scent of city life in all its chaos.

He had time to spare, so he walked to work, lost in thought. Was Levi asleep, his arms and legs strapped to the bed? And Sam—was he somewhere in Brooklyn, worrying? Byron thought of Levi's mother, but decided once more against contacting her. He wasn't going to drag her into a situation that could get her killed.

For now, he'd have to focus on Levi—on drawing him out and helping him heal. If he wasn't already beyond healing.

As Byron hurried across the street with a growing crowd of morning commuters, a wave of guilt hit him. At work, he'd spend the day polishing Cole Industries' pristine public image. He wasn't sure if he felt guiltier for betraying his only living relative, or for betraying the tormented mage he'd left underground.

CHAPTER 12
REFLECTION

Levi woke to soft, anguished crying. He struggled in a heavy fog, trying to figure out who was making the awful sounds. Every blink was a scratch of sandpaper against his eyes, and his mouth tasted like the morning after a bender.

"You're all right," someone said.

Levi didn't believe him, because he was stuck and someone was crying, and his head hurt—and a deep sense of panic grabbed him before he could remember why he was frightened.

"Please. Try to hold still. You're all right."

With a startled hiccup, Levi realized he was the one crying. Tears wet his face and blurred his vision, and when he tried to wipe them away, his arms were trapped, wrapped snugly in something soft that wouldn't let him move at all.

He tried to stop crying. The pathetic sniffles that followed weren't much better than the low sobs he'd been making before.

"Will you help me wipe my face?" he asked tightly, hoping the person was at least semi-invested in his dignity.

A warm, soft cloth dabbed at his face, gently at first, before getting the job done. The next time he blinked, his eyelashes didn't stick together in a messy blur. He could see.

"Are you fucking kidding me?" he immediately said.

Byron Cole stared back at him, having the decency to appear sheepish where he sat in a plastic chair. "Sorry," he said, clutching a towel like a lifeline. "I guess I'm the last person you want to see."

"The last person I want to see—" Levi cut himself off, nervously scanning the room to make sure it was empty before he went on "—doesn't appear to be here."

The absence of Kurt Crane in the room didn't soothe Levi's fraying composure. It hurt to use his voice, he was in an unfamiliar bed, and his arms were tied down with wide, soft restraints. He didn't know where he was, or how long he'd been here, or how he'd gotten here. The air was too thin.

"Don't. I can go get Victoria. She's— This is her place. She has a medical background. She can help you or get you something to sedate you. Please don't panic."

"Sedate me?" Levi shouted. It felt good to get loud, even though his voice cut like razor blades. Shouting made it easier to breathe. "That's not what I want. Have you maybe considered that this is a normal fucking response to the shit you're doing to me? God!"

"Okay." Byron worked at the towel. His eyes darted to the door. He didn't look the way he had on the subway that morning—like a polished Boy Scout or every other financial bro heading downtown.

Now his hair wasn't stiff with gel. It fell into his eyes, coal black and messy—as if he'd been running his hands through it over and over.

"Why are you here?" Levi yanked his arms against the restraints because it felt good. Byron jumped a little when they rattled, and that felt even better.

"That's complicated." Byron fidgeted with the incredibly wrinkled dress shirt rolled up to his elbows. He was younger than Levi remembered.

"Yeah?"

"I didn't think you'd wake up." He hesitated. "I came in here because you were shouting in your sleep, and Victoria's in a board meeting for another hour."

"I don't know who that is, and I don't know why you're here, and I don't know why I'm tied up." Panic swelled again. The bed was more comfortable than the last, but his magic was still hiding like a tail tucked between his legs. He was still hollow and sore. And weak. Would the rest of his life be like this?

"I know," Byron said.

"You don't know anything!" Levi's voice broke, to his frustration. He wanted to be angry, to scare this yuppie asshole, but he was frightened, and the blanks in his memory had begun to fill with memories of pain and Kurt Crane's sweaty face close to his. For all he knew he was being cleaned up for another round with that shithead awful scientist, and he wouldn't be able to take it. He would rather die before he let that man assault the magic at the very core of his soul again.

"You're right," Byron said quietly.

Something snapped in Levi—not a break as much as a release. He couldn't recall the last time someone had agreed with him, and he stopped fighting the restraints and let the exhaustion take hold. "Go on," he mumbled.

"I don't know what you're feeling." Byron spoke with painful sincerity, like a rookie school guidance counselor. "I want to let you out of bed, but I have to wait for Victoria. I know—I *assume*—you're confused. And probably scared."

"How'd you guess?" Levi struggled to muster a glare.

"I don't think you'll believe me if I tell you that I want to help you."

"Crane would have said the same thing." Numbness blanketed Levi, dulling the edge of fear.

"I know what he did." Byron's fingers clenched into fists around the towel in his hands, and the hesitance left his voice. "I object to it. Strongly."

"Yeah, me too," Levi deadpanned. He didn't have a reason to trust anything Byron was saying, but if he was full of shit, he was a great actor. "You're not an actor, are you?" It would explain the alarmingly good looks.

"What?" When Byron frowned, a small wrinkle formed directly between his thick eyebrows. "No. I work in PR."

"Close to the same thing." It was so strange, this tired detachment. Like floating on the surface of a pool of terror and pain. "Wait. Am I high?"

"Super high." Byron's frown deepened. "You've been agitated and having a lot of nightmares. Victoria didn't think you'd be awake considering the dose you're on."

"I am awake." Levi sighed, one of those full-body shudder-sighs that came after a long bout of crying. "And I have to pee, dude."

"Will you fight me if I get you out of those restraints?"

"Do you say that to all the girls?"

Byron's mouth quirked. "Are you going to fight me?"

"You're like . . . what? Six foot?"

"A little taller than that."

"I'm not going to fight you unless you don't let me pee. I'd also really love a toothbrush."

A smile flashed across Byron's face, before seriousness shadowed his features again. He stood and leaned over the bed and unbuckled one restraint, then the other. It happened so quickly, and without any warning, that Levi didn't immediately realize he could move.

He stared at his wrists and his skinny, bruised arms. His limbs ached with disuse, and the metal bands that still circled his wrists weighed him down. Despite his newfound freedom, despair welled up in his chest again.

Hugging his arms across his middle, Levi reconsidered attempting to walk to a bathroom. He was exposed in his sweat-damp scrubs and bare feet, with Byron standing there probably trying to figure out how to spin all of this into heroics for the newspapers in Cole Industries' pockets.

"Hey. You okay?" Byron's voice was surprisingly soft.

Levi lifted his gaze. "No."

Byron offered his hand, the gesture familiar in a way Levi couldn't place. He took a deep breath to shove back a knot of panic when he took Byron's hand. Byron's fingers were cold.

Maybe Levi would have fought, another time. He wanted to. But he was also so tired and freaked out and the call of nature was pretty compelling, all things considered. Fortunately, a tiny bathroom was only a few steps away. Byron helped him walk, patient with his pathetically slow pace, and stood in the doorway, facing the jamb, as Levi relieved himself. The sink had a soap dispenser built into it. He washed his hands and splashed his face, thankful to see nothing but white tiles. If his reflection showed even a fraction of how bad he felt, he never wanted to see it.

"Thank you," Byron said, as he helped Levi out of the bathroom.

Close up, Levi saw the circles under his eyes. Fine lines of exhaustion. "For?"

"Not fighting me."

"I'm not strong enough to fight you right now. That doesn't mean I wouldn't."

"Good."

Levi turned to Byron, puzzled, as Byron helped him lift his shaking legs back into the bed. Someone had taken measures to make him comfortable. The sheets weren't the thin, scratchy sheets from a typical hospital, and unlike the cell they'd been holding him in before, the room had a vaguely welcoming vibe, with buttery-yellow paint on the walls. The cabinets and counter along the wall reminded Levi of the fixtures at his doctor's office. And the bed itself was nicer than any hospital bed he'd ever seen. He settled against the soft mattress as if sinking into an embrace.

Byron returned to his chair beside the bed. "Thank you for saving my life too," he said gruffly.

"I didn't mean to do that."

"I know. I mean, you don't have to say that here, to me. But I believe you."

"Then why are you thanking me?"

"I don't know a lot about magic, but from what I understand, magic has to have intention behind it to work. It can't be half-assed."

Levi crossed his arms. "I don't know as much about magic as you do."

"All I know is part of you didn't want any of us to die, and because of that, we lived. I owe you more gratitude for that than I could possibly express."

"Okay," Levi said, still confused, but inexplicably warmed. He rolled onto his side tenderly, expecting Byron to stop him and get him back into the restraints. When Byron didn't reach for them, he began to relax, lulled by the softness of the bed and the freedom to make himself comfortable.

After a minute, Byron approached the bed so hesitantly that Levi didn't shy away. He held very still as Byron adjusted the blankets around him, tucking them behind his back and up to his chin.

"You're safe here right now." Byron lingered, smoothing the sheets all around Levi but carefully avoiding touching him at all.

And despite himself, Levi believed him.

CHAPTER 13
PRISONERS

Byron didn't move at all for several minutes, worried that the smallest sound would wake Levi. It wasn't that he didn't want to talk to him, but he hadn't expected talking to happen so quickly. The doors opened and Victoria walked in—he hushed her. She pursed her lips until he ducked his head, apologetic. This was her facility. She knew what she was doing.

"I watched the feed." Victoria kept her voice low. "He was friendlier than I imagined he'd be."

"He was out of it." Byron wasn't going to fool himself. After weeks of facing nothing but unkindness at best and torture at worst, of course Levi would respond positively to being treated like a human being. A brief conversation under the influence of strong sedatives didn't mean they were suddenly allies, or even off on the right foot.

Victoria handed him a sandwich. "I'd still call it a win."

"Thanks." Stale pimento and cheese, but Byron was starving and devoured it while Victoria opened a cabinet and brought out the vitals kit. Levi didn't stir when she checked his blood pressure and oxygen counts and took his temperature with a temporal scanner.

"All things considered, he's in decent shape," she said, winding the cords up neatly. "At least physically. Emotionally, there's a lot more at play. And considering how lucid he was, I'm a little concerned his magic burned off the meds. That will make him harder to treat."

"That can happen? Even with the bands on?"

"It's been theorized, but no one's ever been able to test it on a mage of his caliber. CALM suppresses magic, but it doesn't remove it. I've read compelling research indicating that individuals with a higher-than-average magic saturation reject foreign substances in the body."

Byron was struggling to follow along. "But he fell asleep when you sedated him."

Victoria put the kit away and leaned against the cabinets, her arms crossed, gaze thoughtful and calm. It calmed Byron in turn. As long as she wasn't rattled, things were probably all right.

"He did," she said. "But he had a lot in his system. I mean a *lot.* I would have been speaking pig latin if you'd somehow managed to rouse me with that much Ativan on board."

"Speaking from experience?" Byron smiled, trying to picture that.

"Let's just say I have a fear of dental work, and a very generous dentist."

They fell into an awkward silence, both studying Levi, who was sleeping curled up on his side, his lips slack but his brow knitted with worry. Rest softened his slender frame—made him appear younger. More vulnerable.

Byron's chest tightened. He'd assured Levi that he was safe because that's what adults had done to calm him when he was a child, but he didn't have a plan. Only a budding, frightening notion: freeing Levi wasn't going to be enough.

Cole Industries had to be stopped.

Every time Byron let himself consider that, it got harder to breathe. Where would he start? What would the country look like if Cole Industries didn't bind every man, woman, and child with magic?

Absurdly, he wondered what his mother would think of his new views on magic. He couldn't remember her ever speaking about serious things like magic or her brother-in-law's work—only on the kidnapping plots that had been exposed when Cole Industries had first boomed and everyone found out his parents had more than enough money to pay a ransom. He'd seen the stories in the newspaper—copies of the *Times* ferreted out of his father's study—and he'd brought the clippings to his mother, his small hands shaking. *"You're safe with us,"* she'd said, drawing him into a warm hug that made it feel like the truth.

She'd had an uncanny ability to soothe his fears. Normal childish fears—the dark, clowns, the unlikely return of dinosaurs.

He hadn't feared anything like plane crashes, but that was what had killed his parents as they headed home from a weekend vacation at Warren's country estate. After they were gone, Byron had mostly feared Warren, who had dutifully seen to his care and never threatened him or raised his voice.

Byron didn't know exactly why Warren had always frightened him. He'd grown up ashamed of his fear; it made him no better than the children who pointed and stared at people who were different.

He'd missed his mother. Now he missed her again—a small, surprising ache.

"What are you thinking about?" Victoria asked gently.

"Nothing."

"Bullshit. You look like a wrinkly dog."

Byron touched his brow. "I was thinking about growing up with Warren."

"A hardship, I'm sure." Her deadpan tone sent a pang of guilt through Byron. "All those nannies and boarding schools must have been rough."

"He scared me. He still does." Saying it out loud eased the knot in Byron's chest. "I'm pretty sure he doesn't like me."

Victoria's expression softened. "If you weren't frightened of Warren Cole, I'd question your sanity. This is reckless. Our jobs are at stake. Our lives are at stake. I know this is the right thing to do. But God, Byron. We could lose everything."

Somehow, Victoria's fear strengthened Byron's resolve. "Are you regretting this?"

"No. Not exactly. But I'm worried about Eleanor and my team. I'm gambling with more than myself and my business. I keep mulling over worst-case scenarios. We're virtually defenseless, you know. The weapons in this facility are only effective on mages."

"You've been so confident." Byron shook his head, a tired smile tugging at his lips. "What's changed?"

Victoria hummed. "I've been thinking about the things I can't control. Like my team. I didn't hire them based on liberal points of view or rebellious natures. They're good, loyal kids. I wouldn't blame a single one of them for betraying us to Warren and the authorities."

"Then we're careful, right?"

"I can handle careful. You need to handle the rest. Slow down. Figure out a *plan*."

Byron let out a humorless laugh. "Right."

Levi didn't stir, unaware of the casual conversation debating his life, his future.

They needed to find a way to give Levi a choice. If Byron decided everything for him, he wouldn't be any better than the rest of Cole Industries.

"I may have most of the staff transferred to our sister facility in Dubai," Victoria was saying, as if talking to herself. "At least until things quiet down over here."

"That's a good idea," Byron said. "Protecting them."

"Honestly, I believe a few of them would agree with what we're doing, although they'd probably approach it more reasonably. An online petition as opposed to trying to circumvent the law, for example," she said ruefully. "Still. I'm not going to drag them into this."

"Into my horrible plan, you mean?" Byron asked, arching a brow.

"I'm starting to view this as *our* horrible plan."

He couldn't help smiling. "You don't even roll through stop signs."

"And?" She narrowed her eyes.

"And you go to Mass with your parents twice a month."

"So?"

"You're an atheist."

She patted her bun. "What are you saying, Byron?"

Warmth pooled under Byron's skin despite his tension. "I'm saying thank you. I know you're not doing this lightly."

Victoria grunted, but her mouth twitched with a hint of a smile. "Thank me if we survive this."

Byron's gaze drifted back to Levi. His short-sleeved scrubs showed more of his tattoo. The dark swirls and intricate designs were beautiful, whatever they meant.

"I think I'll try his ex again," he said absently.

Victoria's voice thinned. "'Again'?"

"The first time didn't go so well. We didn't have Levi yet, and I didn't know what to say. He asked me if I was wearing a wire, though. I think he has something to hide—like being a mage sympathizer."

"I hope you're being careful."

"You're the one who said it was probably safe to talk to his family. Sam's not even related to him!"

"It seems like a bad idea now that you've done it." Victoria crossed her arms and pressed her lips together. "But if you're right that he's a mage sympathizer . . . He could help us find somewhere to send Levi. Somewhere Levi can hide. Try to find out if the ex has connections."

"I will. If he'll talk to me at all."

Levi stretched and shifted, but his breathing remained steady and he didn't open his eyes.

"Are you and Eleanor getting serious?" Byron blurted.

"God, no."

He raised an eyebrow.

"It's not like I don't want to be." Victoria sighed and gestured around the room. "But all of this. You, that kid. I'm not girlfriend material at the moment."

"You say that every time someone falls for you."

"This time it's true."

"This time it's my best friend. In the entire world." Byron couldn't stand the thought of Eleanor being rejected—even for a damn good reason.

They obviously had strong feelings for each other. That had to be worth something. Worth the risk.

"Byron, I care about you. But I don't give a damn about your thoughts on my love life."

Stung, Byron adjusted his cuffs. "All I'm saying is there will never be a good time."

"Says the perpetually single guy."

"That's different!" Bringing anyone into his life in a serious way felt like inviting a lamb to the slaughter. It would mean gossip sites and Warren and hectic schedules and—

"It's not that different," Victoria said, quietly.

She was right. He excelled at coming up with excuses.

"But I understand," she went on. "We're both married to our work."

"I'm not married to work the way you are. You're passionate and driven. I just found the one way I could contribute to Cole Industries."

"You're good at what you do, Byron. When you care."

"It doesn't matter. I think we're getting divorced from work in a hurry."

Victoria laughed once—a sharp, bitter sound. "Too soon, Byron."

He stood, leaning against the cabinets and bumping his hip against hers. For a moment, it felt comfortable—familial. He almost forgot where they were. As far as Levi was concerned, this was still prison.

"I used to fantasize about staying in bed all day for a week. Binge watching cooking shows and napping."

"Doesn't look as fun in practice, does it?"

"Not in here." The room, all pale hues and tile halfway up the wall, was nothing like the inviting nest of a bedroom he'd created for himself in the apartment. "Maybe I can get some things from his place. I have a key."

"Now who's getting serious?"

He elbowed her. "His pillow, at least. I don't want him to feel like a prisoner."

"He's a prisoner whether he feels like one or not. It's not like we can turn him loose."

"If I was stuck somewhere, I'd want my stuff." Byron had never been imprisoned, but his first years away at boarding school had been close. He'd left all of his toys and most of his belongings back at his parents' penthouse, which was sold while he was away his first year. When he'd asked his uncle Warren where his things were—his stuffed animals and action figures and pajamas and photos of his parents—Warren had scoffed. *"Sold. Given away. And thrown away, I suppose. Why?"*

"You'd risk your life for a pillow?"

"If I get caught, I'll tell them it's part of my report."

"You're being reckless."

Byron gestured at Levi. "I owe him that much."

"If you do it, don't bring more than you can fit in a messenger bag. I don't want the security detail outside to suspect anything. Most people don't attend meetings with luggage."

"Text me AMID's shipping address. I'll ship some of it in a box."

"Do you really think bringing him his belongings is that important?"

"Yes." Byron said it with a certainty—a ferocity—that surprised him.

Victoria stared at him. "All right."

The next morning was a Sunday, and Byron debated whether to go to Levi's apartment or Summons to talk to Sam. He chose Levi's apartment, deciding that a normal pillow and clean underwear were more pressing, or at any rate were the least he could do for Levi.

Before he could unlock Levi's door, the door swung open forcefully and a hand grabbed him by the shoulder before he could react. He immediately found himself in a familiar position, slammed up against the now-closed door with Sam Johnson's hand pressed to his sternum like a vise.

"What are you doing here?" Sam demanded.

"I was looking— I needed to get— It's for Levi," Byron stuttered out, more surprised than afraid.

"Levi's gone."

"He's safe," Byron said quickly. "For now. And I need your help."

"What the hell does that mean?" Sam took a full step back and dropped his arm, giving Byron a chance to catch his breath.

Byron let his head fall back against the door and closed his eyes. "I was going to look for you today."

"Well, you found me."

Byron ducked his head. "I know."

"You better start talking, Cole. I have folks on speed dial who would love to make you disappear before you can make it back uptown."

Knees trembling with adrenaline, Byron sank to the floor and rested his arms on his legs. He'd thought in the split second Sam grabbed him that the authorities were onto him, that someone was going to throw him into handcuffs and haul him down to the precinct. Was this how Levi had felt every day of his life? Afraid? Always waiting to get caught?

Victoria had been right. This was a stupid risk.

Sam pulled up a kitchen chair, sat on it, and watched him, eyes tight with exhaustion that mirrored Byron's.

"You're bluffing, aren't you?" Byron asked.

Sam released a slow breath. "Yes."

"Levi's still in a lot of trouble," he said. "He's somewhere safe where no one can hurt him, but I don't know how long we can keep him there."

"'We'?"

"I can't tell you who I'm working with."

"I don't know how you expect me to believe this." Sam wore tight jeans and a tighter T-shirt; it wasn't a Sunday-morning outfit. He'd probably slept in his clothes. Maybe here.

Several brightly colored bracelets made a rainbow along Sam's forearm. A hollow ache of regret struck Byron. He wasn't that open, that honest, about anything—but he couldn't pinpoint why it had seemed so incredibly important to be not only secretive, but a blank slate. A nice haircut. A nice suit.

Byron glanced at the unmade bed. "I'm gay."

It wasn't what he'd meant to say, and as he said it, he realized he'd never said it to anyone.

Sam rolled his eyes. "I know."

"You know?"

"Don't you read blogs?"

Byron winced. No. He didn't read blogs about himself. Reputation management was part of his job, but he found it too unsettling and humiliating to dive into independent blogs that did nothing more than spread rumors.

Sam raised his brow.

"Listen," Byron said, trying to focus on what was important. "I'm doing everything I can to protect Levi, but I can't do it alone."

"This sounds like a setup. The government puts ads out on Craigslist for shit like this, trying to lure mages out of hiding or talk bound mages into attempting magic."

"You're not a mage. I checked the registry."

"Are you so sure? Levi wasn't on it."

"Yes, I'm sure." He was bluffing, but he couldn't imagine that anyone under real threat of execution would coyly hint at having magic.

"Then what do you need from a regular man?"

"I need to know if you know people. Activists. Other mages in hiding. Anyone willing to fight for Levi." It sounded incredibly stupid out loud, and Byron cringed.

"Fight?" Sam's brow knitted. "Fight who?"

"Cole Industries."

"Why not aim a little higher?" Sam asked, voice thick with sarcasm. "How about the entire United States government? Since that's who's technically holding Levi prisoner." He faltered. "That's who's going to kill him."

"No. He'll die at Cole Industries long before his execution date." Byron's words were heavy in his throat. He watched Sam's shoulders slump. He must have been grieving already, grieving all along. Sam didn't have the luxury of hope.

"What are you proposing?" Sam trained his gaze on the scuffed floor.

"I don't know yet. I need help figuring this out. I need people who understand magic—people who can hide Levi. And teach him how to— I don't know. Use his magic. Safely. Secretly. When he shielded us from the explosion, he looked as surprised as we did. I don't think he knows what he's doing."

Sam's voice went soft, achingly fond. "That's because he has no idea what he's doing."

"I need Levi to fight too," Byron said gently. "If he doesn't, I can't help him."

"You're going to ask a man accused of terrorism to openly use magic? After he's already going to be put to death for using magic?" Sam stared at him. "Why don't you offer him a gun and let him go out with dignity?"

"I don't want him to die."

"That's not what it sounds like to me."

Byron inhaled sharply. "I came here to get him clean clothes and some of his stuff."

"Sure."

Blinking, he sputtered out, "Seriously."

"That's psychotic. You could have gone to Macy's."

Byron flushed. "The point is, would I do that for someone I didn't—for someone I wanted to die?"

"No." Sam's gaze bore into him, and Byron fought the urge to look away—guilt thick in his throat. "But I have no reason to trust you."

"That's what Levi said." Byron scrubbed his hand across his face. "Well, he said something about me not understanding anything he's feeling. Or knowing anything at all."

"That's Levi. He'll tell you exactly what he's thinking." Sam's voice thinned, as if daring to hope threatened to crumble him to pieces. "You're not bullshitting me? You've talked to him?"

Byron tried not to sound too excited. "I told you he's safe! He's resting where they can't hurt him."

For now.

Sam's eyes shone. "Can you tell him I was here? That I'm thinking about him every second? You should grab pickle potato chips. He's fussy about his deodorant too. He's got about ten under his bathroom sink in case they stop making it."

"You really believe me?" Byron half expected someone to burst out of the bathroom, guns drawn. Neither of them had any reason to trust the other.

"It's better than the alternative." Sam shuddered. "They'll kill him. Levi, who wouldn't so much as heat a cup of coffee with his magic. Wouldn't do a damn thing with it."

"You knew." Byron had suspected, but it was another thing entirely to hear Sam all but admit it. How many others were protecting a rogue mage with their silence?

"Yeah," Sam said, challenging, stubborn.

"Can you help? Do you know someone who can teach him?"

"People don't exactly advertise services for magic tutoring. It's against the law. You know, punishable by death?" Sam's attitude didn't mask the change in his demeanor, the unmistakable sheen of hope. Byron probably looked the same way.

His heart beat faster, and he fidgeted with his sleeves. Maybe they had a chance if they could tap into the rumblings of dissidence, the voices Byron had always worked so hard to drown out. If they backed up the questioning, the quiet undercurrent of rebellion, they could change the way people saw—and feared—magic.

They could change everything.

But first they had to get Levi somewhere safe, hidden away.

"If you know anyone who would risk their life for him, maybe for others . . . think about it." Byron picked himself up and dusted his jeans off. A few silvery strands of cat hair stuck to his palms.

"You actually spoke to him," Sam said, sounding dazed.

"Only for a little while."

"How is he?"

"Frightened. Angry. Sleepy. He's on medication that's helping him rest. I have someone helping me, someone on his side. She's trying to make him as comfortable as possible."

"He should have left the city." Sam's voice thickened. He cleared his throat. "I should have talked him into it. He should have been living in a cabin on a mountain in the middle of nowhere. He shouldn't have been there. He shouldn't have done it."

"If he hadn't done something, the blast would have killed him too."

"Quickly. Mercifully."

Byron flinched and nodded slowly. He'd never had a reason to imagine that a sudden, violent death might be preferable to the alternative. He'd never needed to worry that his friends might be tortured and killed.

"Where's his cat?" he asked, trying not to think about the fact that his entire life had been sheltered from the terror mages faced every day—and the fact that he'd directly contributed to the public's fear and hatred of magic.

"Daisy?" Sam asked. "I drove her to Mrs. Camden's house."

"How is she?"

"The cat?"

Byron shot him a look. "His mom."

"She's frightened and angry," Sam said pointedly.

"I don't think she should know about this."

"You think it's better for her to keep thinking that her son could die any moment?"

"Yes. Anything else might be false hope. Or she might want to see him. I don't know her. I don't even know Levi, but I don't think— Well, I wouldn't have wanted my mother pulled into something like this."

"Because she could get killed," Sam said, giving a name to the fear Byron didn't want to voice.

"Right," Byron said, throat dry. His knees went weak, and he let the wall catch him.

The danger was real. Not hushed words. Not Victoria's worries.

Not just real, but the most likely outcome: His death. Victoria's death. Levi's death. Maybe Eleanor's too. Maybe others at AMID. Maybe Sam. Maybe Levi's mother if the authorities went after anyone who might have had anything to do with a conspiracy against the government.

His head spun.

"I'm so sick of all of this," Sam muttered. He began gathering a pile of clothes from Levi's dresser, moving with the ease of familiarity, grabbing a few pairs of boxers. Soft sweatpants. A couple of T-shirts. A well-worn pair of jeans. Socks.

"Shoes," Byron said suddenly, needing something to focus on—something other than the spiraling thoughts about death. Violent, awful death.

"What?"

"He's barefoot. He needs a pair of shoes."

"In that basket by the door." Sam pointed. As Byron dug through a small pile of sneakers to find two that matched, Sam folded the clothes he'd picked out.

"I'm sick of my friends being afraid," Sam said. "Most people who wear the bands can't get a job. Their rents get jacked up. They get beat down, assaulted on the street. And the government won't even call it a hate crime, but it's hate. That's all it is."

"It's fear," Byron said, quietly.

"That's the same damn thing."

"Not to them. It's all about the branding. It's hard to justify hate. When you package it as fear, it makes sense to people."

"Spoken like a real asshole." Sam tucked the clothes into a paper grocery bag he'd retrieved from under the kitchen sink. He held on to the bag, jaw set.

"I know."

Sam shook his head. "I don't understand why you're doing this."

"Levi got me thinking—"

"When he got arrested saving your life?"

Byron gave a tight nod. "When that happened, and afterward. And I've seen things anyone—most people, anyway—would object to. Things they're going to do to Levi and others. So I have two choices: ignore it or do something."

"And suddenly you're okay with magic?"

"I don't know. I don't think I was ever not okay with magic. Scared of what it could do, maybe. But I didn't think it was *bad*."

"Yet you're part of a dynasty that's done nothing but aid in the persecution and torture of mages."

"Not torture. I mean—I had no idea."

"Have you ever been to a bound-mage support group? Listened to CALM men and women talk about what it's like wearing the bands every day of their lives?"

"I didn't even know that was a thing." Byron sat in the windowsill, abruptly weary. How could he have gone so long not knowing, not questioning? Did Eleanor know about support groups? Did they have them for children too?

"It is a thing. It has to be, because your technology takes a tremendous psychological toll. Are you aware of the suicide rate of bound mages? Over half attempt suicide, and those are the ones that get reported."

"Be honest with me," Byron said, his voice thick with frustration. He felt guilty, horribly so, but Sam was making him angry too. "What's the alternative? Lawlessness?"

"Do you know how many Americans carry weapons? Concealed or open carry, tucked under their bedroom pillows, you name it. Why is that all right, when magic—a force that no one's proven to be violent by nature—is regulated to the extent of dehumanizing mages?"

"So magic should go unchecked?"

"Magic isn't unchecked. Do you think mages are genies? Magic comes with a price. Haven't you ever seen a fairy-tale cartoon? Come on."

"I don't know anything about magic," Byron said, realizing how true that was. Sam had told him more in five minutes than he'd learned in his entire life. He was so unbelievably foolish. All this time he'd feared something he didn't understand.

"That's pretty clear."

Byron's anger flared. "How do you know so much?"

"Why would I tell you? Maybe today you're interested in saving Levi. But what happens tomorrow when you realize you're in deep shit? You'll throw me under the bus."

Byron deflated. Sam was being completely serious and practical. Smart. "You don't have any reason to trust me. And there's no excuse for my ignorance, but I want to learn. I hope I can show you that, eventually."

Sam's expression softened. "At least you're aware that you're a stupid asshole."

A small, tired laugh escaped Byron. "Yes, I am."

Sam handed him the bag of clothes, but didn't let go of it. "Bring me proof that he's all right, and I'll think about helping you."

"I will."

Sam let go of the bag.

CHAPTER 14
PICKLE CHIPS

Levi relished waking up in an empty room. A soft orange glow lit his way to the small bathroom. The tile floor chilled his bare feet, and he wondered what day it was, and if winter was already settling over the city. He still wasn't sure where he was, but it didn't feel like prison.

He let himself fantasize that this was a mental hospital. He was here for his own safety after a nervous breakdown—over having a childish belief that he had the ability to do magic. Doctors would take good care of him and then set him free, and he'd return to his aimless, happy existence.

Without waiting for the water to turn warm, Levi dropped his clothes on the floor and stepped into the shower. The first icy shock hit him like a slap, jarred him out of the daydream of being crazy but safe. He wasn't crazy or safe. The bright metal bands on his wrists gleamed, an ugly reminder of that.

Angry shivers ran through his body as he waited for the water to warm up. He rubbed his arms and put his face in the spray and apologized silently to the magic inside of him. Sometimes he thought of his magic as an imaginary friend—a living being that didn't take lightly to being forgotten and suppressed.

"Um, I'm not looking," a deep voice said.

"Fuck!" Levi yelped, ducking his head out of the spray. He wiped his eyes hurriedly and saw Byron Cole in the doorway to the bathroom, hiding his face against the wall and holding out a paper bag.

"Sorry— It's early. I'm sorry. I brought a few of your things. There's soap and shampoo in there. Sam said—"

"Sam?" he shouted, his voice echoing in the tiny bathroom. Byron said something else, but he couldn't hear him over the rush of water, and a wave of horror struck him.

Was Sam in trouble too? Was Mom in trouble? He hadn't asked—hadn't thought to. The bathroom tilted, and he grabbed at the slick shower tiles and slipped, landing so hard on his ass that his teeth hurt.

"Levi!" Byron was there, in his face, soaking wet in all of his clothes. His hair ran down into his eyes like ink, and he didn't seem concerned that the entire building was falling over and spinning. His eyes were wide with fear, though. And he kept yelling in Levi's face.

It was hard to breathe.

Maybe he was drowning. Was the water getting into his mouth? He thrashed from it, kicking and punching at Byron to get him out of the way. This was how people died in crowds, probably, trying to claw their way to the surface, where the air was.

"Levi. Levi! Victoria!" Byron kept reaching for him, and Levi kept kicking. "He needs help!"

When Levi got out of the spray, he still couldn't breathe. His mom. Sam. The dumb kids from Summons. What if they were dead? It was his fault. He pressed his hands against his chest and his belly, trying to push the air out so he could get more air in. Every gasp was nothing, non-air, not enough. He was going to die in the shower with a total asshole yelling at him.

"He's having a heart attack or something," Byron said, sounding frantic and stupid. It wasn't a heart attack—Levi was dying. Plain and simple.

"It's a panic attack." A woman appeared at the edge of Levi's spotty vision. The doctor woman, Victoria. "What happened?"

"I was in here for two seconds. I was handing him his clothes."

"It doesn't matter. It could be a flashback, could be anything. Levi." She reached for him, and he clenched his hands into fists and tried to squeeze away from her. "Levi. Byron! Turn the water off."

When the water abruptly shut off, the bathroom got very quiet. Levi heard his own gasps. He was breathing. He was breathing all wrong, but he was breathing. He lifted his gaze to Byron towering over him and moaned with terror.

"I didn't do anything." Byron sounded almost as hysterical as Levi felt.

"It doesn't matter." Victoria got close and put her hands on Levi's shoulders. Her hands were warm. "Levi. You're doing a really good job. Can you stay here with me, in this bathroom right now? No one is hurting you here. You're in the bathroom, and nothing in here is going to hurt you."

Levi nodded but didn't really believe her. Byron was there, standing over him, and he was with Cole Industries, and he'd talked to Sam.

"Sam." He gasped the name out between hiccupping breaths. "My mom."

"They're safe. You're safe," Victoria said slowly. "No one is hurt."

"They're safe," Levi repeated, nodding. "They're . . . not . . . dead."

"Nobody's dead. Byron brought you clothes from your apartment. Sam helped him. Sam's safe. He wanted you to have your things. Byron, sit down. Sit on the floor."

Levi squinted his eyes open. One of his shoes was sticking out from a sad paper bag next to the toilet. A plastic deodorant container lay next to it. His favorite kind. He had a huge stash of it, just in case. Sam was the only person who knew how particular he was about his deodorant.

"Sam's okay," Levi said.

"I got you pickle chips. Sam said you like them." Byron sat in the bathroom doorway, soaking wet like a dog who'd had a hose turned on him for barking.

Levi began to cry.

He didn't want to, not with these strangers looking at him, but he'd missed having shoes so much, and he'd smell like himself again, and Sam was safe, and he really did love pickle chips, and everything was so frightening, and his magic hurt.

Victoria offered him her palms, beckoning. Struck by the simple kindness of the gesture, he curled into her lap. One of them draped a towel over his back, and it occurred to him dimly that he was naked, but he didn't care. He cried against her, letting her rub his back and comb her fingers through his hair over and over and over. He cried until his face and head hurt, but his lungs felt clear and he knew he wasn't dying.

"Do you want me to give you medicine to calm you down?" Victoria asked a long time later, when Levi's breathing had evened out, punctuated by quiet shudders.

"Please don't." He was tired of the haze, of losing time. "I'm sorry."

"You don't have to be sorry. Have you had a panic attack before?"

"No. I've never had anything like that."

"That's all right. You've been through a lot. I'm surprised it didn't happen until now."

"Can I get dressed?" Levi sat up slowly, holding the towel against his lap. His curls hung in his face, dripping and cold.

"I'm going to help you, if you don't mind?"

It was weird being asked if he minded or not. "Sure."

Byron mumbled something about waiting outside and slipped out of the room, taking another towel with him.

"He didn't mean to frighten you," Victoria murmured. She helped Levi step onto a dry towel and set the bag of clothes in the sink.

"He didn't. It was fine, it wasn't him." Levi's hands trembled when he pulled his boxers on, but he felt better. Wrung out, but in control. "I don't know what happened. That was weird."

His stomach gave a pang at the thought that it might happen again, could happen without warning. He took a deep breath.

"It must have been frightening. I'm sure you don't want to feel sedated—that's normal—but please know that you don't have to suffer if it happens again. I have rescue medications, benzodiazepines that work quickly."

"Why are you being so nice to me?" Levi tugged one of his favorite T-shirts over his head. It had an illustration of a big whale floating in the sky, tethered by dozens of strings like a giant balloon.

"I don't have reason to believe that you deserve anything other than kindness."

He studied her angular, pretty profile as he pulled on a worn-out pair of jeans. "Other than how I blew a bunch of people up and killed them?"

"Were you responsible for that?"

The soft smile that quirked at his lips felt foreign. "No."

She turned to him and crossed her arms. "Levi, I need you to know something. I design and implement weapons specifically made to fight against magic. To kill mages, if necessary."

The flutter in his stomach intensified. His next breath caught in his throat.

"Breathe, Levi. Breathe through it. I'm only telling you this because I want you to understand that I haven't come to this decision lightly. I believe that you've been treated unfairly. That many others have been as well."

"Are you going to shoot weapons at me?"

She pursed her lips. "Only if you give me good cause to."

"I'll try not to do that."

"Good. Now finish up in here. I'll be right outside."

Left alone in the bathroom with the door ajar, Levi took a few minutes to relieve himself, wash his hands, and apply his deodorant. He smelled like himself. Familiar. He'd been using it so long that using anything else made him feel like he was rubbing elbows with a stranger. He grabbed the bag of chips and walked back into the small room. Byron and Victoria were speaking in hushed tones next to the cabinets, so he made himself comfortable on the bed and popped open the bag of chips.

"Hey, these . . . This is my pillow," he said.

Guilt shadowed Byron's features.

"You brought it?" Levi asked, confused.

"I thought it would help."

Levi touched the pillow, a gentle flush warming his cheeks. The case was flannel, much softer than the sheets on the bed. "It helps."

Exhausted and beat up, he only nibbled on a few chips before the soreness in his body chased the brief flare of appetite away. His jeans slipped down when he moved, and he wondered how much weight he'd lost. He'd always been on the skinny side; malnutrition probably wasn't a very good look.

He rubbed his jaw. His face felt vaguely scruffy, scraggly with the pathetic excuse for a beard he'd never really been able to grow. "Can I get a razor?"

Victoria broke off from murmuring to Byron and pursed her lips.

"They make safety ones. You can babysit me."

"I'll think about it," she said.

Byron, still damp and wearing a sheepish expression, was rubbing a towel at his hair. It made it stand up in black spikes every which way. He was handsome and fit, especially compared to Levi's scrawniness. In the grand scheme of how deeply fucked he was, he wasn't sure why he cared how terrible he looked next to Cole Industries' head bro, or what Byron might think of him.

Maybe it was the pillow thing. The pillow thing was nice.

And if he thought back to the last few moments of his normal life, he recalled an instant attraction to Byron. That morning, he'd thought about changing his plans and dragging Byron off to get too drunk to think about anything but hooking up.

His lingering flush deepened.

"Your friend Sam doesn't really trust me." Byron sounded shy, of all things.

"He doesn't have any reason to." Levi waited for a cocky, defensive response. But Byron ducked his head and nodded.

"I think he'll help us—"

"Because he's an idiot." Levi hated the thought of Sam sticking his neck out, but he'd always been so dead set on helping mages, it wasn't surprising.

"But he needs proof. That you're alive."

"So . . ." Levi snorted. "You take a picture of me next to today's newspaper?"

"Sort of." Byron pulled his phone out of his pocket: it was one of those new, stupidly expensive models that worked underwater. "I don't get reception down here, or I'd have you call him. I'll have to take a picture. It'll be time-stamped."

"Cheese," Levi said tonelessly. When Byron lifted the phone and took a quick picture, he flipped him the bird. "That's only going to him, right?" What if it ended up on the news somehow? He didn't want his mom to have to deal with him looking like an unrepentant shithead.

"I'm not even emailing it." Byron tucked his phone back into his pocket. "I'll show him in person, to be safe."

"Email. Man." Levi had never gone this long without the internet. He wondered what had happened to his phone, his inbox, and his social media accounts.

His stomach twisted into a knot at the memory of his final tweet, the last thing he'd posted before deciding he'd be better off keeping his thoughts to himself.

"Are you all right?" Victoria asked, frowning a pretty frown.

"Yeah." Levi pulled the covers up and rolled onto his side, facing away from them. He closed his eyes, as if that would make them disappear, make all of this disappear. "I want to go to sleep."

They didn't say another word, but Levi didn't sleep. Not when Byron slipped out of the room, and not when Victoria eventually followed. Not for a long time.

CHAPTER 15
LIMITED RESOURCES

Byron nursed his ginger ale, wishing it were something stronger. His adrenaline hangover lingered from watching Levi's panic attack this morning. Victoria had been so calm and understanding, and Byron had felt like a fool—unable to do a damn thing to help Levi.

He couldn't bring himself to tell Sam the entire story. Instead, he'd handed him his phone. Sam was still studying the photo of Levi, his soft smile lit by the pale glow of the screen. Byron gave him plenty of time to see that Levi was alive—and feisty enough to shoot an obscene gesture at the camera.

A server with a swaying bob and thick-rimmed glasses brought Sam another drink. When her dress shirt rode up her arm, a bright CALM band peeked out. She hurriedly brushed her shirt back over them and gave Sam a red-lipstick smile before bustling to the next booth over.

Circular booths lined the walls of Summons like honeycomb. Quiet conversations rumbled, a low backbeat to melancholy music. On any other occasion, Byron would have liked it here. It felt homey. Private. A little cool, but not pretentiously so.

He studied the booth they shared and frowned. It was big enough to hold half a dozen people, but Sam had brought a grand total of no one to their meeting.

"Don't look so impressed," Sam said, thick with sarcasm. He placed Byron's phone on the table between them. "I told you I have connections. I didn't say I'd let you meet all of them at once."

"I was assuming you'd start with one. Maybe two. Hell, three to make things really wild." Byron tucked his phone back into his jacket pocket. He was overdressed, but the jacket was armor. It made him professional and older. It helped him pretend he'd gotten more than four hours of sleep in three days.

"Calm down." Sam grinned at him, seemingly bolstered by the photo of Levi.

"This is the guy?" a woman asked, sliding into the booth on Byron's side and cramming up against him. Her eyes shone, bright and keen in a way that reminded Byron of Levi immediately.

He knew in an instant that she had magic, and wondered if it would be this obvious to anyone if they looked closely and cared—if they saw magic as a spark of life and not a ticking bomb.

"I'm Penny." She gave him a crooked smile and adjusted her blue-framed glasses. "And you're wearing an antiglamour device."

"Ah." Byron touched his shirt where the flat pendant rested against his chest. "How can you tell?"

She laughed. "Because you're not staring at my tits."

Her clothes were tastefully bohemian. She could be anything from a guidance counselor to a palm reader for all Byron could tell. "What?"

"You know I don't like you doing that here," Sam said to her, his voice tense. "Byron doesn't need proof."

"That's true. Though he'll have proof enough when the time comes." It was too cheerful to be a threat, but Byron fought a shudder. She pulled her curly blond hair back into a swift ponytail using a ribbon from her wrist, and patted the table with both hands. "So! Sam thinks you're special."

"Those are not the words I used." Sam waved his hands.

"I'm glad he trusted me enough to let me meet you," Byron said.

Penny glanced at Sam and cringed. "He's such . . . a dork. No offense, Byron. You're lovely, but my goodness."

"He's not a dork," Sam said. "But he's naive as fuck."

"Thank you." Byron was so surprised at Sam coming to his defense, the insult caught up to him a shade too late.

Penny threw her hands up. "See?"

"All right, let's focus," Sam said.

"You know Levi?" Byron asked.

"I've met him a few times. He made a strong impression on me."

Byron tried to make sense of her expression. "And that means . . .?"

"We'll leave it at that," Penny said, narrowing eyes that held wisdom—and exhaustion—in a way that showed her age more than anything else. She had to be in her late forties or even early fifties. "I'd like to help Levi any way I can, but I've worked with mages wearing CALM bands, and no one's ever been able to break through them. It's not like he's going to suddenly learn how to use his magic."

"He won't have to break through them if we do this right." Byron glanced around. Speaking so casually and openly about magic went against everything he knew. "Aren't you worried about talking about this here?"

"I'm using an enchantment that will muffle our conversation to any prying ears," Penny said. "Unless Sam has his own club bugged, we're perfectly safe."

"I don't. And the security cameras aren't on right now." Sam showed them an app on his phone that controlled them.

Byron held his hands out. "Wait, I'm still stuck on magical conversation muffling. What?"

She smiled at him.

"I don't know very much about magic," Byron acknowledged.

"Good, you're not supposed to," Penny said. "Let me break it down: I'm skilled, not powerful. I'll have a migraine all day tomorrow for this. A small price to pay for our safety and Levi's life, if you really think you can save him."

"Aren't you afraid you'll get caught?"

"Of course I'm afraid." Penny's voice took on a chill, and guilt washed through Byron. Fear was new to him, but it clearly wasn't new to Sam or Penny. Or Levi.

Sam took a sip of his drink and set it down. "Byron, there's a whole world you don't understand. People who didn't submit to CALM registration. Rogue mages hiding magic, practicing in secret. People like Levi who denied themselves magic to try to stay safe. Your arrogance—Warren's arrogance—it's blinded you to the true nature of magic. It can't be bound forever. It will find a way."

Byron reached for Sam's drink, and Sam chuckled and handed it to him. He swallowed the rest down in a sharp gulp. Whiskey didn't have the smooth sweetness of sake—the hardest liquor Byron typically indulged in. The burn did the trick almost immediately.

"What are you really saying?" he asked, his voice hoarse.

Sam took the glass back, fidgeted with it. "I'm saying that if Levi is somehow freed, or if a pro-magic statement is made—not one of terror, but of hope—people will respond. People who have been waiting for something."

"Are these the people behind the terrorist attacks?"

"No." Penny spoke softly, but her voice reverberated right through Byron's bones. "Mages would never hurt people like that. Magic isn't supposed to kill or destroy. It's breath. It's life."

"But all the evidence . . ." Byron had spent hundreds of hours scouring reports from investigative agencies only to find each missing critical details. He'd always chalked it up to not having government clearance.

When Byron glanced at Penny, she was studying him.

"Did you really think mages were behind those attacks?" she asked.

"Yes." He cringed. The nagging suspicions he'd swallowed down rose like bile in his throat. There'd been more to it all along, and he hadn't had the courage to dig deeper—or listen to the voices speaking up against injustice.

Penny turned to Sam. "You didn't tell him?"

Sam shook his head. He drummed his fingers against the table. "No, I didn't tell him. I wanted to get your read on him first."

"And you believe he's someone who can help us?"

Sam shrugged. "I want to believe him. We've never had a chance like this before."

"How could he not know?"

"I don't know, but if he doesn't, that's our best reason to trust him, don't you think?"

"I'm right here," Byron said irritably.

Penny dragged the ribbon out of her hair and ran her fingers through it. As Sam moved back in the seat, she looked Byron in the eye. "Warren Cole is behind the terrorist attacks."

Byron's ears rang. He was suddenly very grateful for the booth that pressed against his back, propping him up. "My uncle?"

"Not him specifically. I mean, he's not out there setting bombs off."

"But he's paying someone to do it," Sam said. "We don't have hard evidence, but Cole Industries is funding and orchestrating terrorist attacks in every metropolitan area. And if our people have figured this out with limited resources, the FBI and every terrorist task force in the United States are looking the other way."

"But I almost died that morning. On the way to the press conference." Byron's body went hot and cold at once. He could feel them watching him. "If Levi hadn't been there . . ."

"Take the subway instead of the town car," Warren had told him. *"It makes you relatable, a regular person. One of them."*

"Is he going to pass out?" Penny asked.

"My uncle tried to have me killed."

Sam grimaced. "Yeah. Pretty much."

Penny touched Byron's hand. Her fingers were warm. "Sorry, honey."

CHAPTER 16
THE BIG SPOON

Eleanor wrinkled her nose when Byron crawled into her bed after midnight. "You smell like smoke, and you're— Byron, you're wearing your shoes. Take them off. Lord."

He kicked his shoes off. After losing a wrestling match with his shirt, he gave up and dropped his head onto the pillow beside hers. "E, everything is awful."

"You're kind of drunk, huh, kiddo? It's a school night, you know."

"I'm not. I was, maybe a little." His insides still felt like they'd been run through a shredder, and his mind was a foggy mess.

"Not convinced. We'll see how you feel at 5 a.m. when my alarm goes off."

"Warren tried to kill me."

She bolted up and switched on the lamp at her bedside table. "I'm sorry, what?"

The light pierced Byron's eyes, and he shut them tightly and then resorted to covering them with both hands. "I met with Sam Johnson today. And one of his friends. They know things."

"Slow down. Who's Sam Johnson? That name sounds familiar."

"Levi's ex-boyfriend. He owns a club."

"A club owner told you your uncle tried to kill you?"

"Sort of."

"Do you think maybe he's not a reliable source of information?"

If only she were right. He wanted to latch on to that and poke holes in the story. Sam and Penny could be elaborate con artists. Except Byron had gone to them, not the other way around. And they had nothing to gain by lying about Warren. Unless they wanted to use Byron for his connections.

His head hurt more.

"You don't get it," he said.

"Of course I don't get it. The only information I'm getting is through the filter of your nonsense and the vague nonanswers Vic's giving me."

Byron groaned. "I met a mage. A real one."

"As opposed to . . .?"

"Not registered. No CALM bands. Nothing."

"Jesus, Byron."

"I know."

She sank back down into the bed and pried his hands off his eyes. When he rolled over to face her, they were kids again, side by side at a sleepover. He'd always had a daybed growing up, and she'd slept on the lower mattress, within whispering distance.

"Tell me exactly what they said."

"They think Warren's behind the terrorism. Not mages. Not magic-rights activists."

"Why on Earth would Warren do that?"

"To further his agenda. To make people afraid."

"Shit," Eleanor hissed. "That actually makes sense in a horrible way."

"Warren told me to take public transportation that morning. I hadn't thought about it before. I mean, why would I?"

"Are you sure that means something?"

"How could it be a coincidence? He could have made sure I was nowhere near the explosion. But he didn't. He had a reason to make sure I was there."

Eleanor groaned. "The press conference . . ."

"For the Harvest. I think Warren wanted me to get killed that morning so he could sell everyone on the Harvest."

On the ride home from Sam's, he'd played it all out in his head over and over. He'd considered his death from a public-relations perspective. He thought about how he'd spin it, how he'd write it up. What it would mean for the antimagic movement.

The promising heir of Cole Industries killed by terrorists, killed by mages. How bittersweet. What a perfect way to ensure that the people would willingly—gladly—back the Harvest Initiative. Public support of the Harvest would be a fitting tribute to Byron Cole's tragic death. Magic needed to be controlled, stopped, harnessed—now more than ever. Warren would have been not only a philanthropist but a grieving, heirless uncle.

"Byron, that's fucked up."

"But it's brilliant. It would have worked."

"Except Levi saved you."

"Except Levi saved me," Byron echoed.

"Then Warren must *really* hate him."

Byron hadn't thought that far, but she was probably right. Even if Levi hadn't shown so much promise, such a high level of magic, he likely would have been the first subject handed over to Kurt Crane for his sadistic tests. Out of pure spite.

"Warren will never let him go," Byron whispered.

"I'm sorry." Eleanor pushed her fingers through Byron's hair.

"That's what Penny said." Byron frowned, hating being pitied over this. Hating all of it. Warren was his father's brother, his only family. How could Warren have been so willing to sacrifice him? Was the Harvest that important? More important than Byron's life?

Of course it was. Deep down, Byron knew that.

Warren was poised to have a monopoly on a proprietary, revolutionary source of energy. Nothing else would matter. Nothing would stand between Warren and power.

"Who's Penny?"

"The mage. I didn't ask... I wonder what else she does. She dresses like an art teacher."

"I doubt she's a teacher if she's a rogue mage."

"Sam's friends say there are lots of mages who haven't registered. Penny used magic in front of me. Right out in the open."

Eleanor frowned. "That's crazy."

"Is it? Look what hiding magic got Levi. These people know the stakes."

"It's still crazy to me. I don't even jaywalk, let alone break a law punishable by actual death. Does Vic know you were talking to mages?"

"She knew I was trying to find allies. People who can help us with Levi."

"It sounds like you're both going to get killed, and I'm not going to have anyone to hang out with."

"Don't worry, if it comes to that, I'm sure they'll kill you too."

She punched his arm. "I didn't sign up for this."

"Would you, though? Would you sign up for it?"

"I've been thinking about it. I mean, thinking about my kids more than your . . . whatever he is. They're suffering, Byron. The ones wearing bands. They're suffering more than I've wanted to let myself see." She exhaled heavily, breath shuddering. "I didn't sign up for the killing and the dying."

"I don't want you involved, not the way Vic and I are. But I don't know if I can do this without your brain."

"It's a great brain, admittedly." She turned onto her side and wiggled back against him until he caught her up in a spooning hug and had to blow her hair out of his mouth. "When I wanted to know your secrets, I didn't know they'd be this big."

"I didn't either." It was an understatement.

The fan beside her bed droned in the quiet space between them, and he floated, unable to connect to anything but the security of Eleanor and the fact that Levi needed him—whether he wanted the help or not. Every other foundation was crumbling away, from Byron's own family to everything he'd thought he'd known about magic.

"What are you going to do?" she asked.

"I can't let Warren suspect that I know he was willing to off me to support the Harvest. I mean, it's terrible, but at least we're aware of what we're dealing with. We'll be even more careful now."

"Like not going to nightclubs with mages?"

"Well. That's probably still on the menu. We're going to meet up again soon."

"I don't think I'm ready for that."

"You don't have to be." He squeezed her in a brief hug. "Not yet. Maybe not ever. You can help without stepping right into the line of fire."

"Okay. I like that plan."

"I have to focus on Levi. Sam's friends will help. We have to get him out of the bands and figure out how to use his magic."

"What good will that do? Magic will still be illegal, and if you get him free, he'll be a fugitive. A huge terrorist fugitive everyone and their mom would want dead."

"You paint a cheerful picture. Thanks." Byron blew more of her hair out of his mouth.

"You're the one hiding in my bed."

"Hey, you'd want therapeutic cuddling too if you found out you were the target of a murder plot."

"Fair. Also, don't get me wrong, Byron, I care a lot about you. But I'm a little more freaked out that Warren's okay with murder. The annual death toll is something like three hundred nationwide. And thousands injured. That's a lot of people. And not even mages—normal people."

"Mages are normal people," Byron mumbled. He'd been trying not to think about that part, but it was impossible not to. His uncle was a mass murderer. Potentially not out of hatred, but out of greed—the desire to give Cole Industries more business. The clinical nature of the terrorist attacks was much more frightening than the idea of senseless deaths at the hands of a madman or a secret organization trying to liberate mages.

Eleanor didn't respond.

"I know," Byron eventually said. "It's worse than the Harvest and worse than trying to kill me. He's out of control."

"Torture and murder. You've got screwed-up genes."

Byron snorted. "Thanks."

"Don't you think he'll try again?"

Oddly, Byron hadn't thought that far. It was bad enough trying to reconcile the fact that his only living relative was morally bankrupt. "Now that you mention it, yes. I guess I'll go out of my way to avoid being where he expects me to be."

"You better be careful. He could start tailing you, and you'll lead Cole Industries straight to your new mage friends."

"You're right. We'll switch up our meeting places. I'll get a burner phone."

"How do you even know what a burner phone is?"

"I watch TV, you know. Sometimes."

Eleanor chuckled. They fell into a comfortable silence, and Byron had begun to drift off when she spoke. "How is Levi?"

"He was okay until I accidentally scared the shit out of him in the shower." Though Levi hadn't been afraid for his own safety, instead he'd been worried about his mother and Sam. That settled heavy and warm in Byron's chest—another brilliant facet of Levi's personality, another reason to believe he was good.

It strengthened the relentless tug of attraction Byron was struggling to ignore.

"In the shower?" Eleanor asked pointedly.

"It's a long story." Byron's face heated, the memory of Levi's lean body hitting him like an aftershock. "But he was sleeping when I left. I brought him clothes and shoes and his pillow and bathroom stuff."

"That was nice of you. And slightly weird."

"What's weird about that?"

"I don't know." Eleanor shrugged against him. "I'm picturing you rifling through his underwear drawer and his medicine chest."

"Sam helped."

"That isn't less weird."

Byron grunted. *She's right.*

"I'm going to go by right after work," he mused, unable to quiet his mind. "Victoria isn't going to give him any more sedatives unless he asks for them. So he might be up again. I can't imagine how he feels."

"Then ask him." Eleanor yawned. "No more talking. It's about a billion o'clock."

"Love you."

She hummed. "Love you too, B."

CHAPTER 17
SALUTATIONS

Byron's work day crawled by, and his hangover from the night before didn't help. Much to his relief, nothing related to the Harvest crossed his desk. Instead, he spent hours blogging about a Cole Industries project preserving wetlands around one of the factories in South Florida.

"Did you know the Everglades are full of giant pythons?" he said to Charles, the intern. Charles didn't hear him because Charles always wore headphones and listened to mid-nineties rap so loud Byron could hear the dim chatter all day long.

Usually he went heads down into his work and never craved a distraction like music, but lately every minute felt like an hour. He considered finding a streaming station online and decided against it; once he started screwing around online, he'd end up down a black hole of defamatory articles about Levi. He was better off researching the terrifying snakes in Florida.

"They can swallow entire alligators," he said to no one.

Warren was in Las Vegas at a nanoscience conference. While it didn't really mean that Byron was safe, he relaxed slightly knowing his uncle was on the other side of the country. He wouldn't have to visit with him for now.

Byron had never been able to shake an irrational fear that Warren could read his mind, and the last thing he wanted to do was lie to Warren's face again—especially now that he knew how disposable he was.

He waited until five fifteen to leave the office. He was always one of the last to leave, and he didn't want to rouse suspicion by changing his routine any more than he already had. His workers appeared to be over his absences. The receptionist had stopped asking him how he was holding up over a week ago. No one brought him pity-lunches anymore. The postbombing-stress excuse for his spotty work attendance was wearing thinner and thinner.

By six, he was back at AMID, practically jogging to the quiet hallway that led to Levi's locked room. He passed one of Victoria's coworkers and tried to smile casually, but it came across more like a slow cringe in his efforts to be chill. Victoria rounded a corner into the hallway, stopped, and shot Byron a dirty look. She took him by the elbow and led him to her office.

The street view on the TV mounted to the office wall showed typical early-evening congestion. The traffic crawled by and commuters hurried past on foot, all of it eerily silent.

"You're acting like a schoolboy rushing to a date." Victoria crossed her arms and glared like she was about to send Byron to his room. "People are going to ask questions."

"I've always been excited to work with AMID."

"Not this excited. You're *glowing*. Calm down or I'm going to ban you from coming over. I've managed to hide Levi's presence from everyone I work with. Even the late-night cleaning crew. If you screw this up, I will literally kill you."

"Ouch, too soon." He realized what she was saying. "Wait, are you sleeping here?"

"Of course I'm sleeping here. Do you think I have a night nurse on staff?" She pulled her phone out of her pocket and waved it at him. "I have him under surveillance when I'm not in there. It's not perfect, but so far we haven't had any disasters."

"Is he awake right now?"

"Sometimes I'm not sure if you listen to me at all." Victoria shook her head. "He's awake and doing a crossword puzzle. I need you to sit with him for a couple of hours so I can go home and get clothes." She handed him a small remote control. "The panic button on here will send an alert text to my phone. He's already had dinner, but if he's hungry or thirsty, you can find something for him to eat in the kitchen down the hall. Don't let him out of the room. At all. Under any circumstances."

"Got it," Byron said evenly, as if he wasn't nervous about the responsibility. It wasn't technically babysitting, but he'd never so much as dog-sat let alone been responsible for another human being.

She eyed him, let out a slow sigh, and shooed him from her office.

When he arrived at Levi's room, he gave a quick knock before entering the access code on the door and heading in slowly, calling out, "Hey, it's me. It's Byron, I mean."

Victoria hadn't been joking; Levi was sitting up in the bed with a thick book of crossword puzzles. "I have no idea why people do these." His brow knitted in a tight frown. "This is the most boring, stupid thing I've ever done. I want to destroy these crossword puzzles. I really do."

"Hi," Byron said, surprised again at how normal Levi was acting.

"Do you do these?" Levi asked.

"No. I'm more of a Trivia Dash guy. But my roommate always destroys me."

"Does he cheat?"

"She. No, I don't think so. Maybe. Probably not." Byron gestured at the chair beside the bed. "Do you mind?"

"Go ahead." Levi turned back to the crossword puzzle. He drew his lower lip between his teeth and frantically erased something. "I miss sweet, sweet internet."

"That I can't help you with." Byron crossed one leg over his knee.

"What *can* you help me with?"

He didn't think the question was sincere at first, but after a few moments, Levi looked up at him through a fall of curls, his gaze expectant.

Byron's pulse skip-hopped, and he struggled to find his voice. "I want to show you how to use your magic."

Levi waved his pencil like a wand. "If you show me how to use my magic, I can cast enchantments on you."

"I'm wearing an antiglamour device."

"I could blow you up."

"You could."

"Aren't you afraid I will?"

"A little bit." Maybe this conversation wasn't a good idea when he had no medical backup. Plus, Byron had spent his lunch break reading about panic attacks online, and it hadn't taught him as much as he wanted to know. Without Victoria, he couldn't give Levi any drugs that might help him calm down if his anxieties got the best of him.

"You should be." Levi stared at his lap and closed the crossword puzzle book. He sighed softly, his chest falling with the deep breath.

"Why? Do you want to blow me up?"

"Not really, but I didn't mean to save you either. I don't know what I'm doing. It's like in cartoons when someone gets three wishes and they accidentally wish for something stupid and it wastes a wish. What if I think something awful for a second and it happens because of me?"

"I don't think that's how it works."

"But you don't know!" Levi's voice took on an edge that Byron found alarming enough to change the subject.

"Sam took your cat to your mom's house."

"Oh jeez." A small smile flashed in Levi's eyes. "Better get her fixed, then. Mom's got half a dozen toms in her neighborhood. I'm too young to be a grandfather."

"I've never had a pet."

"What? Everyone's had a pet. Fish? Guinea pig? Come on."

"None. My mom was allergic to animal dander, and I spent so much time in boarding schools after—there was never time."

"Well, you saved yourself money, then." Levi stretched his arms out. "Kitty litter nearly does me in. Daisy's a persnickety thing. She likes the fancy stuff."

Byron smiled but said nothing. They fell into a semicomfortable silence as Levi shifted out of bed and stretched his hands toward the ceiling. He folded over, surprisingly limber.

"If I do a little yoga, it almost helps with the constant pain from my pissed-off magic." Levi dropped down to the floor on the opposite side of the bed, where Byron couldn't see him. He grunted and exhaled heavily, and then his butt stuck up in the air.

Byron turned away. A hot flush crept up his neck. "I've never done yoga."

Levi moved forward and folded over, and then stretched up tall and pressed his palms together, as if in prayer. The bands at his wrists shone. "You should try it."

"Right now?"

"No, not right now." Levi laughed as he reached toward the ceiling. His shirt rode up, exposing tufts of hair at his belly. His jeans were too loose, and they hung low on his hips, revealing striped boxers. "Watch a video online. I'm not going to teach you yoga."

He went through the same series of movements again, more fluidly this time. Byron tried to memorize them, but it took several rounds for him to tell exactly what Levi was doing. With each pose, Levi breathed rhythmically, and Byron found himself breathing with him.

After about fifteen minutes of doing the same thing over and over, Levi sat back on the bed and pulled his legs onto it. He was barefoot, but his shoes rested on the foot of the bed, the laces undone. His chest heaved as if he'd been running.

"You're out of shape," Byron realized aloud.

Levi eyed him. "You think?"

"Sorry, that was . . . Of course you are."

"Why are you being so weird?"

"What do you mean?" The flush on Byron's throat came back. He hoped it wouldn't creep as far as his face. His mother had been incredibly fair, and he'd inherited her hair-trigger blush.

"The pillow. My clothes. The fact that you're here. The fact that I'm here. I'm not stupid. I know you want something from me." Levi spoke evenly, but his voice wavered and his fingers worked into the sheets on the bed.

He's scared.

He's scared of me.

"They filmed it—what Kurt Crane did to you."

Levi's expression closed off. His shoulders slumped inward, like a shrug in reverse.

"Crane was trying to use your magic to generate energy—electricity," Byron went on. "I don't agree with his methods. Or any of it. I don't agree with any of it."

"Don't you—don't you work with them?" Levi avoided Byron's gaze. "Aren't those your people? Your whole . . . That's your whole thing."

Byron could feel the tension ratcheting up in the room, and knew he should start talking about literally anything else, but he wanted Levi to know, needed Levi to know. "It is—it was. Listen, I can't explain what happened. You changed something in me."

Levi glanced up, brow arched.

"Okay, yes, that sounds asinine," Byron said. "But I mean it. It isn't only that you saved my life. It's everything. God, I feel like I've been explaining this a lot."

"I hope you didn't Facebook status about this, Cole. They'll kick you out of the family."

Byron laughed, a bark that resulted in comically wide eyes from Levi. "You have no idea how accurate that is."

"Not the Facebook part, I hope."

"No." Byron smiled. "Not the Facebook part."

"I'd heard of you. Everyone has," Levi said. "But I never thought you'd be this weird."

"I don't get out much."

"Yeah, I can tell." Levi tossed him the crossword puzzle book and then the pencil.

Byron caught them in swift succession and tilted his head at Levi.

"You finish a few. Victoria said they'd help me get my mind off things, but they're only reminding me how annoyed I am that I can't look things up on my phone. Rest in peace, phone."

"I guess it was taken as evidence."

"You guess?" Levi rolled down onto his side and propped his head up on his hand. There was something quietly intimate about the way he rested there, so close, and it did nothing for the inappropriate warmth Byron couldn't shake.

"I'm not involved with what the police are doing. I work in PR."

Levi watched him appraisingly, and shook his hair out of his eyes. "You really talked to Sam? In person?"

Byron nodded, careful to keep his expression neutral.

"Did he threaten to kill you?"

Byron kept nodding.

Levi grinned broadly. "What did he say?"

"He said he'll help."

"What?" Levi scrambled up, nearly falling out of the bed.

Byron jumped to his feet, taking Levi gently by the arms to steady him. His heart rate kicked up, set off by the sickly pale of Levi's skin and the low moan of panic on his breath.

"No. No." Levi gasped as if surfacing from icy water. "He can't do that."

"We should talk about this later, when Vic's here."

"No." Levi pushed him with unexpected strength, but it didn't set him off-balance.

He gripped Levi's arms tighter and spoke softly, evenly. "Then you have to calm down."

"Right! Telling me to calm down will definitely calm me down!" Levi yelled, splotches of color rising in his cheeks. At least he was angry and not sliding into blank, crippling fear.

"Sam's a grown-up. This is important to him, and he knows what he's getting into."

"He's gonna get killed. I told him that." Levi's struggle against Byron's hold weakened, and he glared. "I always told him that!"

"He wants to help you," Byron said. "He has friends who want to help."

"It's suicide. I never wanted his help." Levi wilted, but his gaze remained bright.

Byron let go so he could scrub his eyes. "No one wants to watch you die."

"By 'no one' you mean 'the entire world,' probably. You mean *everyone*. Everyone except my friends, my mom, you for some reason, and Victoria, I guess. She seems pretty cool."

Byron sat beside Levi on the bed. The mattress dimpled, and Levi slid toward him, pressed against his side. "Fine. A lot of the world wants you dead right now. But that's not your fault."

"It's partially your fault, though." Levi took a sniffling breath and swore quietly as he wiped his nose on his sleeve.

"I know." Byron frowned at his hands. "Are you okay?"

"In the 'Am I going to have another panic attack?' sense?"

"Yes."

"I'm okay," Levi echoed. He inhaled slowly, as if to prove it. It wasn't impressive.

"I'm meeting with Sam again. Victoria will find a way to get him in here. Maybe a friend of his too. A mage."

"Sam's friends are annoying."

"Well, we're short on people stupid enough to help us, so they'll have to do."

Levi let out a snort that Byron ignored.

"Are you going to be okay with Sam here?" Byron asked. "It's not awkward between you two?"

"We're friends. Why would it be awkward?"

"Because you . . ."

"Because you creeped all over my private life, apparently?" Levi gave Byron a gentle push.

"It's called investigating." Byron fidgeted with his cuffs.

"You said you weren't involved with the police." Levi watched him, openly amused. "Creeper."

"I'm going to assume that means you're not going to be awkward."

"Right. Sam and I were friends, and then we dated, and then we didn't, and now we're still friends."

"Sounds good." Byron reached for the crossword puzzle.

"Mm-hmm." A brief flare of amusement lit up Levi's features, and then it passed like a soft sigh, leaving his expression empty and pale. Even his curls seemed less lively, dull and rumpled from being in bed so much. They had to help him stay hopeful—hopeful and daring enough to test the limits of his magic when the time was right.

Byron gave a crossword puzzle a solid go while Levi alternated between staring at the ceiling and staring at the opposite wall. After a few minutes, he closed his eyes and dozed, his head slowly leaning onto Byron's shoulder until it rested there.

They were still pressed together thigh to thigh, almost companionably. Except that Byron could feel every inch like a cling of static electricity.

He had a strong urge to put his arm around Levi's shoulders.

Now that they were close for the first time, he didn't want to move away. He wanted to hold Levi. He'd been on dates and had sex, but he'd never had the urge to straight up nurture someone. And that was weird.

The crossword puzzle became a meaningless blur as he pictured walking Levi into the shower and washing his hair for him, massaging his curls and kissing the tension away from his neck. Then Byron would hold him while he slept and keep him sheltered for as long as he could.

Levi abruptly shifted his weight—Byron flinched like he'd been caught with porn on his computer screen.

Yawning, Levi sat up and gave him an odd look. He stretched his hands forward, studying his wrists.

"These bands. You'll really take them off?"

"When it's time. Kurt Crane is coming by in two days to check on you. There's no sense taking them off before that."

Levi's breath hitched. He rolled away, giving a squirm that clearly communicated that Byron wasn't welcome anymore.

Byron slipped off the bed and back onto the chair, the crossword puzzle in hand. He stared at the squares and lines, sick knowing he'd announced Kurt Crane's visit without an ounce of sensitivity. Levi had no choice but to endure whatever Crane had planned, and Byron had no way to protect him.

Levi continued to ignore him, even when Victoria arrived freshly showered and carrying a box of warm cookies. Byron didn't blame him. As long as Levi wore the CALM bands, Byron was still the enemy.

CHAPTER 18
THE STRIP

Byron was grabbing an early lunch at a hot dog cart the next day when his phone lit up with a flurry of texts. Before he could read them, the phone buzzed with a call.

"Byron Cole."

At first Warren's assistant, Eric, a young man who was openly scared of Warren, spoke too quickly for Byron to understand. For one awful moment, Byron hoped the news was terrible—a heart attack, an aneurysm. Something quick and painless to take Warren out of the picture.

The truth was worse than that.

"There's been an attack," Eric was saying. "Eight people were killed on the Strip in Las Vegas. Mr. Cole was there—but he's fine. It's a miracle. He climbed out from under a slab of concrete. He's safe!"

"He's safe," Byron echoed.

"Byron? Are you all right?"

"Yes, thank you. I'll call him in a few hours when things have settled down," Byron told Eric. He walked half a block to an electronics store. A few TVs in the window were already playing the news. People were stopping to watch.

Concerned, well-dressed anchors spoke next to live footage that showed a plume of smoke rising from the Vegas Strip. At least it had been early, before rush hour. Byron had never been to Vegas, but he assumed the Strip was quiet in the morning when people were sleeping the night off in their hotel rooms.

He sat down on a concrete bench and fought a wave of nausea.

Victoria texted him. *Did you see the news?*

And Eleanor, two minutes later. *You ok?*

He replied to both numbly, with simple assurances that he was fine, and didn't bother telling them that Warren was safe.

Victoria hadn't been as surprised as Eleanor when Byron told her about Warren's suspected role in the terrorist attacks. She'd sighed and sat down heavily.

"I never fathomed it went that deep, but I knew he was a bad man. AMID needed Cole Industries anyway. We never would have gotten funding anywhere else," she'd said, her voice uncharacteristically small. "Warren's attacks might be orchestrated, but in other parts of the world magic *is* being used as a destructive force. People need a way to defend themselves. I'm sorry, Byron."

He'd worried, for an aching moment, that she'd known about Warren's plans to kill him, but when he'd hinted at his concerns, she'd kicked him in the shin and yelled, "I'm passionate about my work. That doesn't make me a murder apologist!"

Byron turned away from the screen as the news station blurred out bodies and flashed a viewer discretion warning. He'd been close to being one of those bodies—lying among dark stains on the ground, surrounded by broken concrete and shattered glass. Despite having to write official statements on Cole Industries' stance on terrorist attacks, Byron had never grown accustomed to seeing death documented with cold precision. When he'd been sixteen, Warren had invited him to watch a live feed of a rogue mage execution. Byron hadn't asked why Warren had access to the feed, and he hadn't declined the invitation. Even then, he'd known better than to question his uncle.

The mage had been a woman, and she'd died by lethal injection, sobbing uncontrollably until the first wave of sedatives dragged her into silence and the rest of the chemicals stopped her breathing and her heart. Byron had made no sound—done nothing for Warren to see—but Warren had placed his strong hand on Byron's shoulder and held on to him the entire time. Byron had been too scared to close his eyes.

When Warren had asked Byron for his impressions on the execution, Byron had lied. "It was gentler than I expected."

"Exactly my concern. We're considering something with more impact. Firing squads are coming back into style. I'm backing the bill in Mississippi."

Shaking off the memory and tuning out the sound of frightened conversations around him, Byron swallowed against a sour taste in his throat and called into work, telling the receptionist he'd be out for the rest of the day. She murmured an empty platitude, and he hung up on her. He was walking before he made the conscious decision to head back to AMID.

The slap of his shoes against the pavement soothed him and kept him from getting on his phone and browsing Twitter for firsthand accounts of the explosion. Searching wasn't going to find him the answers he needed. Warren was a smart enough man to cover his tracks. This wasn't an amateur effort.

One step at a time. Byron moved with the steady flow of foot traffic toward the entrance to the building that soared far above AMID's underground facility. The offices at the ground level and above used the same security detail in the lobby.

Byron paid closer attention than usual as he headed through security. So many people came and went every day that it wouldn't be impossible to get Penny in to coach Levi. Anyone coming in and out of the building would be on camera, but that was a risk they'd have to take. Getting Levi in control of his magic was the top priority. That way, once they were able to get him out, he wouldn't immediately blow his cover by accidentally doing something spectacular with his magic again.

After they got Levi free, Byron would figure out what to do with Warren.

Victoria met him downstairs and led him to her office. "What a shit show. Are you going to tell him?"

"Why would I?" Byron shrugged his jacket off and held it over his arm.

"I don't know." She leaned against her desk and checked the security feed on her phone. "At least they can't pin this on him, I guess."

"How is he?" Byron gestured at the phone. He dropped his jacket on the small sofa in her office.

"Good. Bored. I got him a few magazines since I can't let him online. It's not that I don't trust him, but it's too risky." Victoria smoothed her sleeves down. "I hate acting as his jailer. We need to start moving with this. He's stable."

"Stable now. But Crane's coming tomorrow."

"I know." Victoria let out a noisy breath. "I'm going to sedate him and hope we don't lose all the progress he's made."

"So not actively freaking out is the best possible status?"

"For now," she said, sliding her phone back into her pocket.

Byron fought a shudder at the thought of Crane at AMID. He had no idea what to expect. There were too many unknowns and not enough to grasp onto.

"We don't know what Levi can really do." He rubbed his eyes where a headache started to build.

"Hopefully more than just shields. Although—a shield built out of instinct, with no training? I'm still blown away he could do that. He's got talent, whether he understands it or not."

Byron nodded. "I don't know that much about the functionality of CALM bands. Can you get them off?"

"Yes. Many of our devices work in conjunction with them, so we've been given full access to the technology."

"All right. I'll talk to Sam, see if his mage friend can help us handle Levi when we take the bands off. I think with the four of us, it'll be safe."

"It won't be safe, but it'll be safer than only you and me."

"Friday, then? That way he has a few days to recover from dealing with Crane, and we have the whole weekend to work with him."

"If he's ready." She glanced at the TV on the wall. The streets were emptier than usual, as if people were afraid to step out after word of the attack in Vegas. "I'm going to have a weapon on hand: a stun neutralizer. I know he won't like that."

"I don't know," Byron said. "He might be relieved. He's worried about hurting us."

"That makes two of us." She shrugged without apology. "There are sandwiches in the fridge. Bring him one, and bottled water? I'm going to go make up a reason for everyone to be banned from the building this weekend."

"World's best boss."

The sandwich options were still lacking. This time, he picked deli turkey with a very sad piece of lettuce on white bread, wrapped in plastic. Byron took it to Levi's room, regretting not bringing something hot from a street cart. He'd been too preoccupied with the news.

"What's wrong?" Levi asked as soon as Byron walked in. He had a different T-shirt on, this one covered in faded gray birds in flight.

"What do you mean what's wrong?" Byron handed him the sandwich.

Levi touched Byron's forehead, startling him into stillness. A hot shiver ran down Byron's back.

"You're frownier than usual." Levi grinned boyishly, his jaw smooth. Victoria must have let him shave. "Don't you ever look in a mirror?"

Levi was one to talk—the circles under his eyes were dark. Exhaustion clung to him. The skin around his eyes was tight like he was trying to hide pain, and Byron suspected the CALM bands had something to do with it. His stomach knotted up at the sight of them gleaming on Levi's wrists.

He handed Levi the bottle of water and rubbed his forehead where Levi had touched him. The skin tingled, a reminder of how infrequently he had physical contact.

"Someone set a bomb off on the Vegas Strip this morning," he said. "A lot of people died."

"Not it." Levi raised one hand, palm out. He took a small bite of the sandwich and chewed like he was gnawing on cardboard. Which probably wasn't far off.

"Very funny. I know."

"Sam thinks there aren't really any terrorist mages in the US. Isn't that a typical American point of view, though? We don't have those, only Europe and the Middle East do, blah, blah."

"Terrorist groups overseas are vocal about their demands. Conflict is typically religiously or politically motivated. No one has ever taken responsibility for the attacks here." It was one of the best points of evidence Byron had to support Sam's theory. Warren was smart and rich, but he wasn't creative—not in the way it would take to fabricate an entire rebel movement.

Levi's brows lifted. "So you're on Sam's conspiracy theory team."

"He makes a lot of good points."

"Like?" Levi took another bite and made a big show out of waiting for Byron's answer.

"Like it isn't natural to use magic for violence. Most of the rebel groups overseas are involved in active conflicts. Awful things that are already happening, and people are using magic as a weapon because they're already involved in violent situations."

"Hmm."

"Think about it." Byron leaned closer. "Would you blow people up?"

Levi hesitated for an unmistakable moment. "No . . ."

"Levi?" Byron rested his elbows on his knees.

The bed rustled as Levi squirmed, shifting his weight around and kicking at the blanket covering his bare feet. "Did you ever wonder why I was there on that train? That morning?"

Byron's pulse quickened, and with a pang of guilt, he reassured himself that the bands were still there to protect him. Was Sam wrong about Warren? Were mages really targeting innocents? Was Levi part of it?

"No. I didn't. Weren't you on your way to work?" But now that he thought about that, it made no sense. Levi had worked and lived in Brooklyn.

"Your uncle." Levi put the sandwich down. "Warren Cole."

"What about him?" Byron's throat felt dry and sticky.

Levi closed his eyes. "You're going to hate me."

Byron struggled to keep his voice even and nonthreatening. "What is it?"

"I was going to go to that press conference, the one about his big new project. I figured he would be there. I wanted to see him in person, see this person who made the things that hurt us. But then I thought—part of me thought—what if I get angry enough, what if I can't control myself? What if I kill him?" He looked up at Byron, stricken. "What if I'd lost control and done it? I'd be a murderer. I'd be worse than him."

Byron stared for several long seconds before relief burst inside of him. Unable to stop himself, he laughed, face buried in his hands.

"What the fuck, Byron!" Levi threw the sandwich crust at him. It bounced off Byron's hands, and that only made him laugh harder. "You're psychotic!"

Byron collected himself quickly, wiping his eyes and coughing to cover the last few horrible chuckles. He picked up the crust and tossed it into the wastebasket in the corner. "Sorry. It's just—wow."

Levi crossed his arms and glared at him. "I've been agonizing about this, and you think it's hilarious."

"It's not that." Byron shook his head. "Warren set me up to die in that explosion. I was supposed to die that morning. He's not . . . He had it coming."

"What?" Levi rubbed his biceps idly, like he was cold. "*You*? How would he . . ."

"He's behind all of the attacks. I'm pretty sure he is, anyway."

"Well, that's fucked up," Levi said. "But it's still not funny. You're nuts."

It wasn't funny at all. Lately, Byron wasn't convinced his mental faculties were entirely in place. He sat up straight and stretched, trying to shake off the giddy relief. "Thinking that someone deserves to die isn't the same as trying to kill them. You never would have done that."

"Uh-huh." Levi rolled his eyes. "Because you know me super well."

"I believe you're a good person."

He huffed a breath. "I would have been too scared to do it, if anything."

"No." Byron shook his head. "You weren't too scared to save all of us, and it had the same consequences."

"Which is fucked up, by the way."

Byron offered him a smile. "Exactly."

"You're not mad that I might have killed your uncle?" Levi's small voice twisted Byron's heart. They could sit here and talk and get to know each other, but it didn't change the balance of power.

Levi was entirely at his mercy. He knew it, and he knew well enough not to trust Byron or trust that he was safe here.

"First of all, it's not like you tried."

"I might have tried."

"I think it's amazing, actually." Byron spoke as gently as he could. "I mean, not really. It would have been horrible if you'd done something to Warren, and you might have hurt others."

Levi flinched.

"But someone needs to stop him," Byron said. "This can't go on."

"None of this can go on. I know you're worried about the people who are getting killed, and you should be, but there are hundreds of thousands of mages stuck wearing these things." Levi held out his banded wrists. "They're losing their rights, they're getting beat up and abused and killed, sometimes. That has to change too."

"I know." Byron fought the urge to cover Levi's hands with his own. "I'm trying to figure out how to do this."

"You tell the truth!"

"It isn't that simple."

"It is, though." Levi dropped his arms to his sides. "You basically lie for a living, don't you? Just do the opposite of that."

"I don't lie, exactly."

"You 'spin,'" Levi said, making air quotes. "Spin it the other way. The good way. I'm not the only pissed-off mage who hates Warren and wants to be, you know, free. And you can't be the only person capable of seeing the truth."

Byron nodded. "That's what I'm counting on. But we have to do this carefully."

"Without blowing people up."

"Exactly."

For the first time since he'd arrived at AMID, Levi's brown eyes held as much fire as they had in the photos in his apartment.

Byron's chest hurt. What would their lives have been like if the explosion hadn't happened? Would Levi have brought him home to his colorful little apartment? Was he the kind of guy who had a one-night stand?

"Why now? I'm not the first person your uncle's hurt."

"I thought you were really cute." Startled by his own honesty, Byron immediately tried to backtrack, but only managed to mumble, "On the subway."

"When they interview you for the Nobel Peace Prize, please don't give them that answer."

Byron gusted out a breath and laughed once. "It's more than that."

"Riiight." Levi grinned and shifted on the bed, sitting with his legs crossed. When he brushed his hair out of his eyes, something fluttered in Byron's stomach. "I thought you were cute too. But also uptight and probably a dick."

"I'm not a dick," Byron said, unaffected by Levi's assessment. His formative years had been a careful cultivation of exactly what Levi had described. If Levi's first impression had been bad, he was pulling it off reasonably well.

"No." Levi glanced up. "You're weird, though. You're really weird."

The ease in Levi's voice charmed Byron. The seemingly aimless young man must have been hiding depths of passion about magic and freedom and justice. Byron wanted to see him unfettered—given the chance to rage and laugh.

He wanted something else, too. Something he didn't want to name. The fledgling secret itched behind his ribs. Could Levi see it on his face?

But Levi was already fidgeting with the sheets again, his brief amusement replaced with a shadowed frown. Byron had the luxury of sometimes forgetting why they were here and what was coming, but Levi didn't.

Reality returned to Byron like a flood of ice water. Kurt Crane was coming to AMID, and there was nothing they could do to stop him.

CHAPTER 19
INVESTED

"You're too quiet," Levi said the next morning, watching Victoria riffle through her medical bag.

Victoria waved him off.

She didn't seem to be a cheerful woman, but she wasn't cold either. Her total silence raised a lot of red flags Levi didn't want to contemplate on the day Kurt Crane was coming here. And coming for reasons Byron and Victoria hadn't explained beyond shady shrugs and half-assed reassurances.

"Is he going to hurt me?" Levi blurted out like a held breath.

Victoria glanced up from the blood pressure cuff she was fiddling with. She stayed quiet long enough for Levi to cultivate a heavy knot of dread. "I don't think so. He's only coming by to make sure you're not being mishandled by my team." She drew a slow breath and met his eyes steadily. "He clearly has a sense of ownership of you."

"Are we all on the same page that that's gross and terrible?"

A small, tired smile softened her features. "Yes. We are."

She carried the bag over to Levi's bed and sat at the foot. Her gray fitted jacket and narrow pencil skirt made her sleek, like a business sea lion. Levi stifled a laugh.

Victoria's mouth quirked. "What?"

"I'm losing my mind, I think. I pictured you at SeaWorld in a show. It's your outfit: it's very seal-ish."

She smoothed the front of her jacket. "I suppose it's good that you're hanging on to your sense of humor."

"Where's Byron?"

"He's at work." She gave him a quick, odd look. "He'll come by later, but we don't want Crane to see him here. Warren knows he's supposedly documenting my studies, but I don't think it's wise to let on how invested he is."

Invested. Levi ducked, unsure why thinking about that made his belly flutter. It wasn't like Byron cared about him in a personal way . . . even if he had brought Levi his pillow. Byron was committed to this whole thing because people's lives and futures depended on changing America's views toward magic.

It wasn't like Levi himself didn't usually care about the rest of his kind, but right now he was more concerned about being in the same room as Kurt Crane again—without any concrete reassurance that he'd be safe.

He flinched when Victoria reached for his arm to take his blood pressure.

"Oh." Their eyes met, and she looked away first. "I'm sorry."

"Don't be," he said automatically. While she placed a stethoscope against the inside of his arm, he took slow breaths, trying to do some yoga breathing to calm the fuck down.

"Pretty high. That's to be expected today." She handed him a thermometer to place under his tongue. The plastic cover tickled his lips. "I suppose that brings us to the plan."

"Plan?" She frowned at him, and he closed his lips tightly around the thermometer until it beeped and she took it out of his mouth. "That's refreshing. I thought we were winging it."

"Today warrants a plan." Victoria paused. "I can sedate you. And I think I should. But I'm leaving it up to you."

"This isn't like having my wisdom teeth out." Levi drew his feet up on the bed and hugged his knees. "I don't know what's better. Wouldn't he be suspicious if I'm conked out?"

"He may be. But if you're . . . unstable," she said slowly, as if struggling to choose the right words, "it would rouse suspicion as well. He knows there isn't much we can do here with a resistant, distressed individual."

Levi rolled his eyes. Byron and Victoria made everything sound so clinical. He knew what she meant—he was likely to flip out again the way he had in the shower, and that wasn't going to help them at all. "Can you give me something to take the edge off and let me try to do this without being asleep?"

Victoria smiled. "Yes. I can definitely do that."

She went to the cabinets along the wall and unlocked one with a key card.

"Wait, like, now?"

"He'll be here in half an hour."

Levi's resolve to face Crane crumbled, and he placed his hand against his belly as if he could shove away the vicious butterflies that had begun cutting through his stomach. Despite Victoria's care, he still struggled to eat, and slept fitfully. His body hurt like he had the flu, and his magic pooled deep in his bones—always cold, always aching. Flutters of fear felt like razor blades in his gut.

"I don't know if I can do this."

She handed him a bottled water and offered a small pill. "This isn't that strong. If you need more before he gets here, I can give you another."

He swallowed it down, finishing the soothing, lukewarm water in several long gulps. "I don't feel anything."

"Wait a few minutes. I need you to get into these scrubs." She pulled dull-blue scrubs out of a cabinet. "They're not the kind that are open in the back."

Grateful for a task to focus on, Levi changed in the bathroom. He folded his clothes neatly and then handed them over to Victoria. It took him a long moment to let go. They were the only thing that made him feel human, and losing that small shred of dignity and familiarity made his throat go tight.

"Better?" he asked, turning slowly.

"Yes, you look more like a prisoner. I'm going to take you to another room down the hall. We . . ." She closed her medical bag and straightened the plastic containers full of cotton swabs and thermometer covers on the table. "We use it to simulate the conditions in typical prisons. I want you to try to stay calm about it. I promise you'll only be in there as long as Crane is here."

"Can I place an order with Byron for tasty snacks when Crane's done?"

Victoria swiped her card and held the door open. "Yes."

Levi stayed close beside her as they walked down the hall. Her shoulders were tight and her steps quick and tense. "Are you afraid of me?"

"I'm wary." She slowed, let him catch up, and glanced down at his bare feet. "You don't have much reason to cooperate with me."

"I don't think I'd be able to overtake you right now, even if I tried to." Levi paused and braced himself against the wall, his lungs tight like he'd been running for fifteen minutes. "I feel like shit."

"I can tell," she said grimly. She offered her hand and he took it, finding her grip stronger and steadier than he'd expected. "The CALM bands aren't good for you. If I had time, I'd want to do tests, find out exactly how they're affecting your system."

"Bonus lab-rat time? No, thanks."

"Of course. I'm sure you're done being poked and prodded," she said, only slightly wistfully.

Levi snorted. "Can't stop your science-brain, I guess."

She opened another door, this time with a keypad, and held it for him. It had a narrow window laced with honeycombed wire, and a slot near the floor. He hadn't expected anything as comfortable as his previous room, but the frigid concrete floor still shocked him.

"Cozy." A low cot bolted to the floor and an aluminum toilet were the only two things in the room.

"I'd say make yourself comfortable, but I know that isn't likely to happen. I need to go meet with Crane and bring him in here. If you can manage it, be respectful. Don't argue. The story is that we haven't started testing yet. I'll do the talking."

Levi sank onto the cot and crossed his legs. His breathing refused to steady, and his hands trembled. "Got it."

"Do you need more meds? It's now or never."

"No. I'll be all right."

Victoria pursed her lips and touched his head. She drew her hand away quickly and cleared her throat. "You can do this."

"I have to."

Left alone in the room lit by a single recessed light on the ceiling, Levi briefly contemplated doing a few sun salutations to keep his mind off waiting, but his legs were shaking too hard. The bare walls stared at him. He closed his eyes, ducked his chin, and focused on his breath, feeling it cool his nostrils as he inhaled, and warm the back of his throat as he exhaled.

Whatever Victoria had given him kept at bay the impulse to throw himself at the locked door, so that was something.

He counted sixty breaths, then gave up on counting and breathed with a quiet mantra instead. When he had made it to a studio, his mantra had been typically simple. *I am here. Breathe.*

Now he breathed in slowly, *Fuck*, and exhaled, *this place*.

The door opened, and he swallowed back a yelp. Kurt Crane walked in first, as sweaty and soft as Levi remembered him. His spotted scalp showed between the lines of his comb-over, and he wore the same lab coat and expression of fanaticism.

"You look very well," he said, opening his arms as if he expected a hug. "What an improvement!"

Victoria followed, meeting Levi's eyes for a moment before frowning at Crane. "His condition has improved, but I'm concerned about his health overall, Dr. Crane. He's been running a low fever, and he's lost five pounds since he got here. He reports general malaise."

"Malaise." Crane snorted. "Stand up for me, Camden."

Levi rose to his feet unsteadily and kept his gaze on the floor. The room was cold, but not cold enough to warrant the way his entire body shook. He crossed his arms to try to still the tremors.

"He was in a coma when I saw him last. I'd call this significant progress."

Victoria hummed a flat sound. "Mr. Cole said you'd be checking his vitals. Was there anything particular you wanted me to keep an eye on? I'm happy to send you daily reports."

"No, no," Crane said warmly, standing close to Levi without touching him.

Levi fought the urge to cringe. Crane radiated keen interest, like a dog with its eyes on a treat.

"How do you feel?" Crane asked.

"Tired." Levi tried to meet Crane's eyes, his breath hitching.

"Nervous?"

"Yes."

Crane clasped his hands together. "I wouldn't go as far as to say you shouldn't be nervous, but I assure you, when we get started at my facility, you won't be conscious for long. No need to dwell on it."

Anger swelled up in Levi's chest. He caught Victoria's semifrantic expression and bit it back. If he could use his magic, he'd use it to crush Crane until he couldn't breathe or hurt anyone anymore.

His ass hit the cot, jarring a grunt out of him. His eyes widened with the shock of being pushed, but he hadn't felt a thing.

Crane hadn't done a thing.

Victoria crouched beside him, steadying him.

"What happened?" Levi mumbled.

"We plan to get started tomorrow," Victoria said over her shoulder. She squeezed Levi's arm gently.

"Don't overextend him," Crane said. "We've made remarkable progress this month. You may need another test subject."

Victoria eased Levi down onto his side, and he curled up and closed his eyes, the room spinning. He'd been okay one moment, but now his pulse was pounding in his ears and his stomach was threatening to empty itself onto the shiny concrete floor. He barely heard the remainder of their quiet conversation, and only realized they were gone when the room went silent.

He coughed out a weak sob, relief warring with aftershocks of anger. He hated Crane for hurting him, for treating him like an animal. He hated Warren Cole for giving Crane the power to do it. He hated Byron for making him do this alone.

"Levi."

He curled up more tightly and cradled his head in his hands, as afraid of the current of magic inside him as he was of Crane.

"Levi. Hey. He's gone now. You're okay. You're safe now."

It was Byron, his hands warm and tender, not trying to pry Levi's fingers out of his hair, but stroking them carefully. "Victoria says I should carry you, but I want your sign-off on that before I haul you back to your room, all right?"

Levi's breath caught on a broken laugh. "Give me a sec."

Byron and Victoria spoke to each other in low murmurs, sounds he'd grown used to. Despite everything, he found them comforting. Little by little, his breathing evened out and he managed to push up to sit and focus on Byron.

"What happened back there?" Victoria asked.

Levi watched Byron, startled to find him rumpled and flushed, as if he'd been running. His hair had clearly been carefully gelled at some point during the day, but now half of it stuck straight up. "What?"

"You dropped like someone hit you with a dart. Do you know what happened?"

"Oh." He focused on Victoria's slender fingers working at her palms anxiously. "I think I accidentally tried to use my magic. Maybe to murder Crane, I don't know. I guess the CALM bands really work."

"They shouldn't work like that." Her brow knit deeply. "I hope they don't work like that."

"Can you walk?" Byron asked. He had his hands on Levi's knees, and Levi wasn't too sure he knew it. Usually he treated Levi like he was a sandcastle about to crumble to pieces.

"Nope."

Byron glanced at Victoria, as if for guidance, and she gestured impatiently. Anxious to get out of this horrible tomb, Levi wrapped his arms around Byron's neck to get things moving.

His stomach gave a swoop as Byron stood with him, strong and steady. Sam had carried him once like this, jokingly, before tumbling him onto the bed. The memory struck Levi like a blow, and he tucked his face against Byron's neck and squeezed his eyes shut against a wave of grief. His life had been normal before. Boring at worst.

The regular bedroom was a palace compared to where he'd been. Victoria stepped out and Byron helped Levi change back into his regular clothes—a pair of soft sweatpants and his T-shirt. He moved comfortably and efficiently, and sighed once Levi was tucked back in his bed.

"I was waiting at a coffee shop around the corner," Byron said. "Victoria let me know the moment Crane left, and I ran over."

"Did you literally run?"

Byron blinked. "Yes."

"It wasn't an emergency."

"She said you fell and she wasn't sure what happened."

"She's a doctor." Levi wasn't sure why Victoria would defer to Byron, who knew how to make things up but probably had no idea how to figure out if Levi was in medical danger.

"I know." Byron frowned. "I was . . . I wanted to come."

Levi slid down the bed and curled onto his side, drawing the blankets all around him and finally feeling somewhat safe again, his knees drawn close and his pillow soft at his cheek.

Byron pulled a chair up to the bed. "Did he hurt you?"

"No. He made it sound like I won't be able to stay here much longer, though."

A flash of something crossed Byron's bright-blue eyes. He aged in that moment, and Levi could see the leader he might grow into if he developed as much confidence as he faked.

"I'll find out," Byron said. *At least he has the decency not to make promises.* "Do you mind if I stay for a while?"

Levi snorted. "I don't really get a say in that."

"I'm asking you because you do have a say. If you need time to yourself, I don't have to be in here."

A smile tugged at the corner of Levi's mouth. He yawned to hide it. "Yeah, you can stay."

Byron's shoulders loosened. He settled into his chair and reached for the crossword book. After scribbling quietly for a few minutes, he spoke as if to no one, his voice soft but resolute. "I'm going to fix this."

Levi didn't believe that he could, but the quiet statement warmed him anyway.

CHAPTER 20
UNBOUND

As Byron waited for Penny in the AMID lobby on Thursday afternoon, a businesswoman walked up to him and extended her hand. "Hi."

He blinked. "Um, hello."

"I'm here for the job interview?"

Byron smiled. People often confused him for someone else. He had one of those faces. "Sorry—I think you have the wrong person."

"There aren't too many Byron Coles around here," she said. "And the longer we stand here chatting, the more likely it is someone's going to remember seeing me here with you."

"Whoa." Byron touched the pendant at his chest, reassuring himself that it was there.

"It's called hair and makeup." Penny wasn't wearing glasses and had her curly hair pulled back in a twisty, fancy hairstyle. Eye shadow gave her eyes a catlike shape, and she wore a sleek charcoal pantsuit and shiny black high heels. He never would have recognized her as the airy, hippy woman from Summons.

"You're right on time." Byron cleared his throat and led her through security, showing the guard his Cole Industries identification and collecting her guest badge.

No one would think twice about a professional visiting for a job interview. And hopefully no one would notice that she never walked back out.

The security guard checked her bag, quickly sifting through a scarf, a wallet, a bunch of tampons, a pair of glasses, and a makeup bag. He waved them through the metal detector, and Byron led the way down the escalators and elevators to the AMID facilities, using his electronic badge to gain access.

Victoria met them at the entrance, mouth hanging open a shade too long as she looked Penny up and down. "Hi. I'm Dr. Victoria Alvarez."

"Penelope Wallace," Penny said with boisterous confidence, extending her hand. "Penny is fine. I've read a great deal about your work."

"Have you?" Victoria shook her hand firmly as she glanced at Byron.

Byron shrugged. He hadn't spent much time with Penny, but she hadn't struck him as a fan of nanoscience. He glanced at Victoria's hip and recognized a small device made to resemble a cell phone on a clip. It was a stun weapon that immediately disoriented magic users. He didn't blame her for carrying it. They'd have very little defense if Penny's idea of cooperating was attacking them and trying to get Levi out of the building.

"Yes, I admire what you're doing." Penny reached back and loosened her hair. It fell in a long, messy tumble around her shoulders, not quite as curly as it had been at Summons. She dug into her purse and retrieved her thick glasses. "Are we safe to speak freely here down here?"

"Yes." Victoria tilted her head. "Though I've been told you have ways to accomplish that on your own."

"Not around recording devices. I trust you're not foolish enough to keep recordings of treasonous activity."

"You would be correct."

Penny adjusted her glasses. "Perfect. As I was saying, I try to familiarize myself with technology used against mages. AMID has a good track record as far as developing humane methods. Stun weaponry, shields, antiglamour devices. You're not invested in torture or punishment. I respect that."

"Byron, I like her," Victoria said with a smile. "Let's get you situated, Penny."

As they walked, Penny wiped her lipstick off on a small handkerchief from her purse and smacked her lips together. "I feel like a damn clown like this. It's so uncomfortable. No offense, Dr. Alvarez. Your lipstick is lovely."

"Victoria, please. None taken."

Penny walked with long, sure steps, her bag swinging beside her. As they passed office doors and long, rectangular windows that overlooked the large workroom, she didn't glance around. It was like she didn't care one bit that she'd gained access to a highly secure facility producing many of the world's most innovative antimagic devices.

"I met Levi a few times when he and Sam were dating. Nice boy. Deeply in the closet."

Victoria squeaked as she walked, her heels click-clacking along with Penny's.

"Sorry—the magic closet." Penny huffed a laugh. "He's good and out, otherwise."

"Are there really those who—sorry if the question is rude, this is very new to me—live openly as mages?" Victoria massaged her wrist. "I mean, without wearing CALM bands."

"Of course there are. Excuse me a moment." Without preamble, Penny took her heels off, tucked them into her big purse, and slid on a pair of flats that had been rolled up. "It's nerve-racking enough walking right into the enemy's lair, let alone trying it in heels."

Victoria glanced over her shoulder. "I know you don't have any reason to trust us, but I want you to know that we're committed to keeping you safe. You're risking a great deal to help Levi."

"I want to help him," Penny said. "But I have to admit it's a little self-serving too. That boy clearly has gifts beyond his imagining. I've never come across that much natural power." Her gaze flickered to Byron. "Though there's no telling how many powerful mages submitted to CALM. Our nation has lost an amazing resource by bottling up all that potential."

"Yes." Victoria paused, taking a slow breath. "But my point was, I hope that we can trust you too."

"I don't plan on doing anything that would jeopardize your efforts or Levi's safety. But I'm sure the sheer number of antimagic devices in this building alone must be a comfort." Penny gestured at Victoria's hip.

"Do you think you can help him?" Byron asked, hoping to shatter the building tension. "Teach him to control what he can do?"

"I can try. I've spoken to others about how their gifts developed. I don't know that there are hard-and-fast rules. If our culture was allowed to flourish, I believe we'd have standards for these things. Guidelines. And I believe we'd police each other—and teach our young people to use magic responsibly."

Byron thought about the things that people compared magic to: Weapons, primarily. Firearms. Even explosives. Listening to Penny talk, it made no sense to compare magic to anything destructive.

"I'd love to have coffee with you later," Victoria was saying, "if you have a free moment while Levi's resting. To pick your brain."

"An interrogation?" Penny tilted her head. "Or a chat?"

"A chat, I swear." Victoria smiled at her in the winning way that often got her what she wanted. "I'm eager to hear about these mages. I only have intel on rebel groups overseas—but they're clearly extremists."

"Or suffering through horrific circumstances and left with no other choice but to defend themselves."

Victoria's look said she wasn't going to give her that much. Byron didn't blame her. He'd seen the results of conflicts between small governments and mage groups seeking control. They weren't pretty. It was difficult to sympathize with those who demonstrated indiscriminate violence, even to avoid persecution. Under no circumstances could Byron's and Victoria's efforts—with Penny's and Levi's help—result in mass casualties.

"I want to know more about what magic is capable of when it isn't used in warfare," Victoria said. "I want to know what we're not being taught in our briefs and lectures."

"Good." Penny nodded and shifted her bag on her shoulder. "I'm glad to hear that. And yes, we can chat as much as you'd like."

They arrived at Levi's door. Penny turned away politely as Byron entered the code that Victoria changed every few days.

Levi was sitting on the edge of the bed, his hair damp and his mouth a tight, nervous line. He was wearing his sneakers. When he saw Penny, he hid an eye roll poorly. Victoria raised an eyebrow at Byron.

Levi hadn't said much about Penny when Byron had let him know they were bringing her down to help him, but Byron hadn't gotten the impression that he outright disliked her.

"Honey," Penny said, "you look terrible."

"And you look like the cat who ate the canary," he said, submitting to an awkward hug and avoiding Byron's gaze over her shoulder.

"I wanted you to embrace your potential, but not under these circumstances."

"Uh-huh." He shrugged away from her.

She put her bag on the rolling tray table at the foot of Levi's bed and clapped her hands together. "So when do we start?"

"There's no reason to wait. We're the only ones here now," Victoria said. "I told everyone they needed to be out for the weekend for a sanitation service. And as you ascertained, the security cameras are not recording. Levi, if you're up for it, we can move to the weapons-testing room."

Levi shrank back. "What?"

"No, not to test weapons. There's nothing dangerous in there right now—it's simply an open space. It's the safest place to let you test your magic." Victoria cleared her throat. "I assume."

Byron knew her well enough to know that it must torture her not to have a strong sense of how this would go or how Levi's magic worked, precisely. Science had managed to narrow down the wavelength of magic—hypothesized to be a form of energy that could only be manipulated by those with a genetic predisposition. But little was known about magic's practical applications.

Even less was known about the limitations of magic—at least by people like Byron and Victoria. Penny spoke of enchantments, but he wasn't even sure what that really meant. Did she use actual magic words, spells?

Every bit of credible research and meaningful funding had gone into shutting magic down, into finding ways to block it—and to siphon it.

"What's the point of letting me test my magic?" Levi's fingers dug into the sheets.

"I'll let you take that one, Byron," Victoria said.

"Well." Byron swallowed. "We're working that part out. Sam's researching rural areas where mage sympathizers should be able to keep you off the radar. But we can't take that step until we know you can test your magic and control it. No more displays on the news."

"Yeah, but . . . rural." Levi grimaced.

"Rural has more of an appeal than *dead*," Penny said.

Levi's breath quickened and he nodded shakily.

"Hey." Byron waited until Levi met his gaze. "You ready?"

Levi exhaled heavily and gave a small smile. "Yeah."

Shame washed over Byron. Levi deserved a much better ally than someone who had actively encouraged hatred of his kind.

Victoria touched Byron's back briefly, as if she could sense his hesitation.

They walked in silence down the empty hall and onto the second-floor scaffolding that circled the large, open room for testing weapons. Byron had never been invited to observe testing, but knew that the government had a very limited number of mages working for them as test subjects.

The test subjects were volunteers—men and women who had opted into government service for a chance to be released from their CALM bands, even briefly. According to Victoria, her team went out of their way to make sure they didn't face unnecessary discomfort during testing. But it wasn't a painless process. How many mages had been harmed in this room?

They walked down to the main level in a single-file line, the stairs rattling under their feet. Victoria led the way, and Byron walked behind Levi at the rear. Levi took the steps haltingly. He seemed to grow weaker every day despite being in better care with AMID than he'd been at the Cole Industries containment facility.

Byron caught Levi's elbow when he took a heavy step, and Levi glanced back at him, lips parted in gentle surprise. He offered Byron a quick, unsteady smile before his gaze shifted to Byron's grip.

Byron hadn't let go.

"This place is creepy," Levi mumbled as Byron released him.

For the most part, the large circular room was empty. The sealed concrete floor gleamed. Another heavy door led to the lower floor of the facility, but there were no observation windows at ground level.

Victoria walked to a rolling cart covered with small machines and a laptop. "I'm going to set this to record the magic levels. It won't affect anything, and you won't feel it."

Levi stared at the floor. His hands trembled.

"Levi," Victoria said carefully, "I know you have no reason to trust my word, but I promise. These machines won't hurt you."

Penny slung an arm around Levi and turned her sharp gaze on Byron. "What happened to him here?"

"Not here." Byron's skin went cold at a flash of memory—Levi's mouth contorted with agony. He shuddered. "It wasn't here."

Levi shrugged her off and crossed his arms. "It's fine."

Penny lowered her voice. "If you're upset, we don't have to do this now. It's much more difficult to control magic when you're not in control of your emotions. I don't want you to hurt yourself."

Levi gave a stubborn shake of his head. "I want to try."

She drew in a tight breath. "Then you have to calm down first."

"Right. No pressure." He took a step away from her and closed his eyes, shivering.

"Do the yoga thing you did before," Byron suggested.

Levi blinked his eyes open at him. "Here?"

"Here is fine," Victoria said. "It's going to take me five minutes to get this program up and running. Do whatever you need. Jog around, meditate." She turned to Penny. "If you want, I can show you how the program coordinates with these sensors."

Byron sent her a silent thank-you for distracting Penny, who was clearly not helping Levi settle down. The women spoke in hushed tones by the equipment as Byron approached Levi, trying to keep his hands down—despite a strong urge to wrap his arms around him.

"Do it with me so I don't feel like an idiot," Levi said. "Come on, arms up. Feet at hips' distance. There you go." He lifted his chin and watched his fingers.

"What does your tattoo mean?" Byron asked, stretching and feeling stupid. His shoulders ached immediately.

"Nothing. I let the artist freehand it. I wanted something beautiful, that's all." Levi glanced from his hands to Byron. "Get your shoulders out of your ears."

"My shoulders aren't in my ears." Byron lowered them, fighting against the tension there. When Levi bent over, Byron followed, and grimaced at how far his reaching hands remained from his toes. The next movements were semifamiliar from watching Levi, but they felt uncomfortable and strange. Byron had none of the ease Levi moved with.

They did three cycles, and by the third, Byron almost had the hang of it. Levi was out of breath, and his skin glowed with a faint sheen of sweat, but his arms hung loosely beside him. "We better do this, because I've got about two more of these in me before I pass out," he panted.

Byron couldn't tell if he was joking, and made a mental note to ask Victoria if Levi was supposed to be this exhausted.

"Perfect timing," Victoria said, smiling over at them. She approached Levi with a small metal tool like a futuristic skeleton key. "This opens your CALM bands. It won't hurt to remove them. You can hold this first if you'd like."

"I'm not five years old. It's fine." Levi thrust his arms out. The bands were completely smooth. He turned his palms up, revealing the tiny notch on the underside.

Levi's fingers were shaking, and Byron reconciled himself to the fact that there was simply no way of getting around his anxiety. At least he was calmer than he'd been before doing his yoga.

It only took a few seconds for Victoria to unlock each band. They expanded with a mechanical whirr, and she covered them with her fingers. "As soon as I pull them away from your hands, your magic will be released. Some mages report dizziness, disorientation. Sit down if you need to."

Levi bowed his head and closed his eyes. "Got it." His hair fell in his face, trembling as he shivered.

Victoria drew the cuffs away, and Levi's body jolted back like she'd touched him with a live wire. He cried out and collapsed, one knee striking the floor hard before Byron caught hold of him and pulled him down, cushioning him from the concrete with his legs and lap.

Penny crouched, eyes wide. "It's all right. He's all right.

It didn't look all right. Levi took huge, gulping breaths. His arms moved in jerking motions that seemed random until Byron saw that he was rubbing his wrists against his chest and against each other as if trying to relieve a terrible itch. He moaned—not with pain, but pleasure.

Heat echoed through Byron. The skin on his back prickled with sweat.

"It's all right," Penny repeated, wiping her eyes beneath her glasses. "He can feel his magic again."

Levi's movements abruptly slowed, became something else entirely. He writhed against Byron's lap. Penny covered her mouth, a faint flush lighting her face, and when Byron looked up at Victoria, desperate for guidance, her gaze fixed on her computer screen.

"Levi," Byron said hesitantly, brushing Levi's messy hair out of his face. Levi shook his head and turned into him, burying his face against Byron's chest. His hot breath tickled. Whatever Levi was feeling, he clearly wasn't aware of his surroundings. He made himself smaller and wrapped his arms around Byron, making soft noises that fell somewhere between joyful cries and quiet weeping.

At a loss, Byron rubbed small circles at Levi's back. Levi's skin was warmer than before, more alive. How much had those bands been hurting him?

It took a long time for Levi's breath to even out. "Sorry," he mumbled, a heated vibration against Byron's skin.

"It's cool. I've got you."

Levi rolled out of Byron's lap and onto his back to the floor. He drew his knees up and threw one arm over his face to shield his eyes. His face was wet, and Byron knew it was literally the most inappropriate time for it, but he felt his dick swelling and shifted his sitting position to hide it. He pulled the wrinkles out of his shirt, touching the place where Levi's tears dampened the fabric.

Penny cleared her throat. "How you doing down there?"

Levi let out a weak laugh and rubbed his eyes. "Like I'll die if they put those back on me."

The *they* hit Byron like a slap. But he had no right to be hurt by it. He wasn't Levi's friend. He was barely his ally. His good intentions didn't exonerate him.

He glanced at Victoria, and she was frowning. Foolishly, they hadn't discussed what would happen after this little experiment—what would happen when Crane returned for another checkup.

Levi was watching him. "If we do any magic, I want to do it from the floor. I am now made of putty."

"In a bad way?" Victoria asked, in the carefully casual tone doctors used when they were asking how often patients smoked or had more than three drinks per week.

"In the best way." Levi sighed. "I don't want to move."

Penny laughed. "Son, I've never seen anything like that."

"We release bound mages here a few times a month." Victoria's voice was thick with guilt. "The reactions aren't usually that dramatic. But the unbinding of magic often manifests as a significant . . . release."

"She means you give good sex face," Penny said.

Levi snorted and flicked at her, like a little boy tossing spitballs across a classroom.

Several things happened very quickly.

Penny cried out, toppling backward, one hand clasping her upper arm.

Victoria snatched a blocky gun out of the equipment cart and aimed it at Levi.

And Levi scrambled to sit up, his palms sliding on the concrete, his eyes wide and scared. "Oh my God."

"Levi!" Victoria said his name firmly and slowly, as if speaking to a child. "Don't panic. This will stop you immediately if you hurt her again."

Byron rushed to Penny, helping her sit up and shrug out of her jacket. Together they rolled her sleeve up hurriedly. He expected to find blood, but whatever Levi had done hadn't broken her skin. She bore an ugly dark-red bruise the size of a quarter.

"Levi," she said shakily. "Levi, I'm fine. It's only a little mark."

Levi had scooted away until his back met the wall. His fingers pulled into tight fists jammed against his thighs. "Did I just shoot a fucking magic missile at you? What the fuck!"

"Yes." Penny laughed nervously and rubbed the spot. Byron eased her back into her jacket. "Better than you blasting my entire arm off."

"Let's avoid any playful imaginary projectiles from now on," Victoria said, her stun weapon still trained steadily on Levi. "This thing will knock you out for several hours, and we don't have that kind of time."

"How did that happen?" Levi asked hoarsely.

Penny let out a sigh. "Taking the bands off must have triggered your magic to swell. You were holding it in for so long. For your entire life. You can't go back to that. Your magic won't let you. It's free now. It wants to sing."

"Preferably with the volume down," Victoria muttered.

Levi opened his hands slowly and studied them. Despite having gone pale, he glowed with a healthy flush. The circles under his eyes were gone. He was once more the man Byron had checked out on the subway what felt impossibly long ago.

"Penny." Levi curled his fingers into fists again. "Help me."

CHAPTER 21
IN BUSINESS

Victoria might as well be pointing a toy gun at Levi. He wasn't worried about whatever it had the ability to do to him. He was worried about hurting them. Hurting Penny again. He'd never really liked her—she'd made him feel ashamed and shitty for not psychotically doing magic all over the place like she did. But he didn't hate her, and he definitely didn't want to hurt her.

He was worried about hurting Byron too. Byron had been wide-eyed and freaked out, but he'd held on to Levi when Levi had been consumed by the magic sparking through him. Levi could still feel where Byron had touched him and soothed him, and he wasn't sure what to think about that, or why it felt good. He filed that away for later.

Everything was so fucked up. The danger wasn't Victoria's weird weapon, it was *him*.

And he could feel the raw power in him. His magic flickered under his skin, shimmering like the warped edges of a fire. It wanted to escape.

"Let's start over. Did you use magic before, at all?" Penny asked. "Anytime in your life."

"Once, when I was little. Another time alone in the woods. The shield thing, and right now," Levi said slowly, thinking back as if he might have somehow forgotten something as huge as using magic—something he'd avoided his entire life. "That's it."

Penny stood unsteadily and walked over to where he was trying and failing to hide thanks to the stupid circular room. Byron followed her like a bodyguard, which was ridiculous considering how defenseless he was. Both of them crouched out of reach, as if Levi was a dangerous animal.

It made him feel like shit.

"What do I do?" His voice stuck in his throat, and he was on the verge of tears. He needed to know how to control this. His magic sparked and danced, so much louder than he'd ever known it to be before he'd made the shield. He'd ignored it for long periods of time, days—weeks, even—because it had simply been part of him. An afterthought. Now it screamed, bright with joy and longing, and it scared him. It scared him a lot.

"Magic needs intention, focus," Penny said. He tried not to notice the way she massaged her right arm. "You didn't want to hurt me, but you must have slipped out a little bit of intention when you moved your fingers."

He rubbed his head. "I don't get it."

Byron watched them silently, and Victoria—over with her machines—had lowered her gun. But she still held it at her side.

"You have to want things," Penny said. "You have to coax your magic to help you get the things you want. I know it sounds like it doesn't make sense, but once it clicks into place, it's as effortless as breathing."

"Like those Magic Eye books, with the hidden pictures?" Byron asked.

Penny closed her eyes for a long moment, clearly not impressed with his help. "Except it's not unlimited. You're using energy from within. You're using a part of yourself."

"Can you show me?" Levi asked.

Penny glanced over at Byron and Victoria, and they both nodded. "I'm going to bump my magic against yours," she said. "Those of us who remain free can identify each other this way. It's like sonar with bats, I suppose. I haven't consulted a bat on that one."

Levi chuckled, grateful for release, but the sound died in his throat when her magic reached him.

It felt like being touched everywhere—all at once. Invisible fingertips dragging through his hair and over his skin and sending shivers through his body.

No sooner than the sensation started, it went away.

Penny was watching him, brow arched. "Felt that, huh?"

"Did we just make it to second base?"

Byron gave a strangled smile, and his neck turned pink. It was . . . really cute.

"That was only hello," Penny said. "Second base would blow your mind."

"Did you feel the same when you did that?"

"I felt a reverberation when we connected. That's how I know you have magic too."

"Fancy," Levi said. "Do I try it now?"

"Let's keep your magic off me for a bit. Let's try something else—nothing elemental, please. You're not a superhero."

"No fire, wind, or water. Check."

"Watch this." Penny braced herself against Byron's shoulder, and shook her hair. In seconds, it turned long and bloodred, her skin darkened—and she became a completely different woman.

"Holy shit," Levi said.

Byron frowned. "What? What's happening?"

"Uh, the part where she just morphed into a different lady?"

Victoria laughed quietly. "It's impressive. But Byron's wearing an incredibly expensive personal version of our antiglamour devices. It shields him from illusional magic."

"Good thing it doesn't shield him from shields," Levi mumbled, too distracted by Penny's amazing transformation to think about much else. "How do you do it?"

Penny sat down again, and as she moved, her body briefly shimmered before she was herself again. "You need to memorize the details of someone else, or you'll resemble a cartoon. I can't turn into anyone I want. I have a couple of female looks, and a male look. I've never been able to hold an illusion for longer than an hour, and that knocks me on my butt."

"But how do you actually do it?" Levi asked, frustrated.

"Intention, intuition," Penny said. "You've been suppressing your own magic your whole life. You don't have faith in what you can do, and you're not giving yourself the permission to be creative, or to trust yourself."

"All right, I didn't ask for a psychiatric profile." She was irritatingly right, though. He'd spent so long being afraid of his magic, afraid of getting caught and being killed, that anxiety gripped him even talking about it, let alone using it.

"Try it. Study him first." She pointed at Byron.

Levi glanced at Byron. That was easy enough. He was a good-looking guy—chiseled jaw, black hair in need of a trim, pale-blue eyes, fair complexion. Broad shoulders. Tall. Probably stupidly ripped under his expensive clothes.

Byron adjusted his sleeves, the faint blush along his neck deepening. He wasn't the asshole Levi had expected him to be. He was actually sweet. Even a little shy. Intensely awkward for someone so gorgeous.

Levi caught himself smiling at Byron. His face heated. "Um, got it. Now I wave my inner magic wand?"

"Close your eyes and picture yourself in a mirror. Your reflection is Byron. It's all in your head, Levi. Let go and believe."

"I do believe in fairies, I do, I do," Levi said, snickering to himself. He closed his eyes and took a long, deep breath, determined to give it a try despite how impossible it sounded. He hadn't seen a mirror for so long it wasn't too difficult to picture Byron in his reflection instead of his own dark eyes and pale skin and big mouth and the curls he kept long because he knew people liked to touch them. He liked being touched. Unapologetically.

"Nothing's happening, Levi," Penny said. "Are you focusing?"

"Not really." He stopped thinking about his own face and tried again. This time he pictured himself growing taller, pictured his shoulders set back, strong. Pictured Byron's face—a face people trusted. Levi wondered what it was like walking through life as a guy in a catalog for fancy suits. Powerful.

Levi had power too. Not the kind privilege and wealth gave Byron, but living power. It buzzed, wanting to be used, wanting to sing.

Maybe he could do this.

"Aha!" Penny exclaimed. She clapped her hands, and Levi opened his eyes and blinked at her, startled. "What?"

"It worked. Only for a few seconds. But it worked."

"Really?" Byron asked. He crouched, studying Levi. "He did it?"

"It wasn't quite you, but it was very good," Victoria said. "This is fascinating. I've never seen this type of illusion in person. Fantastic. Can you imagine the applications?"

"Spying?" Penny asked. "Fraud? Con artistry? There aren't too many good applications. It's not my favorite use of magic, but it gets the job done."

"I was thinking of acting." Victoria adjusted her skirt. "I'm a theater fan."

"I didn't know that," Byron said.

"Well, I am. I had tickets to take Eleanor to see *Hamilton* before all of this," Victoria waved around the room, "happened."

"I still think you two are moving too fast," Byron mumbled. He looked back at Levi. "How do you feel?"

Levi shrugged. "Like I probably need to do that in front of a mirror to believe anything even happened."

Doing something magical without hurting anyone bolstered Levi. The panic that had threatened to choke him after he'd hurt Penny was still a dull, itchy sensation in his gut, but it was manageable. For now. As long as he didn't think about the bands.

He willed himself to focus on the sound of Penny's voice when she said, "That's the kicker. We can't see our own illusions. I'm telling you, you have to trust yourself."

"I want to try something I can see." Levi tried to remember what the shield he'd stopped the blast with had looked like or felt like, but that memory came through strobed with terror. He'd known the moment the flames danced away from them that he'd only postponed his own violent death.

Byron scooted closer to him and kicked his shoe gently. "Hey."

"What?"

"You were getting kinda . . . drifty for a sec."

Since when did Byron fucking Cole have the ability to read him that well? Annoying. "Yeah, so, something I can see."

"I've spoken to enough mages to know that we all have unique talents," Penny said. "Just like one person might be good at math and another might be good at fixing cars. You'll have to play and find out what comes most naturally to you."

"Moving things. Stopping them from moving." Levi sighed. "I tipped a whole bulldozer over when I was a kid. I stopped the fire. I made leaves fly around. And I hit you with an invisible spitball."

"I think you're right," Penny said. "Illusions come very easy to me, and I can distort perception a little. Garbling conversations, muffling them. I've never been good at projectiles of any sort."

"Here." Byron pulled his wallet out of his pocket, drew out a business card, and handed it to Levi.

"An attorney?"

"No, not for . . ." Byron made a face. "For moving it. I don't think you can hurt us with thick paper."

"Oh." Levi found himself grinning. He stood up—still wobbly, but stronger than before—and walked to the opposite side of the room. When he dropped the business card, it fluttered to the floor facedown. If he could turn a bulldozer over, he could turn a piece of paper over.

I can do this.

It fluttered, like wings flapping weakly, and flipped over several times.

"Oh my God, cool!" He clapped his hands together. "Shit! That is cool."

Penny, Byron, and Victoria had smiles that matched his own. Warmth flared in his chest. He imagined the card moving like a toy car pushed across a bedroom floor. It slid, rustling, slow at first, and then more quickly.

His focus narrowed the way it did when he was on his yoga mat at home, struggling with long holds and arm balances. One of his coworkers had turned him onto yoga a few years before, claiming that it was similar to meditation, and it had worked surprisingly well, and surprisingly quickly. The near-nightly insomnia and anxiety he'd faced worrying about his magic and agonizing over the idea of turning himself in to the CALM program faded to a level he could manage. He'd stopped missing work as much, started meeting people again.

His magic soothed him as he pushed the card around, no longer eking it back and forth but gliding it in smooth circles, and then patterns. And then the card lifted into the air like a navy-blue butterfly.

"Awesome," he whispered.

The card rose high above him, nearly to the ceiling. He let it go, watching it drop back in a wavering free fall—until he stopped it a few inches from the ground. The card spun in figure eights before he shot it back up toward the ceiling, and then swept it in broad circles around the room. It buzzed as the edges flapped, protesting the high speed that business cards weren't really meant for.

He was tired, sore all over, with a burn like the ache of muscle after a difficult pose. But his magic soared freely along with the card. He didn't want to stop. Didn't care.

It wasn't until Byron caught him from behind that he realized he'd started to fall. He blinked hard and the business card fell to the ground, lifeless.

"It's been an hour," Byron said, taking the brunt of his weight. His voice was warm, body solid and good close like this. Levi didn't mind when his legs gave out completely and Byron scooped him up like he weighed nothing at all.

"Overdid it a little, honey." Penny gave his foot a friendly shake. "Magic taxes us, like physical exertion. Never forget that."

"Ugh, stop talking." He dropped his head to Byron's shoulder.

"Is this normal?" Byron asked, his voice rumbling softly against Levi's body. He sounded worried, and Levi wanted to tell him to chill out, but he was too tired. He heard Victoria and Penny chattering near him, talking about harvesting something and staying calm.

"N'sleep," he mumbled, letting Byron's swaying embrace lull him into the dark.

CHAPTER 22
UNIQUE TALENTS

Byron carried two extra chairs into Levi's room, and the three of them sat quietly, watching him sleep. Despite having no medical experience beyond a CPR class at boarding school, Byron had bunked near enough roommates in school to know that no one slept in the unnaturally still, silent way Levi did now.

Victoria had checked his vitals, and his blood pressure had been low, but not dangerously so.

"This is outside of my capabilities," she'd said apologetically.

Explaining what he knew of the Harvest Initiative to Penny only added to Byron's concerns. She had wept quietly, openly horrified over what he and Victoria had seen on tape in Crane's lab.

The Harvest Initiative wasn't revolutionary. It was a nightmare.

More than an hour passed, and Levi hadn't twitched or sighed. His chest rose and fell with an uncannily steady rhythm.

"Is he going to be okay?"

Penny sighed. "He may have recovered physically from what they did to him, but his magic hasn't," she said, voice grim. "He should have been tired after exerting his magic like that. Exhausted, even. But not like this."

"This is still from Crane's machine?" Byron asked.

"It can't be anything else." Penny shook her head at Byron. "Your uncle is overestimating the resources he's working with here. Magic isn't infinite."

"Doesn't magic regenerate?" Byron needed to know that Levi would wake up with the same unfettered delight in his own abilities. The alternative was too horrible to consider.

"I don't know. Usually. Maybe not in extreme circumstances. I feel awful when I use too much magic, but I get better in a day or so. It's like a terrible hangover. But we're talking about artificially ripping magic away." Penny shuddered. "It's like removing someone's life force."

Byron had never felt this ignorant. Would he always have question after question? "Are you saying Levi won't recover?"

"I think he'll recover." Penny glanced at Victoria, who nodded at her. "But if he's like this from only a brief test of the machine, imagine how much worse it will be—how bad it would be for a mage who isn't as powerful as he is. Some of us have hardly any magic at all."

"I've thought about that," Victoria said. "Kurt Crane first made waves theorizing technology that could permanently strip magic away."

Penny inhaled sharply.

"As far as I know, he never completed a successful test of it. I've only heard rumors, but people say he killed everyone he tested on." Victoria turned to Byron. "Do you know anything about that?"

Byron breathed through the pressure in his chest. He knew less than Victoria. "I've never heard of that research," he said, tripping over the last word. It wasn't research. It was *murder*.

"It seems like Crane is using his previous work as a foundation for the Harvest. Based on what he's tried before, siphoning a great deal of magic from a powerful mage would likely have deadly consequences. Honestly, I don't know why they're testing the technology on Levi. He's a terrible candidate. Magic that strong doesn't play well with others."

"Because Kurt Crane doesn't care if it kills him," Byron said. That much had been clear in the surveillance video.

"He's blinded by his own arrogance," Victoria muttered. "I'm sure even if he didn't consider Levi a good candidate, he'd want to use him anyway—harvesting a powerful mage would be a feather in his cap."

Byron's dread became a living thing clawing at his insides when he considered dealing with not only Crane but Warren—who probably hated Levi. Warren, who would be home from Vegas soon. Who would ask for a report on how weapons testing was going. Who might want to visit. Who would expect to see Levi in the CALM bands.

"Crane is a problem," Victoria was saying. "The North Brother Island facility will be up and running soon. Maybe by the end of next week. If Crane's fixated on Levi, he's going to want him over there."

"How many others will be tortured?" Penny glanced at Levi. "I care about him, but I hope you understand that I'm concerned for all incarcerated mages. If it isn't Levi being tortured by those machines, it'll be someone else. Do you understand that they're innocent people?"

"And children," Victoria said quietly. "The cutoff age for being arrested is thirteen. Younger rogue mages are permitted to register without penalty. Anyone over thirteen is considered mature enough to willingly hide mage status."

"We have to approach this from two directions," Byron said, trying not to think of children being forced to submit to what Crane did to Levi. "We have to go public. Show that mages are being wrongly accused. And people need to know their stories. See them as human."

"You're suggesting mages out themselves?" Penny asked.

"Online. We can use social media—put the message in front of younger people who may be more open to social change. Let the rogue mages speak for themselves, introduce themselves. There aren't enough resources to go after all of them at once, but there will be a risk."

"Byron, this is crazy," Victoria said.

"It isn't, Vic. It's the only way. If we out the Harvest and drum up support for mage rights, we'll have the public behind us when we take down the North Brother Island facility."

Penny took her glasses off and wiped them. "When we what?" she asked delicately.

"We're going to have to destroy the Harvest machines."

"That's the craziest thing you've ever said." Victoria rubbed her temples. "We don't have an army."

"We don't need an army," Byron said. "We need a plan. I've researched Crane's reputation. He doesn't like to share his glory so he works with a small team. Once the facility is up and running, staff on the island will be minimal. If we can get Levi in there and visit ourselves, we should be able to sabotage it from within."

"Sabotage?" Victoria asked.

"Well." Byron cringed. "Destroy, basically."

"Are you talking about blowing up that new factory on North Brother Island?" Penny put her glasses back on and stared at him. "Because I'm with Victoria. That sounds absurd."

"What else are we supposed to do? Calmly ask Kurt Crane to put aside his life's work because it's not nice to mages? He . . . I'm telling you, he *delighted* in hurting Levi. To put it crudely, I think he got off on it. But even if we somehow got to Crane, Warren would find someone to replace him. The Harvest Initiative is the future of Cole Industries. It's the next stage in magic containment."

"What did you mean, 'get Levi in there'?" Penny asked.

Victoria shot Byron a troubled glance before turning to Penny. "He's on loan to us. When Cole Industries wants him back, there's nothing I can do to stop them. It would put everything we're trying to do at risk to deny them access to their own prisoner."

"You're going to give him back?" Penny's voice thinned and a livid flush crept across her cheeks.

Byron glanced at Levi, still sleeping, and swallowed back a wave of nausea. Not only would Levi have to submit to the CALM bands again, he'd be in the care of those who had tortured him—who would eventually put him to death one way or another.

"We have to," he said, struggling with the words. "But the plan is to get him out of there—for good—and hide him safe and far away from the city."

"I have a pair of disabled CALM bands here. We can put those on him if he thinks he can control his magic enough to fake being bound," Victoria said. "No one would know the difference. They're GPS enabled, but the suppression system is offline."

"Why don't you ask him what he wants?" Penny ran trembling hands back through her hair. Her voice was a low, deadly rasp that made Byron's skin prickle up in goose bumps. "He's not a tool or a weapon. He's a person."

"And what if he says he wants to go into hiding *before* Crane and Warren take him back?" Victoria asked. "How can we simply let him leave with so much at stake?"

Penny's voice was steel. "If you tell him he can't leave, then you're just like all of the others persecuting our kind, treating us like we're disposable, like we're not human."

Byron's chest hollowed—she was right. He was planning to use Levi. Robbing him of a choice. Guilt grabbed him by the gut and shook him. He took a slow breath to steady his voice.

"It's true," he said, ignoring Victoria's sputter. "Victoria and I aren't much better than Crane and Warren. Levi gave his life to save mine, and I'm sitting here making plans for his life without involving him."

"Then what?" Victoria's voice broke, raw with anger. "We help him escape and cross our fingers?"

"No. We ask him what he wants to do." Byron scrubbed at his face. "Like Penny suggested. Let him decide if he wants to help take the Harvest Initiative down."

"He's never wanted this." Penny glared at him. "He refused to try to use his magic. He wouldn't meet my people."

"But he's gone this far," Byron said. "He knows what he can do now. He'll want to help."

"That's easy for you to say," she spat. "You won't be the one walking into a house of horrors."

"I don't have the right to ask you for your patience," Byron said carefully, suddenly tired. "But we're floundering here. We're doing all we can do for now. I can't wave my hand and change the entire country's mind on magic. I need your help. I need you to rally your people. We have to tap into existing circles—the magic sympathizers gathering online. We have to work together."

"We're risking our lives too," Victoria said. "We risked our lives unbinding him. He may not know what he's capable of, but I do. And you do."

"We don't need to get into a who's-sacrificing-the-most pissing match." Byron shifted in his seat. "I'll ask him if he'll cooperate. If he says no . . . we'll cross that bridge when we come to it."

Victoria's jaw clenched and her nostrils flared. Silence stretched for so long Byron began to wonder if she'd back out of everything, if he'd pushed this too far.

Her breath gusted out. "I'll get the disabled CALM bands ready. And I'll heat something up for us to eat."

The atmosphere shifted, as if a rope of tension had snapped. Byron offered them a grim smile. "Thank you."

"I'll help. I could use a snack." Penny winced and touched her arm where Levi's magic had struck her. "The wheels are falling off a little over here."

When they had left, Byron walked to Levi's bed and sat down beside him. He felt for Levi's pulse at his slender wrist, not really knowing how to find it, but eager to assure himself that Levi was warm, that he lived and breathed. Levi's heartbeat fluttered steadily below his fingers. Byron glanced at the door once more before brushing his thumb across Levi's palm. His own heart raced.

"I want to help you," he whispered. "I'm trying."

But Penny was right. He wasn't trying hard enough.

CHAPTER 23
A TERRIBLE PLAN

On Friday morning, Byron steeled himself to talk to Levi about having to send him back to Cole Industries. His stomach ached with nerves. He'd slept on Victoria's small office couch to give her an overnight break to see Eleanor. For most of the night, he'd tossed and turned—thinking about Levi, thinking about Eleanor being dragged into all this, thinking about Penny calling them out, thinking about Victoria feeling betrayed by his insistence that they ask Levi's permission.

By the time he got to Levi's room with breakfast, he was more interested in taking a nap than having a difficult conversation. The last thing he expected to see was Levi pacing right inside the door.

"You're awake," Byron said. Not only awake, but lively. Energetic even.

"I want to do more magic! Can we do more magic now?" Levi asked. Upon closer inspection, he didn't appear well rested—just wound up. Exhaustion smudged the skin below his brown eyes.

"Sam's coming by tonight." Sam had insisted on seeing Levi in person before reaching out to any more of his activist contacts about finding a place to hide Levi. Byron couldn't blame him. He would have needed to see Levi too. "Do you want to wait for him?"

"Oh." Levi chewed on his lip for a moment. "No. I want to try more now."

"Victoria won't be back for a few more hours. I don't think I'm supposed to let you do that without her around, or Penny at least."

"So she's your boss?"

Byron handed him a muffin and a cup of coffee. "No, she's not my boss."

"But she's the boss of you."

"I know what you're trying to do, and you're not going to goad me into letting you play around with magic."

Levi spoke with his mouth full, grinning. "Yes, I am."

"How do I know you're not going to clobber me over the head with a spell or whatever?"

"Because I could do that in here." Levi rolled his eyes. "Also, I have no idea how to get out of this place, and I'm assuming it involves locked doors. I don't think I can magic-think my way through a locked door."

Could you, though?

Weren't locks just intricate little machines? If Levi had the ability to move things with magic, he could probably move the internal workings of a lock. "Well, I'm on Team Not-Clobbering-Me-Over-the-Head-With-Magic. For all of those reasons."

It took Levi about a minute to devour the muffin. He sipped at the coffee and made a face. "This is terrible."

"At least it's not decaf."

Levi shuddered and made a dramatic scene of finishing half the coffee. "So what happened yesterday?"

"You passed out. And then you slept for about thirteen hours straight."

"Sounds like a typical Sunday night." Levi grinned.

"Well, it's Friday. And you scared the shit out of me."

Levi's smile faded, and Byron couldn't quite get a read on his expression. "I did?" he asked.

"You looked like you were about to drop dead."

"I was tired." Levi shrugged. "I can still feel my magic today. But it's . . ." He gestured with his hands as if pulling taffy. "Stretched out. Thin."

"That's not going to convince me to let you try using it again."

"Byron." The way Levi said his name made something twist in Byron's chest. "Yesterday was the first time I've ever used my magic freely. There's no silencing it now. You can't stop me, but I'd rather do it with your help than alone in here."

"So, basically, you want to show off."

Levi laughed. "You're so weird."

"You've mentioned that." Byron tried to keep a straight face.

How does he get to me like that?

"Come on. Take me to that circle room so I don't break anything in here."

If Byron hadn't been wearing his pendant, he would have thought that Levi was controlling his mind. Despite his better judgment, and with his pulse hammering, he led Levi out of the room. "This is only because I know you'll try something either way, and you'll probably break all of Victoria's nice things if you do it in your room."

"What's the deal with her, anyway?"

"What do you mean 'what's the deal'?"

"She makes weapons that fight magic, right? So why is she suddenly into helping me?" Levi kept up with Byron's long-legged pace, but huffed softly, clearly putting a lot of effort into appearing fine.

"Victoria is a brilliant scientist. She's helped pioneer weapons that are used to resolve and minimize conflict. Some people do use magic as a weapon, and it's only fair to have a defense against that."

"I guess," Levi nodded in thanks as Byron held the door open for him, and they stepped out onto the scaffolding and headed down the stairs. "Don't get me wrong, I like her. But it's confusing."

"She's putting a lot on the line, but she knows it's for a good cause."

"Well, yeah, I agree."

Byron walked behind Levi, and watched him struggle down each stair with his hands on the rails at either side.

"I believe there are others like me and Victoria, who simply need their eyes opened. My roommate—she's dating Victoria, apparently—she's a perfect example. She thinks mages should be freed, that there's a better option than the CALM program."

"Sam was always saying that and trying to tell me about the underground groups, magic sympathizers and activists. There's more out there than you think." A frown crossed Levi's face like a shadow. "I guess I shouldn't be telling you that."

Byron ignored a pang of hurt.

Levi stepped onto the ground floor and spread his arms out wide, shoulders stretching back. "He never understood why I wanted to be left alone."

"Why was that?" Byron tried to sound casual. This wasn't the conversation they were supposed to be having. He was supposed to be asking Levi to do something far worse than talking to a few mage-rights activists. Guilt simmered behind his ribs.

Levi turned. "Because I was afraid."

Sam was willing to put his job and his freedom on the line for mages, but he still wasn't taking the same risk Levi or any other mage was.

"I would have been too," Byron said.

Levi was watching him. "Are you afraid right now?"

"Should I be?"

"I hope not." Levi gave a faint, crooked smile. "But maybe you *should* get that stun gun Victoria had."

"I don't know how to use it."

"Wow," Levi said, brow arched. "Even I know that's incredibly pitiful. You should probably have her give you lessons in that shit."

"I'll put it on my list." Byron opened his arms. "So? For your first trick . . ."

"Got any more business cards?"

"I think we have established that you can fly business cards around. How about a more practical application? Like self-defense."

"Throwing business cards at people?"

Byron laughed softly. "No. How about stopping me from approaching you?"

Levi paled. "I don't want to do anything like that. What if I do something awful, like . . . squeeze you or flatten you."

"Penny said you have to use intention. I hope you're not going to intentionally flatten me, because that sounds horrific."

"I don't know." Levi shook his head slowly. "This is a bad idea."

"Well, you started the bad-idea train." Byron took a step toward him, and Levi stepped back. "Don't back away, stop me."

"No." Levi took another step back, and then another, nearly losing his balance as Byron came at him more quickly. "Stop!"

Byron stopped, not because he wanted to, but because he'd walked right into an invisible wall. He simply couldn't move forward. Not another step. He lifted his hands and pressed, like a mime in a box, and found that the wall extended up and out.

"Are you fucking with me?" Levi asked shakily.

"No, check it out." Byron knocked. The wall didn't make a sound, but it gave a little, like an overfilled ball. His fist bounced away from it. "You're stopping me. It's a shield, I guess."

"Wow," Levi breathed, the tension on his face smoothing to a joyful, soft smile.

"'Wow' is right."

"Try pushing against it." Levi stepped closer, peering at the blank space between them as if he expected to find something there. "Come on, harder."

Face heating, Byron pressed and then shoved. It wouldn't give.

Until it did without warning, and he pitched forward right into Levi, who caught him—barely—and cackled bright laughter. "Gotcha," he wheezed out.

Byron's heart was already racing from the thrill of Levi's magic, and his pulse picked up even more as Levi squirmed and slowly seemed to realize he was tangled in a messy embrace with Byron.

Levi straightened, his arms around Byron's waist, his gaze meeting Byron's—all big brown eyes and wonder—and pushed up onto his toes to kiss him.

"What?" Byron said, the sound lost in the kiss that Levi deepened the moment Byron's lips parted. Byron knew it was wrong. He was taking advantage. It wasn't fair.

But he gripped Levi closer, like he'd wanted to all morning, without being able to put a name to the mix of longing and frustration and worry. Levi hummed, and Byron groaned, swept up in the sweetness of it, in Levi grabbing and kneading at him. They didn't kiss in a coy, first-date sort of way.

They kissed like parting lovers.

"Please," Levi said against Byron's mouth. He kissed Byron's jaw and his throat, and touched his shoulders and his arms. "Please, please." He stripped his shirt off, the swirling tattoo extending up his shoulder and nearly to his collarbone.

"What?" Byron asked.

Levi laughed, breathy and warm. "Jesus Christ, Byron. I don't know. Touch me. Please."

It wasn't a tall order. He was beautiful—his chest dotted with faint moles and freckles, his stomach flat and fit, with a reddish-brown thatch of hair that extended up toward his navel. Byron touched him, finding a ruddy nipple with his forefinger and stroking it until Levi hissed. His eyes had closed, and his fingers flexed, as if he wasn't sure where to put them.

"Turn around," Byron said.

"Wow. You move fast." Levi did as Byron said. More rusty freckles dotted his shoulders. Byron dipped and kissed them, then the back of Levi's neck where his curls tickled Byron's nose. He rubbed his hands briefly at his slacks to warm them, and smoothed his palms in a long, slow press along Levi's tense shoulders.

"Oh," Levi exhaled.

Massaging Levi's shoulders and neck gave Byron a chance to dial back the aching, tight need that had him wanting to drop to his knees to pry Levi's jeans down his slender thighs. "Why did you kiss me?"

Levi snorted. "Good question."

Byron pulled Levi against him, continuing the massage but showing him exactly how his body had responded to the kiss and the touch of Levi's smooth skin. Levi shivered harder the more Byron touched him, until he was trembling all over and reached back to grab at Byron, as if he needed him to keep his balance.

"You feel good," Byron said, amazed at how rapidly Levi had stripped him of his ability to communicate intelligently.

Levi turned around with a quick wiggle and kissed Byron again. "You're annoying. Why do I like you?"

Byron huffed a laugh. He hooked his fingers into Levi's belt loops and walked backward until his back met the wall. It helped support them, since his knees were getting weaker by the second. Levi felt amazing against him, hot and never quite holding still. His hands roamed over Byron's body, mapping him, and when they briefly brushed against Byron's rock-hard dick, Byron hissed like he'd been burned.

That made Levi grin wickedly into the kiss.

"This isn't magic practice." Byron rolled his hips against Levi.

"It's fun, though."

It was.

They kissed until Byron's lips felt hot and used, and his chin stung from Levi's pale stubble. The kiss became slow, sensual. It was scarier then, something intimate. Something real.

Byron ducked away. He met Levi's questioning gaze and caught Levi's wrists, pulling Levi's hands from his body gently. "I don't think we should do this."

"He says, half an hour into a make-out session," Levi said, his gaze going hollow in an instant. "Fine."

When Levi stepped back, Byron's arms ached from the emptiness. Levi walked to his discarded shirt, pulled it on quickly, and crossed his arms, lost and disheveled.

"It's not like that," Byron said weakly.

"I know. It's complicated. I'm from the wrong side of the tracks, you're my babysitter, we'll probably all get executed soon. I got it."

"Crane will be back here on Wednesday," Byron blurted.

Levi froze. "No."

"There's nothing I can do to stop that. We'll do everything we can to keep you safe from him, but I can't deny him access to his own patient."

"Prisoner," Levi spat.

Byron closed his eyes. "It's not just that. I . . . We have to give you back to Cole Industries."

"No." Levi took a ragged breath. "No, you don't."

Byron scrubbed both hands at his face. His lips still stung from Levi's stubble. "They're coming here for you. Soon. Maybe before next weekend. We can't keep you here."

He'd never forget the betrayal on Levi's face. It was worse, a thousand times worse, than the hurt that had crossed his face after the explosion when he'd realized who Byron was.

"And you kissed me like that? Knowing you were going to give me back like a toy you don't want anymore?" Levi asked, his voice breaking before it could reach a shout.

"You kissed me!" Which wasn't the point at all, but Byron ached, and he didn't want to be a grown-up when everything was so unfair.

"Because I like you. And I thought I could trust you!"

A cold, unnatural wind kicked up around Byron. The hair on his arms stood on end. "Levi," he warned.

"I know." Levi sank unsteadily and sat cross-legged, hugging his middle and staring at the floor. "I'm trying not to."

"Listen to me, Levi." Byron waited for Levi to look up. "I know I said we need to give you back, but I'm not going to do it unless you agree to go."

"Why the fuck would I do that?"

"Because we have a chance here!" Byron steeled himself, trying not to shout. "A chance to save people. A lot of people. You're . . . you're the only chance."

Levi took a slow breath. When he blew it out, the wind died down. He trembled. "What do you mean?"

Byron crouched, but didn't approach him, trying to ignore the wetness in Levi's eyes. "Cole Industries has a new facility on North Brother Island. That's where they want to take you. It's where Kurt Crane is going to—he's going to torture mages."

"Then it's the last place I want to go."

"We'll send you with fake CALM bands on. You can use your magic to free yourself and damage the machines. We'll come in from the outside and help you. Together, we can take the place out."

"Take the place out?" Levi asked dubiously.

"Think about what you've done already. You're strong—stronger than you know. Those machines are delicate, and it won't take much to break them. We could set Cole Industries back years. Stop them forever if I can pull off my end of things."

"Your end?"

"Well, the PR stuff." It sounded incredibly weak out loud. "Changing people's minds."

"This is all a really terrible plan." Levi wiped his nose. "What's the alternative?"

"I don't know. I'll have to talk to Victoria. Maybe we can stage a breakout; you can knock us out or something. You won't have much of a head start, but it might be enough. Sam's working on a safe house. You know, the whole rural thing."

"You'd let me go?"

Byron sighed. "I'd try to."

Levi scrubbed his eyes with the back of his hand. "You can't act like this and tell me we can't kiss. I'm scared." His voice broke. "God, you suck."

Byron didn't think. He scrambled across the floor and bowled Levi over, cushioning the back of his head with his palm, and embraced him.

Levi grabbed at him and sighed out a ragged breath, his hands tangled in Byron's shirt, holding on like he was afraid of falling.

"I'll do it," he said.

CHAPTER 24
LIABILITIES

The click of heels against metal registered with Levi a few seconds too late. He froze with Byron's lips against his.

"I was worried I'd find you two in here," Victoria said. "But this isn't what I was concerned about." She was standing at the top of the scaffolding stairs, her arms crossed tightly.

Byron still had one knee firmly jammed against Levi's crotch, and Levi had a fistful of Byron's hair. They remained close, nearly nose to nose, like a couple of teenagers caught on the couch.

"It's my fault," Levi said, figuring unwise make-out sessions were a tiny offense compared to terrorism and illegal use of magic.

"You're in no position to make that call," Victoria snapped. "You're also not in a position to give consent."

Byron recoiled at the mention of consent. His blush would have been cute in any other situation.

Levi let go of him and squirmed back. Victoria's sudden appearance had startled his erection into a half-chub he tried to hide with a hand draped casually across his crotch.

"Things got out of hand." Byron appeared to be having the same problem. He sat awkwardly, one knee bent as if trying to block Victoria's line of sight. "It's not his fault."

"You're damn right it's not his fault." Victoria came down the stairs quickly, like a descending ghost in a horror movie. She wasn't yelling, but it was still scary as hell.

Levi crab-walked back to the wall and felt pretty bad for Byron, who was going from bright red to a sick shade of pale.

"Do you think this is a game? Our lives are at stake, and you're acting like he's your personal . . ." She sliced a furious hand through the air that probably would have taken their heads off if she had magic to back it up.

"I came on to him," Levi offered weakly.

"That's not the point," she snapped. "He's capable of brushing off your advances."

I'm not sure of that.

Byron managed to stand up. He tucked his shirt in, clearly not aware that it somehow made him look even more guilty. "This was a mistake."

Victoria's eyes flashed with murder.

Levi was with her on that one. "Don't start that shit again," he told Byron.

She shot him a succinct *shut up*.

Levi shrugged. "If I'm supposed to be your magical Trojan horse and take out a whole evil laboratory, I think I'm entitled to a couple of shady transgressions," he said.

That took the raging wind out of her sails. She stared at Byron. "He said yes?"

"I'm right here," Levi muttered. He didn't like the idea of them talking about him behind his back, like he was a child—or worse, like he wasn't a person.

Byron nodded, his shoulders set back stubbornly. "He'll do it. He'll help us."

Victoria's dumbfounded stare shifted from Byron to Levi.

Despite Levi's irritation, the pride in Byron's voice sent a warm flare through him. Maybe Victoria was right about him being incapable of making good decisions about Byron.

Did her surprise mean that she didn't have much faith in him, or that his decision to help them was incredibly stupid?

"I'm sorry we kissed," he said abruptly.

Byron's brow knitted in an unhappy little frown. "Are you?"

"Oh my God." Victoria blew out a breath like she wanted to grab Byron and shake him. "This isn't about your feelings."

"I didn't mean it in a feelings way." Levi sighed sharply. "I don't regret kissing you, Byron. But Victoria's right, I guess. It's stupid to think about any of this right now."

He didn't entirely believe that, but a small, angry part of him wanted to get Byron back for deciding they were making a mistake just as Levi had started to trust Byron. Or at least trust Byron to hold him and help him feel like a human being and not a time bomb.

The satisfaction he'd hoped to derive fell flat when Byron nodded, mouth tight with pain, as if he'd agreed to have his nonexistent pet put to sleep.

Kissing had been so much simpler than this—no doubt or shame or confusion. It had been right. Weirdly right. Normal, even. The only normal thing he'd done since his entire life had been torn apart.

"I'm not going to police you two, but I hope you will reconsider a physical relationship," Victoria said.

"I understand." Byron crossed his arms. A muscle in his jaw twitched. For someone who bullshitted professionally, he was pretty transparent with his emotions.

"I used magic to stop Byron from moving," Levi said, trying to distract Victoria. "I guess it was a shield."

Victoria went to her equipment cart and opened the laptop. "I don't know what's worse—you two necking like teenagers, or you two practicing magic in here without any help." Her fingers tapped idly on the keys, not quite typing.

"Probably the magic was worse." Levi made a face. "I think."

"No one says 'necking' anymore," Byron said.

She shot him a side-eye that likely wilted the remnants of his arousal. It definitely obliterated Levi's.

"Did you really agree to this?" She glanced at Levi.

"The kissing? I told you it was—"

"The plan," she snapped. "Going back to Cole Industries. Helping us shut down the Harvest from within." She fussed with her hair, even though it didn't have a single flyaway. The gesture comforted Levi—she was human too, scared too.

None of them seemed very sure about what they were planning.

But any plan was better than inertia. Giving in to the same old shit would mean his death, and the more he considered it, the less he wanted to die like this—helpless, humiliated, condemned.

"To be honest," Levi said, "I'm trying not to think about it too hard."

He'd only agreed because Byron had given him a choice, and he liked having a choice. But he didn't have much faith in his ability to pull off a James Bond move from within. If anything, it sounded like a faster, slightly less helpless way to get killed.

Why did Byron believe in him? Levi wasn't their only choice. Not really. There'd always be another mage willing to risk getting caught. Someone committed to the cause, someone who hadn't been afraid for years and years. Someone who hadn't broken up with a great boyfriend out of shame over being too scared to use magic.

"You're going to have to think about it," Victoria said gently. "Maybe soon. Do you understand that?"

"Of course I understand that!"

She winced. Shame flooded through him—he was still too unstable, too quick to anger.

"What if I can't figure out how to control my magic well enough?" As if called by his doubt, Levi's magic flared in his chest. Warm. Certain.

Powerful.

"We'll keep practicing," Byron said. "But I don't think you're going to be low on intention."

Levi exhaled a mirthless laugh.

"I'm going to have you fitted with CALM bands that don't really work," Victoria added, a stubborn steadiness to her voice. "They're compatible with all systems except those that measure magic output. Kurt Crane's team will have access to that sort of technology, but no one else at Cole Industries will. You should be safe until Crane . . ." She touched her bun and avoided his eyes. "Until he hooks you up to his machines again."

Levi's chest went tight as he glanced aside. Byron's face was etched with misery that echoed his own.

"We should be able to track you too." Victoria pointed at her computer screen. "It's GPS enabled, but that particular set is tuned into my system as well. Once you're free, I'd suggest ditching the bands."

"Or tying them to a semitruck or a stray dog. That's what someone would do in a movie."

Victoria blinked.

"Why did you deactivate a set of CALM bands?" Byron asked, watching the screen over her shoulder.

"It crossed my mind that Cole Industries might eventually become a liability to me and my people when our research is done. After handover, they won't have a need for AMID. They'll be able to replicate what we created." Victoria went silent for a long moment. "I knew I'd need a mage on my side if Warren turned against me."

"You never told me that," Byron said.

There was nothing apologetic about her steady gaze. "Let's get back to work."

CHAPTER 25
ON BOARD

Two hours into practicing shield after shield with Victoria and Byron, Levi stumbled and caught himself against the wall. This time, they stopped before he completely passed out, but as soon as he reached his bed, he fell asleep.

Byron carefully pried Levi's sneakers off and placed them at the foot of the bed. He'd noticed Levi checking to make sure they were close by whenever he was resting—and keeping them in the bathroom with him when he showered.

As Levi slept, Byron logged on to the AMID wi-fi with his laptop and started searching for mage-rights activists online. Victoria had assured him that her researchers spent a great deal of time studying the methods and movements of dangerous magic users. Byron's searches wouldn't raise any red flags.

It was extraordinarily easy to find magic sympathizers once he started looking.

Three minutes of searching located an anonymous blogger posting essays about living with concealed magic. She claimed to be living in the United States. Another blog, under the pseudonym Byrd, chronicled the day-to-day life of a young mage who had fled Iowa for life in Australia, where magic laws were notoriously lax. Byrd never shared his exact location, but he uploaded videos that appeared to show wild animals obeying his every command.

A message board displayed screen cap after screen cap of social media accounts that had since been deactivated for pro-magic updates. Relatives raging against arrests. Bound mages detailing constant headaches, weakness, anxiety, and sickness.

Everywhere Byron searched, he found the undercurrent of dissent they needed. Even antimagic message boards gave him hope. The screen caps of forums presented as evidence of a rampant mage problem showed a quiet underground support network.

Discussing the rights of mages wasn't entirely against the law, but it fell into a gray area—not just frowned upon but scrutinized by the authorities. It was well documented that the Department of Occult Supervision performed audits over offenses as simple as pro-magic status updates on social media.

But the DOS didn't have infinite manpower. If enough people spoke out, they wouldn't be able to go after everyone.

His pulse jumped around in his wrists as he typed in search after search, each uncovered site fanning the flames of hope. Maybe they could really do this.

A chime went off on his phone, reminding him that it was time to meet Sam in the lobby. He logged out, put his computer away, and checked on Levi once more. He didn't know what he was looking for beyond steady breathing, and reached for Levi's forehead. At the last minute, he pulled his fingers back.

Victoria's warnings hadn't been unfounded. He had no right to touch him.

Levi was sleeping, limbs cast out across the bed. The worry line that usually darkened his expression had faded. His mouth was gently parted. Byron imagined his ease had something to do with balance. Levi used magic to the point of exhaustion—but surely his magic also fed something inside of him, fueled his soul.

The fact that Levi appeared healthier didn't mean he'd healed from the emotional torment of being arrested, tortured, and held captive though. Byron still held all the power. It was unethical to pursue a physical relationship with Levi.

"Keep telling yourself that," Byron mumbled. No matter how much he tried to convince himself that what they'd done was wrong, his feelings were genuine. This was more than simple desire.

And that's terrifying.

He needed to talk to Eleanor about this. She'd know what to do—hopefully. Up until now, his relationship angst had consisted mostly of how to politely extract himself from text message conversations after first dates. Nothing had ever felt this serious—this real.

Byron was thinking about Levi's fingers gripping him, when he reached the lobby and found Warren Cole making his way through the lobby, cane in hand. His pulse jumped to a dizzying buzz. Swallowing against dryness in his throat, Byron scanned the room and saw Sam standing at the desk flirting with a female security guard. He was speaking a little more loudly than he needed to, asking the young woman for walking directions to the Empire State Building.

Stupid. This had been so stupid.

He shouldn't have let Sam insist on coming to see Levi. Shouldn't have given into his own eagerness to make Levi smile. He'd let his emotions compromise rationality. This was a totally unnecessary risk, and he'd already come close to blowing everything before the hard part even began.

Byron's chest twisted with guilt and cold, deep fear.

"Uncle," he called, taking slow strides to meet him. Forcing his legs to stop trembling. "How are you? Eric called me about Vegas as soon as it happened . . ."

"Indeed." Warren made his way to the leather chair in the reception area by the security desk and sat with his arms spread to each side like a king on a throne. "He also told me that you'd call to check in. I imagine you must be terribly busy here with Dr. Alvarez's trials."

"I didn't think about how much this observation would distract me." Byron took a seat beside him. "I'm sorry I didn't call."

"You never consider appearances enough, Byron. How many times have I told you to fake interest if necessary? You should have called, checked on me, expressed concern."

"It wouldn't have been faking. I'm interested in your safety." He lied smoothly, having learned long ago that Warren expected him to appear gracious, strong, and sincere at all times. When he'd turned ten, Warren had given him a letter opener with his initials engraved on it. Byron had clutched it tightly, disappointment welling in his chest. All he'd wanted was a LEGO set. Warren had sent him to his room without supper that night, telling him that he didn't need vision to see that Byron was being an ungrateful brat.

Subsequent decades of bullshitting were finally working in his favor.

Warren made a noncommittal sound. "And how is Mr. Camden?"

Byron's skin heated. "He's been ill since he arrived." He swallowed. "They've only done a few trials. Nothing too serious yet."

"Why?" Warren tilted his head slowly. "Don't they think it's wiser to strike when he's weak? You don't want a dangerous, healthy mage on your hands. You want his wings clipped."

"I don't make the rules," Byron said, trying to smile. "I'm here to document things. And it's been tedious and dull. So much bloodwork, tests. A letdown, if I'm being honest."

Feigning boredom did very little to calm the anxiety stinging through Byron's body like ice-cold water in his veins. He hadn't seen his uncle face-to-face since learning that Warren wanted him dead.

Has he already planned a new way to kill me?

"Dull?" Warren chuckled. "Perhaps I can remedy that."

Byron struggled to keep his voice neutral. "Oh?"

"There are so many exciting things on the horizon. I'm sure I can show you something that you won't find dull."

"I would love that." Byron studied his hands. His fingers were clenching the fabric at his thighs, knuckles gleaming white. "Did you want to come downstairs? I'd be happy to guide you."

He could only hope that Victoria was watching the entrance feeds and would somehow have enough time to make Levi appear adequately restrained and bound. Blind or not, Warren had a way of observing his surroundings.

And he'd definitely know if Levi was gallivanting around expecting Sam to show up for a display of unbelievably illegal magic.

"No, no. That's quite all right. I don't have any interest in observing a sick criminal doing nothing. I was visiting my physician on the fourth floor, and I've had more than enough socializing for the day. You can walk to me to my car. You're on your way out, I assume?"

Byron took his uncle's hand. Would Warren feel the rush of his pulse? "Yes."

Warren immediately shook off his grip, taking Byron's forearm tightly instead. The door opened automatically, blasting sour exhaust and street sounds at them. Warren's driver was idling at the curb.

"It's hot today," Byron said, squinting. He hadn't been out in the sun in a couple of days, and his eyes teared up from the glare.

Warren made a disapproving sound. Probably in response to the small talk. If there was anything Warren hated more than open displays of weakness, affection, or sympathy—it was small talk about the weather.

Byron helped Warren into his car and closed the door when Warren waved him off without a word. He didn't take a full breath until Warren's car turned the corner.

Sam met him at the front door of the building with a worried frown. "That's who I thought it was, right?"

Byron's guilt over kissing Levi warred with the adrenaline of having Warren so close by—so close to catching them in the act. He cleared his throat as he reached his hand out to shake Sam's. "It was. But I don't think he suspected anything. Thanks for coming on such short notice," he said, not quite as steadily as he would have hoped.

Sam nodded. He glanced nervously at the security guard he'd just gotten directions from. Byron tried to give him a reassuring smile as he showed the woman his ID, and they passed through the metal detector without an issue. "So much for tourism," he told her with a wink. "I tried to tell him he wouldn't have time to walk over there before our appointment."

"This place is terrifying. And I'm used to being in a courthouse," Sam said under his breath. He wore a sleek suit that hugged his broad shoulders.

Byron noticed the guard giving Sam a double take, her cheeks flushing pink. He looked more model than former attorney. He must have been charming in the courtroom.

They rode the elevator in silence, and Byron didn't speak again until he'd unlocked the last set of doors to take them into the AMID facility. Sam hesitated for a long moment as Byron held the door open for him.

Once they were inside, Byron changed the settings to permit only biometric entry.

"There's nothing to worry about down here." He was reassuring himself more than anything. His legs were still weak from Warren's unexpected appearance.

"That's what Penny said. But I feel like I'm entering a lair anyway." Sam shuddered.

"It's a little lair-like, but Victoria's in charge. And we're not under surveillance."

"Does Levi ever get out in the sun? He can't stand being cooped up. You should have seen him when we had snow all the way into April. He actually took up whittling for a few weeks."

"Whittling is a sure sign of cabin fever." Byron smiled and ignored the question. Levi hadn't seen the sun for weeks, and he hadn't complained about it. How much did he miss? How much pain did he keep to himself?

"How is he?" Sam asked, pulling Byron out of his thoughts.

"He was sleeping when I came up to get you. He practiced his magic earlier." Byron grinned, recalling Levi's infectious joy. "He's getting really good."

"I can't believe it." Sam followed him through the small, empty reception area and the next set of security doors. "I could tell he was talented. I just knew it. But he wouldn't do anything with his magic before. He never tried," he said, not sounding accusing but wistful.

"Penny told you about the way he moved things? With magic?"

Sam nodded. "Kinetic magic. Amazing. That particular ability is rare."

"Isn't all magic rare?" Byron asked.

"Yes and no, I guess."

"'Yes and no'?"

"There's no way of knowing how many people practice magic in secret, like Penny. Or resist practicing it entirely, like Levi."

Byron sighed. "Can you imagine how much more we'd know if magic was cataloged and studied, instead of all of this?"

"It's difficult for me to think about it." Sam glanced at each door as they passed. They were labeled only with nickel-plated numbers, like hotel doors. "This place isn't as creepy as I expected," he said.

"Victoria isn't a mad scientist. AMID is committed to peacekeeping efforts."

"Spoken like a spin doctor," Sam said, smiling faintly.

Byron stopped in front of Levi's door. "Victoria's working in another area of the facility, but she has Levi's room under surveillance with a feed to her phone. If anything happens, she can lock doors remotely and call for help."

"I'm not here to break him out," Sam said. "But I won't say it didn't cross my mind."

"You wouldn't be a good friend if it hadn't crossed your mind," Byron said softly.

Sam met his eye, surprise briefly lighting his features before he gave a small nod.

"It's me," Byron said as he pushed the door open. "Sam's here."

After giving Byron another brief, inscrutable look, Sam peered into the room and then crossed it in three long steps. He launched himself onto the bed and into Levi's outstretched arms.

"Sam!" Levi said, laughing sleepily. He scrubbed his eyes against Sam's shoulder as the mattress dipped with Sam's weight. "You dressed like a fancy businessman."

"I was an attorney for almost ten years, you know," Sam said, voice thick with emotion. He rocked Levi in the embrace and petted his hair.

Byron watched his feet, ostensibly to give them privacy. Something suspiciously close to jealousy twisted in his belly. He tried not to listen to them, but it was impossible not to in the small room.

"How are you?" Levi asked. "How's my cat?"

"She's fine. She's with your mom."

Levi's voice broke. "How's Mom?"

"Worried about you. Unhappy. I've been talking to her every night. She's seeing a therapist. She got a new phone number so the reporters would stop calling." Sam shushed gently when Levi exhaled a quiet sob. "She's so proud of you for what you did, Levi. She says you're a hero."

They didn't speak for a few minutes as Levi composed himself. "What's going to happen to my place?" he asked. Before Sam could answer, he said, "Byron! God, sit down. You're being weird."

Byron shuffled to the chair beside Levi's bed. As he sat down in it, his knee a few inches from Sam's, he realized how close the chair was to the bed. Would Sam find that suspicious?

But Sam didn't even glance at him. He watched Levi, and kept touching him—rubbing his back, fussing with his hair as if reassuring himself that Levi was alive and whole. Seeing them together, it was clearer how much older Sam was than Levi.

Had that factored into their breakup? Byron tried to picture dating someone older, and found he couldn't picture dating anyone at all. Although an unbidden, warm image of Levi pressed against him surfaced—so vivid he feared they could sense his thoughts. He flushed.

"I talked to your landlord, and they're putting your place up for rent pretty soon. We've started a little fund for you. It'll cover getting your stuff in storage for a while, but it'll be too suspicious if we try to pay your rent for you."

"That's okay. That's perfect." Levi smiled and wiped at his eyes with his palm. "You're nuts doing this. Trying to help me."

"Eh, you know me," Sam said.

"Obsessed with magic and social justice?"

Sam laughed. "And you."

Levi's grin faded. He glanced, for a split second, at Byron—meeting his eyes before mumbling, "You must be, to come down here."

"It's not that bad," Sam said. "I was expecting padded walls or chains. This is like a swanky rehab facility."

"Cole Industries has a monopoly on the whole chains-and-torture thing." Levi said it jokingly, but his gaze went distant. "It's not nice like this."

Sam pulled him back into a tight embrace. "You won't have to go back there."

"Well . . ." Byron interrupted hesitantly, and regretted it when Sam turned to him—and put his entire body between Levi and Byron.

Levi put his hand on Sam's shoulder. "No, it's okay. Not actually okay, but okay. We have a plan."

Sam kept watching Byron. "We have a plan?"

"It's not technically a plan, exactly, yet," Byron said. "Cole Industries is going to want him back soon. There's nothing AMID can do to stop them, but we can send him back equipped to fight them when the time is right. At the Harvest facility."

"You're asking Levi to go back into the custody of people who hurt him and want to kill him?" Sam asked, voice steely. "On the off chance that he might be able to get away?"

When Sam put it like that, it didn't sound like a very good plan.

"Basically," Byron said. "I mean, it isn't an off-chance thing. He's going to practice so he can take out the machines."

He pictured Levi stuck on an island with a bunch of burning machines and his heart sank. That sounded even worse.

"Penny said you'd have things to discuss with me, but I didn't expect anything this stupid." Sam shook his head. "I don't know how you expect me to agree to this."

"It's not up to you." Levi's breath shuddered. "None of this has ever been up to you. This is a choice *I'm* making."

Sam turned toward him and grabbed his wrists. "You're choosing this now? When your life is at stake?"

"My life was always at stake! Always!" As soon as he shouted, Levi deflated. He made no motion to pull his hands from Sam's grip, and Byron fought the urge to pry Sam away. "I thought you'd be happy about it."

"How could I be happy about this?" Sam asked, voice loud, filling the room. "I'd be happy if you were escaping today. There's a safe house in Arizona—far from any cities. All you have to do is get there."

"I'm going to make a difference," Levi said. "If I run away now, it'll happen to someone else after me. Maybe I can do something to stop that, or even delay it for a while. Then I'll make a break for whatever rural place."

Sam frowned but released Levi's wrists.

Levi shifted away from him and crossed his arms. "Arizona sounds awful, by the way."

"This wasn't my plan for you. I always wanted your magic to be free, but I never wanted you to get killed," Sam said slowly.

"Well, no shit. I'm fucking scared, Sam. And I don't like this." Levi's words rushed out breathlessly. "But I want to do it. I'll burn that whole place down if I can. And I need you to get your shit together and help Byron get all of us the fuck away from here after that. At least until the rest of the world catches up. "

"I'm sorry." Sam watched his fingers curl and uncurl. "I shouldn't have blown up. I'm not happy, but I'm . . . I think you're amazing." He reached for Levi's hand, and Levi let him take it. Sam kissed his knuckles and let go. "Will you show me your magic?"

A smile broke out across Levi's face—boyish and bright. Byron ached in that moment, wanting to stop time, to preserve the flash of joy there.

"Yes!" Levi's pillow hovered over the bed, floating eerily, and then soared to smack Sam in the face. He laughed, guileless, and Byron wondered how the hell he was going to let him go.

CHAPTER 26
DISTRACTED

Byron walked Sam up to the street level during evening rush hour when he could slip out with the crowd leaving the upstairs floors. After their awkward handshake, Byron lingered on the sidewalk, unwilling to go back where Levi was sleeping soundly—and he'd undoubtedly end up staring at him. Instead, he began walking, letting the staccato beats of horns and the *whoop* of sirens pull him out of his head.

At nearly midnight, after hours spent wandering aimlessly and picking at street food, he hailed a cab.

He'd always enjoyed cab rides—the obnoxious drone of the ads on the backseat screen, the reliable white noise of traffic muffled by glass. This time he found little comfort. Each sluggish mile took him farther uptown from Levi.

Too troubled to concentrate on anything, he closed Trivia Dash on his phone and spent the rest of the ride studying the black screen.

When he got home, Eleanor was sitting on the couch in pajamas and a fleece blanket. She paused something on TV and patted the couch beside her. He left his shoes by the door and all but collapsed next to her.

"I kissed Levi." He hadn't intended on opening with that. It tumbled out of him, lifting a weight he hadn't realized was pressing on his sternum.

"Yeah, I heard." Eleanor put her arm around him. "Victoria texted me. She's not thrilled with you right now."

"I did manage to catch that when she was yelling at us for it."

Eleanor laughed.

He glared at her, and she kept giggling, catching her breath, and laughing harder. His lips twitched, and he pushed at her playfully. "Damn it, E. It's not funny." His voice broke with amusement.

"I'm picturing your face." She wheezed a breath, snorted, and laughed more.

"You're such an asshole." Byron coughed, trying not to laugh, but it caught a hold of him, and he found himself chuckling softly, the sound drowned out by Eleanor's giggling.

It took a few minutes for her to calm down. Finally she wiped her eyes and rested her head against his shoulder. "So. Was it good?"

The breath sucked right out of Byron's chest. She lifted her head questioningly, all traces of amusement gone.

"It was," Byron said, quieted by the sharp pain of longing.

"Oh shit." Eleanor's eyes widened. "You're falling for him."

"It's not that dramatic." But she was right. That was the root of the unease weighing him down. He didn't like leaving AMID, leaving Levi there—where Levi would eventually wake. Alone. Not only because he was worried about Levi's well-being, but because he didn't want to miss a moment they could spend together before—

He couldn't think about it.

Eleanor touched his face. "Yeah, I think it's pretty dramatic, kiddo."

Byron sagged against her. "I don't know what he's feeling. I'm sure he was scared and lonely. And I shouldn't have done it."

"You sound like you're trying to talk yourself out of it meaning anything," Eleanor said. "Typical Byron operating mode, high-stakes version."

"But Victoria had a real point—I shouldn't get physical with him. He's our prisoner. I'm basically a prison guard. It isn't right."

"I haven't been down there, but I doubt Victoria's running a prison. Aren't you guys nice to him?"

"That's exactly it. Listen to what you're saying—since when is the baseline expectation being nice? Yeah, we bring him muffins and sandwiches and he has a hot shower. He's also locked in a small room, and hasn't seen the sun for weeks. He's under twenty-four-hour video surveillance, and Victoria has an arsenal of weapons that can render him unconscious in seconds. He can't leave. His apartment is getting rented out. His cat is living in another state. And he kissed me. Me!" Byron caught his breath. "Why did he do that?"

"Either he likes you, or he's got Stockholm syndrome." Eleanor smiled weakly. "I don't want to sound flippant about this, but you're a good person, Byron. It's not like he kissed someone who's outright abusing him."

"But sort of vaguely abusing him?"

She narrowed her eyes. "That's not what I said."

"So you don't agree with Victoria?"

"We're dating. That doesn't make us a lesbian hive mind." She yawned abruptly and covered her mouth. "I know you care about that kid. You have since the day you met him. If he cares about you too, or even just wants to mess around, I don't see how that's the end of the world. I'm a lot more worried about a SWAT team breaking down our door and arresting us than I am about you two smooching each other or whatever happened. Oooh, did more happen?"

"No." Byron felt a flush spread across his face. He unbuttoned his shirt and stripped down to his undershirt.

"Not for lack of wanting it to, huh?"

"I don't press you for details about your sex life."

"That's because you're terrified of my nethers."

Byron laughed and shifted the blanket to cover both of them. "Disinterested, not terrified. I'm sure they're lovely."

"Wasn't today the big visit-from-the-ex-boyfriend day?" Eleanor asked sleepily, making herself comfortable against Byron's side like a kneading cat.

"It was."

"Weird timing for smooching."

Byron nodded. "It didn't really seem premeditated. We were practicing magic."

"Filed under things I never pictured you saying."

"It's so sexy." Byron groaned miserably. "He's . . . he's not a big guy. But when he's using his magic, it's like he's ten feet tall. I don't think he has any idea what he looks like. He gets all serious, like he's concentrating but faraway, and his mouth opens a little, and I don't know, I can't explain it."

"I look like I'm concentrating when I'm in the bathroom," Eleanor said. "And I'm pretty sure there's nothing sexy about it."

He elbowed her. "I'm being serious. I know he could hurt me. He could probably kill me—maybe even accidentally. But his magic doesn't scare me. If people could only see that it's a natural thing. It's beautiful."

"Slow down, there. You might be able to convince some people that CALM bands are screwed up and the Harvest is a billion times more screwed up, but I don't think you're going to get the whole world to fall head over heels for your mage crush."

"You are the worst."

She grinned and turned off the TV. It left them in the darkness of their small living room. A clock displaying a silhouette of the world ticked steadily above them, and the distant late-night traffic clanged and whooshed. Everything was so normal, so *home*, that Byron felt like he'd woken up from a bad dream.

A bad dream Levi had very little hope of escaping.

"I want this for him," Byron whispered.

"Couch snuggles?" Eleanor asked sleepily.

"Normal, boring life."

"Our life hasn't been normal or boring lately."

"You know what I mean. No one will ever treat him like he's normal again. I mean, he can move things and make shields, but he's not a walking nuclear warhead. It's so stupid. Everything I've ever believed is so stupid."

Eleanor was quiet for so long he thought maybe she'd fallen asleep. When she spoke, it was soft, tired. "I know," she said. "And we're pretty smart people. How did we buy into all of this?"

"Because the truth was never presented to us. I think that's all people need: Truth, honesty. None of the fear-mongering. I've been searching online, and people are reaching out. They're waiting for something to happen."

"I bet no one was talking about blowing people up for the sake of magic rights either," Eleanor said bitterly.

"No. No one was plotting terrorism. At least not where I could see it." Dread washed over him. He'd been so busy thinking about the Harvest facility on North Brother Island—of destroying the machinery there—that he hadn't put much thought into the attacks. How long until Warren came up with his next plan?

The Harvest was so extreme it needed another push—another reason for the American people to stand behind it. And Byron's death would suit its cause perfectly.

The death of an innocent. A name and a face to invoke every time someone questioned the ethics of harvesting energy from living humans. *Remember that boy*, they'd say. *Did anyone wonder if it was unethical to blow him up?*

"Sam is going to help us coordinate a guerrilla social media blitz as soon as they take Levi back," Byron said, shaking off the thought of his own obituary. "If we can call mages in hiding to action—the young ones especially—we can get momentum. People will listen."

"People might listen, but will they change their minds? You're talking about deprogramming lifetimes of fear."

"It'll happen. Every person who sees what I've seen, what Sam has seen, and his friends and their friends have seen—they'll believe that magic is good. Inherently good."

"Levi might be inherently good, but if mages are normal people like the rest of us, you have to acknowledge that not everyone will use magic for good."

"So? That's like saying not everyone will use knives or fists for good. We're not banning those things."

Eleanor squirmed against him. "Hey, hey. You're preaching to the choir. But I'm trying to keep you grounded. Magic isn't all glitter and smooching. Victoria's been telling me about the shit that's gone down overseas when magic is weaponized. People aren't messing around."

"I know. But we can't just—"

"Throw the mages out with the bathwater." She yawned again. "Trust me, I understand. Your uncle has to be stopped."

Another pang of fear hit Byron. "I think I have a mental block about the part where I have to confront him."

"I don't think you should confront him in the traditional sense of the word. I bet he always has a dozen bodyguards within earshot."

Byron made an unhappy sound. "I don't want to think about it right now."

"Thus all the kissing. I don't blame you. And between you and me, Victoria is a tiger in bed these days. You're not the only one getting distracted via creative—"

"Eleanor!"

"I'm just saying." She pried herself off the couch and tugged Byron's sleeve weakly. "Come on, sleepyhead. Go rest. You have mages to kiss tomorrow."

"I still don't think this is funny."

"I don't either. But laughing at you beats the alternative."

He kissed her forehead and trudged off to his room, stripping the rest of his clothes off and leaving them in a messy pile near the hamper. When he put his phone on the charger by his bed, he noticed that it was obscenely late. Was it dark and quiet at AMID? His sheets were cold, and he imagined Levi trying to sleep in his underground prison, waiting for his brief reprieve to end.

As he watched the pale-orange glow of streetlights flicker through a crack in his bedroom curtains, he decided he didn't care what anyone else thought. The world was changing or ending, and either way he was going to kiss Levi again.

CHAPTER 27
ESCALATION

Warren called Byron at 7 a.m., rousing him from a restless sleep. He'd been dreaming about fire, and adrenaline flashed through his body as he sat up.

"You sound out of breath." Warren's voice held a smile. "Did I interrupt something?"

"No, no. Nightmare," Byron said quickly.

"I was hoping we could meet this morning. I'd like to get your thoughts on a new media initiative."

"New media initiative?"

"Something to warm up the public before we get another press conference on the books."

The last press conference had been Byron's death sentence. He sat up and scrubbed his hand across his chest. "I'd love to hear about it."

"I want to focus on the development of North Brother Island. How we're bringing in jobs with the ferry we're commissioning, and the nature specialists overseeing the bird sanctuary. Maybe a little retrospective of the island's history. A feel-good piece. People are wondering what we're up to over there."

Byron wondered if he was imagining an emphasis on that last bit—a subtle shade of accusation. Maybe it was his guilty conscience. "I think that'll go over well. I can reach out to my contact at CNN to see if we can get it on the homepage. Didn't you have a video team on the island the other day? We can offer them B-roll to accompany the piece."

"Yes, that would work nicely," Warren said. "I'll meet you in an hour in the lobby."

Warren's high-rise condo was a thirty-minute commute from Byron's on a good day. He glanced at his clock, sniffed his armpits, and grimaced. "Perfect. I better jump in the shower."

Warren chuckled. "Sure you don't have a girl squirreled away in your bed?"

It was a long-running joke between them that Byron didn't find particularly funny. He'd opened up to his uncle about his sexuality in his late teens, but Warren had shrugged him off, smiling and saying that every boy went through experimental phases. Since then he often asked Byron if he'd met any nice girls, or if he had a woman keeping him up late at night.

"No," Byron said, forcing a grin so his voice wouldn't fall flat. "I'll see you in an hour."

He showered quickly, wishing he had more time to stand in the water and think. Showers centered him. Normally he'd wash his hair and jerk off in the steam. It probably wasn't as beneficial to his health as Levi's bendy yoga was, but it did the trick. He resented the missed opportunity for release—especially on a Sunday morning. Especially when the thought of Levi was making his pulse quicken and his body heat.

He wanted to hurry to Levi. He wanted to pretend like none of this was happening. He wanted to shield him somehow. He wanted to bring him home, to lead him to his bed, to fuck the tension and fear out of him. His conflicting urges churned like waves knocking around in a harbor.

Half-hard and uncomfortable, Byron threw his clothes on and made a mental note to drop his dry cleaning off. He grabbed a bagel, texted Eleanor and Victoria to let them know where he was going—in case he died in a surprise terrorist attack on the way there—and hurried to Warren's building across town.

They met in the exclusive restaurant on the first floor of the building, an old-school room that oozed status and wealth from every Italian leather seat, inlaid marble tabletop, and crystal vase. It was cold to Byron, and a touch ostentatious. His parents had been enormously wealthy, but they'd shied away from status symbols. They'd always owned nice things—very nice things—but everything had been functional and comfortable. His mother had always said she preferred spending money on experiences and education.

Warren, on the other hand, relied on common symbols of success. Byron spotted him waiting in the secluded booth he reserved for breakfast every morning. He stirred a cup of coffee and nodded a silent greeting as Byron slipped into the booth.

"Good morning," Byron said.

"Try the chocolate croissant. Carlos added a hint of spice to it. Delicious."

Dutifully, Byron picked a croissant off the platter of pastries between them. He thanked the server who placed a napkin onto his lap, filled his coffee cup, and poured him a glass of mineral water. The pastry was good, but felt like wadded-up paper in his mouth.

Tension hung in his throat, threatening to choke him.

"You're quiet," Warren said. "A lot on your mind?"

"I was thinking about what you mentioned this morning. About North Brother Island." Byron had spent the ride over fixated on one particular detail. "I'd like to contact a wildlife specialist to do an interview."

"Why?" Warren asked. The bloodred vase on the table reflected on his mirrored glasses when he cocked his head to the side.

"Like you said, a feel-good piece. A human-interest profile—someone who's benefited personally from the upgrades to the bird sanctuary thanks to Cole Industries' funding."

"Ah yes, I like that. Good." Warren finished his coffee and set it down. He cradled the mug in his well-manicured fingers. "Which reminds me, I'd like you to come to the island when we bring Mr. Camden over."

Byron's heart began to beat so wildly, he was certain Warren would hear it thudding. "Oh?" he asked, letting the sound slip out as casually as he could manage.

"Since you'll be covering the Harvest phase-two launch, I think it's important for you to witness it in action. I've spoken to Dr. Crane, and he says it's perfectly safe to have observers. No radiation or anything of the like."

"I'd enjoy that." Byron sipped at his coffee to soothe the dryness in his throat.

"I thought you might." Warren lowered his chin as if he had the ability not only to see him, but to scrutinize him. "I was thinking about what you said the other day, about wanting to see the boy suffer for nearly getting you killed. Perhaps it will give you closure to see his magic being put to good use—permanently."

"Of course. I'm very curious to find out exactly how the technology works." Byron tried to smile, but it felt more like a twitching grimace.

"Excellent. I'll send a team to collect him from AMID in the morning."

"Tomorrow?" Byron asked, his voice a little too sharp.

Warren frowned. "Is that a problem?"

"No." Byron swallowed. "Dr. Crane must be ahead of schedule."

"He's incredibly motivated."

"I'm sure." He stared at the pastries, feeling sick. "I expected him to check in later this week."

"Well, that won't be necessary now." Warren paused, his disapproval thick in the silence between them. "Obviously."

"Perfect." Byron gave what was meant to be a happy sigh but sounded more like being punched. "Victoria—Dr. Alvarez—mentioned that she got more data than she anticipated from her initial round of testing with Camden. When do you need me at the new facility? I'll clear my schedule."

Warren's fingers skimmed over the display on his braille-enabled smartphone. The tiny bumps and symbols rose and fell, almost too quickly to be seen.

"Tuesday evening," he said. "We'll run our systems at night for the first few months. That's our compromise with the city until they're convinced the tourists and commuters in the river are safe from our *mad scientists*."

Byron laughed awkwardly.

"That's where you come in," Warren said. "You'll show everyone that what we're doing is perfectly safe, and in the best interests of every United States citizen."

"I look forward to it, sir." Byron's breakfast hung in his stomach like lead. From Monday morning to Tuesday evening? That was far too many hours for Levi to be unaccounted for, forced to hide his magic, and likely tortured by Crane's equipment. But an invitation to

North Brother Island was exactly what Byron needed. It was their best chance. There was no other way.

"I'm glad to hear that, my boy." Warren reached across the table, and Byron took his hand. It was warm. He cringed, knowing his own hands had gone clammy and cold from the thought of having to send Levi back in less than twenty-four hours.

"You're crucial to the success of this project," Warren said, squeezing Byron's fingers.

Byron fought the urge to yank his hand away from the strong grip. "I'm glad I can make a difference."

When Victoria met Byron in the hall at AMID, she had Levi in tow. It surprised Byron so much that he briefly lost his train of buzzing thoughts and stared.

"Oh," he said.

"Sometimes I wonder how you write for a living." Victoria checked her watch, tapping the screen.

Levi shrugged. "I had a panic attack and—"

"Why didn't you call me?" Byron blurted to Victoria.

She narrowed her eyes. "Because you texted me that you were on your way to see Warren. And something tells me he wouldn't take well to you dashing out of a meeting to handle something I had completely under control."

"She did," Levi offered. "Have it under control, I mean. We've been walking laps around the place. Nobody else is here today." He did appear a little out of breath and pink in the cheeks. Victoria, of course, was completely unruffled.

"Team building off-site." She shrugged.

Byron's initial worry subsided, and a heavy knot of guilt took its place. Levi was trying hard to stay calm—and nothing Byron was going to say would help that. "That's good," he said absently. "Can we go to the testing room?"

Victoria gave him a small, suspicious glance, but nodded. "Sure. We were heading there anyway." She set the door locks back to biometric entry and walked ahead of them, her shoes snapping in staccato clicks against the polished concrete floor. "I tell you, I'm getting used to having the facility to myself. I might send my entire staff to Dubai more often."

"When you said off-site I figured you meant upstate. That's a hell of an expense," Byron said.

"Fortunately I don't particularly care about my budget at the moment."

"What's going on?" Levi asked, brushing against Byron's elbow as they walked. "You had to see your evil uncle?"

Byron didn't want to talk about Warren. He wanted to tell Levi about the three-legged poodle on the way over, and how traffic got held up for a parade, but small talk would buckle under the weight of the truth.

We're out of time.

The only ember of hope was the fact that he had an invitation to the Harvest facility. An invitation that would take him right to Levi again, if Levi could somehow hold on for nearly forty-eight hours.

"Jeez," Levi said jokingly, filling the silence. The amusement didn't reach his troubled eyes. "That serious?"

Victoria glanced back at them, concern written plainly on her face.

"I have a lot on my mind." Byron wanted to get to the security of the training room. Less to break, more ways to subdue Levi if he lost control of his magic once Byron told him the truth.

As Victoria walked away, Levi grabbed Byron's arm. Byron resisted, trying to drag him along, but Levi tugged harder, murmuring, "I could make you stop, so stop."

Byron stopped. Victoria continued to walk, and he had a feeling she was giving them space. "What?" he asked.

Levi shrugged. "I don't know. I wanted to talk to you. Isn't that dumb?"

Byron pulled him close, ran his fingers up into his hair, and guided him into an urgent kiss. Levi went still for a moment, and then responded as eagerly, his hands gripping Byron's sleeves and anchoring him. It was hard, openmouthed, and frantic.

"Levi," Byron said, gasping it out, trying to hold him tighter, needing more of him in his arms.

Groaning softly, Levi dragged his teeth on Byron's lip and deepened the kiss. It went from urgent to something hotter—something needy. Byron backed Levi against the wall and rolled his hips against him, and felt Levi's dick against his own.

Levi broke out of the kiss and knocked his head back against the wall. "Fuck. I need . . ."

"I know," Byron said. "Wait—one second." He left Levi there staring at him and jogged around the corner, nearly bowling Victoria over where she stood, glaring like she wanted to set fire to him with her eyeballs.

"What are you doing?" she hissed.

"Wait in the testing room? Please?" he asked, trying to ignore the way her eyes widened even more. "Please, Victoria. Do this for me."

"Do me a favor and don't desecrate my hallway. Room three is unlocked. I will be having coffee in the weapons room and *hating* you."

He didn't bother answering her before he returned around the corner. Levi remained where he'd left him, panting against the wall and visibly hard. "Um," he said.

Byron took him by the hand and dragged him into the unlocked room. He palmed at the wall but couldn't find a light switch. The door closed behind them, leaving them in a quiet space lit only by a dim nightlight. Equipment he'd probably never understand cast long, pointy shadows, and all he wanted to understand was why Levi made him feel like this.

Levi shrugged out of his shirt and fumbled with Byron's buttons.

"Here," Byron said. "Let me . . ." He tried to unbutton his shirt, but Levi made it difficult, getting in the way and kissing him, laughing softly under his breath, the sounds like little moans. When Byron finally dropped his shirt to the floor, Levi pressed closer, warm and solid against him.

"Are we in trouble?" Levi asked. He hissed when his bare back met the cold door.

Byron dropped to his knees slowly, kissing his way down. "Probably." He tugged Levi's jeans open and pulled them down his wiry thighs.

"Oh my God." Levi swallowed audibly. His fingers sank into Byron's hair, fluttering like a moth's wings. "What are you doing?"

"Honestly, it's been a while. But I think I remember the gist of it." Byron rubbed his cheek against Levi's erection over his boxers and exhaled a low laugh when Levi's breath hitched.

"Is this all right?" Byron asked, face hot and thankfully hidden in the dark.

Levi exhaled a sound between a laugh and a long hiss. "Yes. Yeah. Yep."

Byron eased Levi's boxers down and ran his mouth along the silky-smooth skin of Levi's dick until he reached the blunt, warm tip.

"I'm STI-free, in case you were wondering," Levi mumbled. "Mr. Irresponsible Cocksucker."

Byron hummed a thank-you that made Levi shake. He ran his hands up the backs of Levi's thighs, palmed his ass, and sucked him off with more enthusiasm than skill. Not only had it been a while—he'd only done this a few times.

Levi's fingers twisted in his hair, helping him set a slow, steady rhythm. He let out soft moans and trembled, and his dick went from hard to impossibly hard, bumping the back of Byron's throat and tasting like clean skin and salt. Byron's eyes watered and his jaw ached, and he never wanted it to stop.

When Levi started yanking Byron's hair, Byron knew he was close. Levi let out a garbled warning, but Byron didn't pull back, instead swirling his tongue at the smooth underside of Levi's dick and sucking harder. *Come on, come on.*

When Levi came, it was a lot, hot and sticky at the back of his throat, but he didn't slow until Levi's fingers patted at him frantically.

"Stop," Levi moaned. "Stop, stop, oh God."

Byron caught Levi when he sank to his knees and found Byron's mouth for a deep, filthy kiss. Levi's cheeks were wet, and he exhaled a shuddering breath, resting his forehead against Byron's.

"Well. That happened," Levi whispered.

"You're beautiful."

"That's what you tell all your secret mage lovers."

Byron kissed him again, more softly this time—a quiet nip that resulted in a sweet smile from Levi. He started when Levi's sure fingers found his pants and unbuttoned them. It was awkward—Levi still tangled in his jeans, and Byron off-balance and too hard to think.

They both laughed, breaking apart. Levi pulled his jeans back up and helped Byron out of his slacks.

"Are these briefs like six hundred thread count?" Levi asked, palming Byron's crotch.

"That's sheets." Byron then lost the ability to talk.

"Whatever, rich boy." Levi pushed Byron onto his back. The polished concrete felt like ice against Byron's shoulders, but Levi's mouth was like fire when he pulled Byron's briefs down and licked his dick in one obscene, wet stroke. He found his balls, kissed them and nosed at them, and Byron had never been this happy to be completely outclassed. Levi made it wet and slow, using his hand and his mouth. Byron's entire being twisted up—wrung into nothing.

"Levi," he breathed, pressing his palms against the floor to keep from getting his fingers tangled in Levi's curls. His hips bucked, and he damn near lost consciousness when Levi let out an amused hum and didn't skip a beat, making it feel so good it hurt.

His orgasm started to build, too soon, an edge like a roaring wave that crested without warning. He came with a shout, back arching, hips jerking again and again as Levi swallowed him and kissed him and licked him, catching all of it.

Byron reached out with wobbly arms when Levi moved up his body and collapsed along his side, panting. "Hey." It was little more than a raspy wheeze.

Levi tossed an arm over his torso. "This floor is fucking freezing."

"It's pretty bad."

"I guess we have to move."

"Walk of shame in front of Victoria. I'm not looking forward to it," Byron said.

Levi rubbed his cheek against Byron's shoulder. "Maybe we can stay in here forever."

"Except the floor. So cold."

Levi sighed. "True."

Byron curled to sit, helping Levi up with him, and kissed him again, gently, touching his face and his neck, rubbing his chilled skin. He knew it was only from the floor, but his heart twisted with concern.

Reality snapped into place, and Byron fought a wave of dread and grabbed his discarded shirt. They moved together in the dark, collecting clothes and getting dressed with awkward hops and huffs of frustration.

Once they were dressed, Byron stood there, the weight of what he needed to tell Levi rooting him in place. Levi watched him in the low light and sighed.

"Those were bad news blowjobs, huh?" Levi asked.

Byron gathered him close and nodded.

CHAPTER 28
SEE THINGS DIFFERENTLY

Levi could still taste Byron when they walked into the ugly weapons room. Victoria scowled at them from whatever she was working on at her laptop. Her blatant irritation, clearly warranted, soothed his guilt in a weird way. At least they weren't going to pretend like he and Byron hadn't hooked up in a creepy, dark room seconds earlier.

"We got waylaid," Byron said.

Levi cringed, and then cringed more when Victoria muttered, "'Laid' being the operative word?"

"You guys are making this weird," Levi said.

"I wanted no part in this." Victoria waved them over delicately. Her nails were hot pink.

Levi was about to comment on how well the color matched her bronze complexion when he saw a pair of CALM bands on the table beside her computer. "What the fuck."

His throat went dry and his body tensed, coiled to bolt.

"No, no," she said, glancing between Levi and the bands. "These are the fake ones. They won't affect your magic."

Byron placed a warm hand on Levi's back, probably trying to comfort him. Instead, Levi felt pushed—pushed toward the CALM bands, pushed toward having his magic bottled up and choked again. He startled away, drawing his hands close to his body to remind himself not to lash out at either of them.

"Give me a sec," he snapped.

"That's fine," Victoria said, talking to him like he was a dog threatening to bite. "There's no rush."

"There's a slight rush," Byron said.

Levi closed his eyes.

"Define 'rush.'" Victoria didn't sound so calm or soothing this time. Levi needed calm and soothing. He moved to cover his ears, but Byron spoke too quickly.

"They're coming for Levi tomorrow. In the morning."

The silence following Byron's words was a roaring waterfall. Levi's face went flushed and hot, like he was about to pass out. Instead of dealing with that embarrassment, he sat down right where he was, cradled his head in his hands, and reached for a long, deep breath. He needed oxygen. The room was full of it, even though it felt like it was being sucked away.

"No." Levi struggled to breathe and shook his head. "No."

He needed to be left alone for a little while. For however long it took him to process the fact that he had one more night here, where he was at least relatively safe. One more night before they came for him and he was back to being a criminal and a prisoner and a lab rat and a dead man.

"I can't," he whispered, squeezing his eyes shut.

"Levi." The edge of pain in Byron's voice made Levi look up.

Byron and Victoria were pressed against the wall, arms and legs cocked at awkward angles. Victoria had her head turned to one side, and she was gasping for air. Levi stared at them for several seconds before he realized why they were like that.

It was him. He was pushing them away.

"Shit!"

"Levi, you need to let go," Byron choked out.

Intention. That was the key. He needed to intend to release them, but he was flustered and scared and his magic was the only power he had left, the only thing that was still his. Reining it in felt like pulling in a parachute while speeding toward the cold, hard ground.

But he didn't want to hurt them. Not Victoria and Byron.

They dropped to their knees, hunched over and coughing. Byron went to Victoria and rubbed her back. "Are you all right?"

She sat down with his help. "Yes. Just shaken up."

Levi pressed his hand against his mouth to muffle a sob. His eyes welled up with tears. How could he face Cole Industries with his magic in check if he couldn't even hear bad news without hurting two people who wanted to help him?

And the one person he wanted to be close to despite every good reason not to.

"Levi, hey. Hey." Byron crossed the room to crouch beside him. "We're fine. Hey . . ."

Levi shook his head. When he blinked, tears fell.

"Look at me."

People paid big money for polished concrete floors like the ones at AMID. The industrial-chic thing was huge, and Levi could see why. There was something beautiful in the swirls of pale gray—the flaws beneath the gleaming surface.

"Levi, please," Byron said.

Levi glanced up, and steeled himself when Byron reached and touched his shoulder. They didn't explode. His magic didn't push Byron away. But Levi did swallow against the taste of more tears.

"Come here." Byron opened his arms, and Levi sagged into the embrace and let himself be held.

"I don't want to go." Levi felt childish. He was twenty-one—a grown-ass man, not a blubbering kid. But he couldn't think past the knot of fear that only released, ever so slightly, as he cried. For himself. For Byron and Victoria. For his mom and Sam. For every mage who'd been executed before him—the deaths in the news he'd always felt distantly responsible for, as if he could have saved them all if he'd only been brave enough.

He had the chance to do it now, to try to do something courageous. And he was terrified.

"I don't want you to go," Byron said fiercely.

"Here." Victoria sank down beside them and handed him a brown paper towel, the kind from bathroom dispensers. "It's scratchy, sorry."

Levi took it and blew his nose. He hiccupped a weak laugh. "Better than snotting all over Byron."

"Hazard of the job." Byron smiled, but his blue eyes were sorrowful.

They huddled together in the middle of the big room. The absurdity of sitting on the floor with a beautiful antimage weaponry scientist and Byron Cole—corporate shill and giver of endearingly earnest blowjobs—startled a giggle out of Levi. "Are we really doing this?"

"I think it can work." Byron gathered Levi close, pressing his mouth against Levi's hair. His breath tickled. "Warren asked me to come to the Harvest facility. And I have a plan to get Penny out there too."

"What about me?" Victoria asked.

"I need you to stay here with Sam, and Eleanor if she's up for it. The shit's going to hit the fan, and Cole Industries will try to spin it immediately. You can tell the truth. Online. The media. Everywhere you can. To everyone who will listen."

"So . . . career suicide," she said.

"I'd take that over literal suicide," Levi said.

She lowered her eyes. "I'm sorry. I know."

Levi sat up and used the paper towel to wipe his nose again. He shoved it into his pocket and rested back against Byron. It felt comfortably intimate to sit like that, bracketed by Byron's arms and legs.

"I have a couch in the other room." Victoria's mouth quirked with a small smile. "And plenty of chairs."

"Chairs I could use as scary projectiles."

"You didn't throw my computer. Which I am profoundly grateful for, by the way."

Byron's chin wiggled against Levi's shoulder as he spoke. "It's a good thing, too. Because we're going to need that webcam."

Levi blinked. The last time he'd used a webcam, it had been to make an incredibly amateur solo porno for a boyfriend who'd moved to the south of France. "Why?"

"You're going to make the rest of the world love you."

Levi examined the laptop dubiously and couldn't place why Byron's words sent a heady thrill through him.

Byron kept his hand on Victoria's cart so Levi wouldn't see his fingers shaking. He hadn't expected to be nervous, but everything hinged on each one of these small steps going right. Levi had to pull this off.

"My name is Levi Camden." Levi glanced at Byron, voice catching, and Byron gestured for him to keep his focus on the tiny spot where Victoria's webcam rested.

"I'm twenty-one," he went on. "Um. I'm from Brooklyn. I've been waiting tables for a few years. I like art and going to shows. I don't wear robes or wave a magic wand. I have a mom." He smiled. "She's pretty great. She's cat-sitting for me right now. My cat, Daisy, weighs about nineteen pounds. She's a pillow with claws."

Levi paused, inhaling audibly. His breath shuddered when he exhaled. "I've known I've had magic my whole life. I knew about registration. I mean, everyone does. I knew it was against the law to hide from the registry. But I knew wearing CALM bands would be like . . . like . . ." His gaze went distant as he rubbed his wrists absently. "Actually, I didn't know. I was afraid it would feel terrible, but nothing I imagined was as bad as it really felt. If you've ever held your breath too long, you know you get that freaked-out feeling that makes you breathe again. Having my magic bound felt like that, every single second. It made me tired and sick too. Like having the flu."

He glanced at Byron again, and Byron nodded in encouragement.

"Every mage wearing those bands is in pain. They've learned to live with the pain because they have to. They have to try to have jobs and survive. Little kids, old people: all of them are hurting because people think that CALM bands are harmless bracelets that stop magic from doing bad things. People are being tortured. So maybe you can imagine why some of us won't do it. We hide our magic and force ourselves not to use it, even though magic isn't a weapon. It isn't bad." Levi wiped his eyes. "It's beautiful. I wish everyone could see that. It's as natural as the tide. People used to think that was magic too. Just like the sunrise and fire."

Byron smiled, pride soaring through his veins.

Levi lifted his chin stubbornly. "I might be dead already when you're watching this, but I want you to know something. I want you to know that Cole Industries isn't protecting you from anything—they're just making money off your fear. The new program, that building out on North Brother Island, they're using it to torture men, women, and children. People who have never done anything wrong in their entire lives. People who never used magic to hurt someone."

He lifted his hand, and his gaze went faraway. His expression lost its hard edge, and something close to a smile ghosted across his lips as he made a pen hover in the air over his palm. It swirled in lazy circles. "Mages can do things you can't do. That's all. Is that really so scary?" He caught the pen and focused on the camera again, his smile fading. "Is that what you want people to die for? Is that why you want to take all their rights away? Take their kids away?"

His breath quickened, and his breathing became uneven. Byron fought the impulse to hurry to him, but he didn't want to get in the shot unless Levi fell apart.

"I'm afraid." Levi gasped a few more breaths, and spoke shakily. "I'm afraid of what's going to happen to me and to people I love, and to people I've never met. I spent my whole life being afraid that people would find out what I was, and I never even used magic. I had no idea it would feel so good. And right."

He let out a soft, bitter laugh. "I had nothing to do with that terrorist attack or any other attack. All I did was stop it from killing a bunch of regular people and first responders. And trust me, I didn't mean to. Call me a coward, but I'm not sure I would have given my life to save people who probably would have hated me if they'd known what I was. But today . . . whatever day this is, I've lost track down here . . . today I'm making that choice. I'm risking my life to tell you the truth and try to stop innocent people from being tortured. I hope you'll think about that if you're ever given the choice between fearing magic and believing that magic is simply something you can't do. Something that—that can be used for so much good. Choose to be unafraid. I think you'll see." He scrubbed his hand at his eyes. "I think you'll see things differently, that way."

He sighed and hugged his middle. "That's all," he said softly, looking away, his mouth an unhappy line—as if he'd spoken his last words. "Thanks."

Victoria hit a key on the computer and brushed her knuckles under each eye. "Got it," she said. "You did great."

"How do you feel?" Byron asked.

Levi blew out a heavy breath. "Like that won't matter."

"Maybe it didn't seem like much," Victoria said, "but no one's ever said something like that publicly. Not a mage, anyway. I think it will open a lot of minds."

"Especially if we get others to participate. Make it a social campaign, use a hashtag. Invite others to share their stories when we share your story. There's potential there. It could go viral."

"You make it sound like you're trying to sell something online," Levi said. He walked up to the computer. "This is my life."

"You want to watch?" Victoria asked. When Levi nodded, she played the video. They stood together and watched it, Levi slowly leaning into Byron's side.

Byron put his arm around him. "I was an anchor for the morning show in college, and I hated being on camera. Now I have to do it for work, and I still hate it."

"Why? You have TV-guy jaw. I look like a meth addict." Levi frowned. "I look sick."

"This isn't a beauty pageant," Victoria said. "It's supposed to be real. And you're recovering from physical and emotional trauma."

"Yeah, for like fourteen more hours. Then it's right back to trauma-land." He paused the video. "Can you give me something to help me sleep tonight?"

"Yes," she said. "And something stronger right before they get here too. It'll tide you over for a few hours, at least. I wish I could do more."

"Don't worry about it. I don't think a little Xanax is going to do the trick once the shit hits the fan," Levi muttered.

"You ready to get these bands on first?" Victoria held them out.

Levi tensed against Byron, but offered his wrists. "Guess I better get used to pretending like they're working."

"That's the idea," she said, giving him a gentle smile. It took seconds to snap them on. The locking gears whirred briefly, and the bands immediately tightened to become seamless cuffs encircling his wrists. "Is that all right? Not pinching?"

"Not pinching or working." Levi heaved a sigh. "Much better than last time."

"Can you remember any of that?" Byron asked. "The first time they put them on you, I mean."

Byron remembered vividly. So vividly that he saw it every night when he tried to go to sleep. The closer he got to Levi, the more it hurt to picture him limp on the street, dying.

"I remember agony and not being able to see." Levi shook his head and touched both bands. "They're so small for being able to do so much."

"When they're enabled, they actually send a minuscule current through your body at all times," Victoria said. "No one knows exactly why it works, but that's the case with many pharmaceuticals. We throw things against the wall to see what sticks. In this case the disruption within the body and the surface tension binds magic."

"That's like saying cyanide makes you sleepy," Levi said.

"You're sure your magic is still working right now?" Byron asked.

Mischief briefly danced in Levi's eyes. An unseen touch ran up Byron's legs, following the curve of his ass, and then up his back—like dozens of tiny tapping fingers, gently tickling his skin. "I'm pretty sure it is, yes."

Victoria snorted and closed her laptop. "I'm going to get this edited and ready to upload. Byron, you know the way to Levi's room." She picked up her shoes and carried them hooked on two fingers. Stopping at the lower-level door, she turned to Byron and Levi.

"I'll bring the meds by in an hour." She hesitated, as if wanting to say more, and slipped away.

"This has been a day." Levi shrugged him off like he'd suddenly noticed that Byron still had his arm around him. "Do you think I should practice a little more?"

"I think you should rest," Byron said.

"What if I can't figure out how to break the machines?"

"They're delicate. We're talking about advanced technology, not a sawmill. Anything you break is going to cause a chain reaction."

Levi nodded, brow knit. "Won't Crane's people shoot me or something? As soon as I do it?"

"You can create shields. Shields that stop huge explosions. You have to focus on protecting yourself. The only thing that can hurt you is an antimagic weapon, and they'll have those, but I'll be there too. I'll do anything I can to protect you."

"No offense, but you work in PR, not . . . weapon-y stuff."

"Hey, I work out. Sometimes." Byron caught Levi by the waist and pulled him close again. "I kickboxed one time. It was to music, but it felt pretty badass."

"So what you're saying is, I'm totally screwed." Levi grinned crookedly, his lips a few inches from Byron's.

Byron kissed him once and took his hand before leading him up the stairs. "Don't tempt me."

"Yeah, right." Levi swatted Byron's ass. "Confess. You've never topped."

"I've thought about it," Byron said, glad to be facing away from Levi when his face heated.

"Your semirugged exterior is so misleading." Levi kissed Byron's hand, his tongue glancing across Byron's skin.

Byron shivered. "Semirugged?"

"That haircut is more bellhop than badass."

"Harsh." Byron grinned. In a normal world, this would be the part where he'd take Levi up to the street, buy him dinner, and ask him all about his life and his friends and what he watched on TV. And what he liked in bed. Then he'd take him home and show him his ugly flower-print couch and his cramped bathroom and his big bed.

"What?" Levi asked, giving him a funny look.

Byron blew out a slow breath. "I want you."

I want to be with you.

They walked down the hall to Levi's room, Levi bumping against Byron playfully. "Sorry, bud. This is not the part where I lovingly teach you how to do me."

They entered the room, and Byron pulled Levi against him. "But is it the part where we agree to have smoking-hot sex if we live?"

"Why are you so weird?" Levi kissed him. "I mean, really, you're the weirdest person I've ever met. And I live in Brooklyn."

"I'm taking that as a yes on the rain check."

Levi laughed and then sobered. A fine tremor ran through him.

Before he could speak, Byron shook his head. "Don't lose faith. Please. Please." He touched Levi's face and pressed their foreheads together. "We can do this."

"You'll be there? You promise?"

"As soon as I can. And I will set fire to that place myself if I have to."

"I bet it's going to have all kinds of firewalls and sprinkler systems. We better stick to my magic." Levi shivered.

"You have to wait for me and Penny or they'll kill you. Do you understand?"

"I don't have a ton of faith in your ability to stop them from killing me."

"Levi . . ."

"I understand what you're saying, but . . ."

Byron braced himself.

"If it's too much and I can't take it, I won't care about surviving," Levi whispered. "I'll bring the machines down around me, and that'll help. It'll help some, at least."

"Try to hang on."

"For you?"

"Yes," Byron said, not caring if Levi didn't believe him or if it was selfish or stupid.

Levi drew back and stared at him, eyes wet. "See? Weird."

After pacing outside the bathroom while Levi showered, Byron tried not to hover too closely. His fingers curled and uncurled.

"It's an injection," Victoria was saying. "Is that all right?"

Levi was sitting in bed now, his back against the wall where a headboard should have been. He wore a pair of sweatpants and a clean T-shirt from his apartment, and his hair was still wet.

"Yeah. I always get my flu shot. And I had allergy shots as a kid. Mages—" Levi's mouth twisted with a humorless grin "—they're just like us!"

"What are you allergic to?" Byron asked as Victoria swabbed Levi's upper arm with a cotton ball and rubbing alcohol.

"Cockroaches."

Byron cringed. "How do you even find that out?"

"From eating them," Levi said. "Obviously."

Byron stared.

"Ew, Byron! From the dust of their little roach corpses. Jesus Christ."

Victoria shook her head as she quickly finished the injection. "Sorry to break it to you, but you live in New York. A tenth of what you eat is actually cockroach."

Levi laughed. "I didn't have a bad allergy. Just used to make me wheezy when I was little."

"Fortunately you're not allergic to sedatives." Victoria snapped her medical kit shut. "You should feel pretty mellow shortly, kid. I'll be here tonight if you need me. I'm going to come in at six and give you a smaller dose. I doubt it'll do much, to be honest. But you should sleep tonight, at least."

If the medicine did its job, he'd get far more sleep than the rest of them—at least judging by the lines of tension around Victoria's eyes.

"Thank you." Levi rubbed the spot where she'd injected him. "I know you're trying to help."

Her eyes welled up, but she blinked the tears away and collected her things, clumsier than Byron had ever seen her before. She switched the lights off on her way out, and they were alone again.

Levi sighed and sank down into the bed. He patted the space beside him. "You gonna stay?"

"I can't be here when they come for you."

"Well, that sucks."

"I know. But my uncle will be suspicious if I'm here and not at work."

Levi yawned. "I hope he doesn't blow you up before you get to the island to help me out."

"Me too."

When Byron climbed into the bed beside him, Levi threw one arm over him and pressed close, loose-limbed and warm like he was waking up from a long nap. "So. The drugs aren't kidding."

Byron petted his hair. "Good."

"What are you allergic to?" Levi asked.

"Pollen, I guess. I get a stuffy nose sometimes."

"Maybe it's cockroaches."

"I'll ask my doctor," Byron said, grinning and wrapping one damp curl around his finger.

Levi hummed a low sound. "How did you end up normal?"

"I thought you said I was weird."

"Normal compared to your evil uncle."

"I've been on Team Evil Uncle until very recently, you know," Byron said. "But Eleanor has always helped. You guys would like each other. She says I'm afraid of commitment."

"Are you committing to me?" Levi snickered softly. "We just met."

"I've never made it past a second date," Byron said. "So planning a third date that involves destroying a billion-dollar facility is basically getting married."

"When you put it that way, it does sound pretty serious." Levi yawned again, his mouth against Byron's shoulder. "I hope Sam isn't mad I didn't run away."

"Sam loves you," Byron said plainly. "I don't think he'll be angry with you for your choices. I wouldn't either, if you decide you want to be with him when this all blows over."

"I broke up with him, like, forever ago," Levi said. "And I told him I don't want to get back together. Even though, oh my God, he's good at fucking. Like, so good. No offense. I mean, you haven't done it yet so who knows. Am I doing the no-filter thing? I got my wisdom teeth out once, and I was so worried I'd say something dumb or do magic and get killed 'cause of impacted molars."

Byron smiled, painfully charmed by Levi's quiet babbling. "Did you say anything dumb?"

"My friend took a video of me in the recovery room. I kept saying that Daisy needed her teeth brushed. She did, actually. They gave her cat drugs to do it. I hope my mom's giving her the right food. She's an old lady cat."

Byron sank down lower in the bed until they were face-to-face. He kissed Levi's lips lightly and smiled when Levi stared at him.

"I like you," Levi said. "I'm glad I met you."

"Don't." Byron's chest ached. "Don't say it like that."

Levi squinted. "I don't think the drugs are working. I'm still scared."

"Me too." Byron pulled him closer.

"Oh." Levi frowned and shifted, burrowing against Byron's chest.

Byron drew the blanket up over them. His phone alarm was set for 5 a.m. They had several hours to stay like this, cocooned under a thin blanket in the dark, and there was no use talking through the fear. Nothing he could say would matter. Nothing would be enough.

He stroked Levi's back in small circles, over and over and over, as Levi cried himself to sleep.

CHAPTER 29
BLINK

Levi felt Byron slip away early in the morning. In the haze of sleep, he let himself pretend it was for a normal reason, like heading to the airport early for a business trip, or getting up to make breakfast. He curled in the warm spot on the bed and continued dozing until Victoria woke him up with a gentle pat.

"Hey there." She'd turned the lights on, but they were dimmed, haloing her face. She had her hair down, and it was long and wavy. It made her seem younger.

"I thought the bun was a permanent thing on your head," he said. "You're really pretty. I mean, you were before too."

"Don't tell Byron you saw me with my hair down."

"Intrigue." He stretched. "I like it."

His stomach ached—the low, fluttering hurt that came with nerves. As soon as he recognized it, it got worse, and he breathed in sharply, trying to will away the panic for a few more minutes.

"I can't give you what I gave you last night or you'll be out of it, and it would pose an interaction risk if they sedate you." She handed him a bottle of water and a small white pill. "This is one of mine, actually. If that makes you feel better."

"Oooh, the secret lives of scientists." He took the pill and swallowed it with the whole bottle of water, guzzling in long pulls like a college kid downing a beer. When he'd caught his breath, she took the bottle and handed him the clothes he'd had on in the last place. The bad place.

"Sorry," she said. "Just like before. They can't see you in your street clothes."

He took the bundle into the bathroom, relieved himself, washed his face, and changed. His toothbrush sat there, but he didn't use it. Maybe they'd check him for suspicious minty freshness.

"What about my face?" he asked, cracking the door so she could hear him. He touched his jaw, and tried not to think about Byron mouth against him. "I shaved yesterday. Will they think that's bad?"

"I doubt it," she said. "You were AMID's first long-term detainee, so I have some wiggle room as far as protocol is concerned. I gave them daily reports on your health and results of initial experiments we weren't doing. You don't need to know any details. If they ask, tell them we'd take you down to the weapons room, and we did tests that made you tired or made you pass out. That it's all foggy."

"That shouldn't be hard. Everything's been foggy since the explosion." He stepped out and handed her his folded clothes. "My shoes are under the bed. Can you give Byron my stuff so he can hang on to it?"

She smiled. "Yes. Though I can't promise he won't make a nest with it and sleep on it until we have you back."

"Because he's weird."

Victoria put everything down on the table and hugged Levi abruptly. She was short and slender, but strong. Her hair smelled like floral, expensive shampoo. "You've changed everything, Levi. Thank you."

"No cheesy good-bye-shaped things," Levi said, gently extracting himself from the hug. "Get your hair up and your game face on."

She dragged her teeth at her lower lip. "I need you to be in the other room and bound to the bed when they get here. It could be soon, so . . ."

"So you have to do it now." He took a deep breath. "Okay."

They walked in silence down the hall to the sparse room he'd stayed in when Crane had visited. It was just as oppressive as before, but this time he would have given anything to stay here rather than leave with Warren Cole's people.

Her fingers trembled as she drew a set of soft restraints from her bag and began attaching them to the legs of the metal cot fastened to the ground. "I'm—"

"I know. You don't have to tell me." Levi shifted around, trying to get comfortable, but he was already too tense with anticipation. Restraints were restraints. The honeymoon was over.

She placed the first carefully. It wasn't too tight, and the fake CALM bands weren't hurting him. He had to focus on those small wins now.

"All right, kid," she said, fastening the second one. "I'm leaving your legs free. I'm going to tell them you were extremely docile. Maybe they'll let their guard down a little."

That sounded like wishful thinking. "Maybe," he said, avoiding her gaze.

The familiarity they'd developed didn't feel so familiar or good now that she had him tied to a cot. She seemed to pick up on that too, because she patted his shoulder a few times and began bustling around the near-empty room as if she had to straighten up. After a minute, he stopped watching. All of the square tiles on the ceiling were symmetrical except for one line along the left side of the room, where they looked like they'd been cut to fit. It bugged him. And the two overhead lights weren't centered.

The air filtration whirred softly, the only soundtrack to Victoria's fidgeting. "I need to go now." Her voice was thick with apology, and something more. Something that made him smile through the sting of tears.

"See you soon." His arms coiled, and he forced them to relax. Panic thrummed in his chest. He couldn't stop this now, even if he wanted to. Even if he couldn't do this—couldn't possibly go back to Crane.

I can't do this.

"Hang in there." She cringed, opened her mouth, closed it again, and left the room.

The walls and doors were so thick he could only make out the low thumps of doors slamming now and then. Left alone and restrained, he had nothing to do but strain his ears, wondering if each distant sound meant strangers were coming to take him back to Cole Industries. The air unit continued to whisper.

Whatever Victoria had given him wasn't doing much. Or maybe it was. He was tense and scared, but it wasn't taking over. He could still think straight.

With his legs free, he bicycled them slowly, trying to improvise a half-assed supine yoga routine. It helped him control his breathing for now. Long, full breaths. In and out of his nose. Every few minutes, a deeper breath blown out his mouth. The arm restraints actually gave him a little leverage. He could almost work himself back into a shoulder stand.

When the door opened, he shot his legs out, trying to look casual and not like he'd been stretching one out to the side in a gentle hip opener.

A man and a woman he'd never seen before surveyed him warily, and his breath caught in his chest. All the confidence—or denial—he'd built up left him in a rush. Victoria walked in behind them, a tablet in her hands.

"I don't think you'll need the wheelchair," she said to them, ignoring Levi. "He followed direct orders without delay. I noted general weakness and malaise, but I'm sure he can walk to your transport unassisted."

"Dr. Crane wants him sedated," the man said. They both wore lab coats and khaki slacks, and he carried a black leather medical bag. "He reported combative behavior."

"I'm telling you that he hasn't been combative at all."

"He's restrained," the woman said, as if Victoria hadn't noticed.

Levi turned his head to the wall opposite them.

"That's protocol with any mages we have on loan," Victoria said. "Studies strongly suggest a suicide risk, and I don't have the manpower to have him under around-the-clock watch. I'm not suggesting you disregard Crane's orders, but you may want to note a behavior change."

"Why is that?" the man asked, sneering.

Levi had a feeling Crane's people weren't big fans of Victoria's people.

"Because protocol always has room for improvement," Victoria said sweetly. "And I've found it's far easier to work with a noncombative subject."

The man put his bag down and retrieved a syringe. He uncapped it and handed a rubbing alcohol applicator to the woman, who couldn't have been much older than Levi. "Let's see how noncombative he is."

She approached Levi as if expecting him to pounce, claws out.

"Mondays, amirite?" he asked.

Her eyes widened as she pushed up his short sleeve and rubbed the cold, wet tip of the applicator against his arm for several seconds. She had pale skin and small hands. "They're not my favorite," she finally murmured, glancing at her colleague nervously, as if she'd broken a rule by talking to him.

The man pushed by her and injected Levi without warning. Levi gasped. He should have known better. No one else was going to treat him the way Byron and Victoria had.

The man capped the syringe and dropped it into the sharps box attached to the wall next to the bed. Levi couldn't blame him for being a dick about it. He'd probably spent his entire life being told mages were dangerous and inhuman—not people who liked a little warning before being injected with something.

Or maybe he'd lost someone in a terrorist attack. Maybe he saw Levi as the poster boy for the fear that gripped New York every day.

"Sorry," Levi said, his tongue thick. He blinked slowly, trying to remember why he was sorry. Not for what he'd done. For everyone. Everything was so sad, so broken.

"If you'll sign these release papers," Victoria was saying, her voice gone faraway. Down a tunnel, in the dark.

Levi blinked.

Blinked.

Blink.

Byron was still at home when Victoria texted.

They have him.

He wanted to text back and ask how Levi had done, but if it had gone badly, she would have told him. He let the read receipt suffice as a reply and turned back to his computer. At work, they'd be monitoring his internet use, so he had to finish his research here.

He was going to be over an hour late to work after getting pulled down a rabbit hole online, but it was worth it. Now he had a bunch of links to cross-reference with Sam's—dozens of places to post Levi's video to the moment he gave Sam the go-ahead from the island.

He ached to post anonymously right away, to tell the desperate, frightened mages and their loved ones that hope was coming—that things were going to change. But he couldn't risk giving Cole Industries any indication of what they had planned.

Instead, Byron was going to walk into what was clearly a trap.

Warren had never brought him in on experiments in the past. He'd made enough backhanded comments about Byron's naivety and youth to show that he didn't consider him capable of witnessing violent work. Whatever Warren had planned for him, Byron could only hope it was supposed to take place after they brought him to the new facility.

Eleanor handed him a cup of coffee and a plate of scrambled eggs.

"Hey, why aren't you at work today?" he asked.

She sat on the easy chair next to his desk. "Funny story. I got fired on Friday. The asshats who got me suspended took it all the way to the superintendent. Said I was poisoning kids' minds with a subversive, pro-magic agenda."

"Shit, E." He sat back in his chair. "You should have told me."

"You have all of this happening. I didn't want to . . ." She had one of her work outfits on—a long skirt and a cardigan—but she wasn't wearing makeup and she had dark circles under her eyes.

"Does Victoria know?"

"I told her this morning. Anyway, it's fine. I don't want to work for dicks." Eleanor gave him a weak smile. "And this frees up my time this week for an actual subversive, pro-magic agenda."

"There's more at stake than your job with this."

"If you get busted, do you think they're going to let me go? We live together. Our cell phone records alone will be incriminating." She shifted and shrugged. "I might as well go all-in."

Nauseated, Byron took a sip of his coffee, struggling not to spill it. His mind reeled.

"Careful there."

"This is my fault. I'm so sorry."

"Get over it. What's done is done. I want to help. That's my choice."

"You can work with Sam and Victoria tomorrow," Byron said reluctantly. At least that way, she wouldn't be near the immediate danger. "They're getting a hotel room with a view of the island and setting up a command center there with computers. If the hotel wi-fi fails, Vic and Sam can use their phones as hot spots."

"We'll probably get arrested within an hour."

"Maybe. Think you can help make that hour worth it?"

She grinned. "Yeah. I have a little pent-up rage. I'm ready to unleash it on the internet."

"Good, because we'll need more than this video. But this is a solid start. And I'm giving you guys the log-in information for the Cole Industries accounts, so you can send this out from their Twitter."

He pulled up the video of Levi on his computer. For a few minutes, they watched Levi speaking quietly—alternating between hesitant and certain.

"He's cute," Eleanor said, eyes creasing with a sad smile. "And it's really compelling. I think people might listen to this."

"It won't make a difference if it's only him. We have to convince people to speak up. Lots of people."

"I know what the kids are down with these days. You wouldn't believe how many phones I had to confiscate in class. We can post to those networks and apps too. You might have a better chance with young people if you use the platforms they use."

Byron gave her Sam's number and forced down a light breakfast, hating the need to go about his normal business when he had no idea what was happening to Levi. Unless Warren volunteered information, he'd have no way of knowing how Levi was for nearly two entire days. His pulse buzzed like a saw.

"Have you slept?" Eleanor asked, watching him guzzle his lukewarm coffee. "Like, at all?"

"Not last night. I tried to. Levi slept. I stayed with him."

She frowned at him. "You need to be sharp tomorrow. Sleep sometime before then, okay?"

"I will." It would be a betrayal, but he needed to rest so he could give everything he had tomorrow at the Harvest facility. He packed up his computer. "Call Sam. See if he can meet up with you today or tomorrow morning. Maybe you two can hash out more ideas? I'll be home tonight, and we can talk about it."

"Do your hair, Byron. It's sticking up like you shoved your finger in an electric socket."

Byron touched his hair and winced. It did feel particularly . . . fluffy. Despite being straight, it had a tendency to stick in every direction if he didn't keep it under control. "Thanks."

"You need to act normal today."

"Relatively so?" he asked, thinking about Levi calling him weird. It made him smile.

"Wow."

"What?"

"I've never seen you with that look on your face before." She smiled back at him. "Try not to do that at work either, or people will start asking you if you got laid last night."

When his face flushed, she shook her head and laughed. The sound faded immediately though, like the echoes of a dream. They stared at each other in silence. Reality sank in, cement around Byron's feet. He took a breath that whistled in his throat and ran his hands through his hair, as if smoothing it down—fixing that one thing—might give them better odds of survival.

Byron set up his phone on a bendy stand to record the bird expert who had come to his office to do an interview for Cole Industries' social media campaign.

He asked basic questions and let the middle-aged man ramble about black-crowned night herons and how with Cole Industries' help, he hoped to bring them back to their former nesting grounds on North Brother Island. Over the next hour, Byron learned more than he'd ever wanted to know about bird habits and different types of egrets. Despite himself, he found most of it interesting. The city had never seemed like a place where birds would find any sanctuary, but apparently the East River attracted wildlife.

If he'd been creating the video in earnest, it would probably have proven to be a very successful campaign for Cole Industries. Even people who didn't identify as environmentalists liked feel-good stories of job creation and lifelong dreams to protect rare species.

As soon as he'd escorted the bird expert out of his office, Byron compressed the video and sent it to Penny. She'd have a lot of homework and practice to do overnight.

That left him the rest of the day to finish his to-do list.

Byron steeled himself to update a landing page on the Cole Industries site with information on zero-energy housing in Alaska—the sort of press-friendly efforts that boosted Cole Industries' public image. When he finished that, he began his real work.

His final work for Cole Industries.

He wrote copy for pages that would remain unpublished until Sam pulled the trigger on them. He wrote about Warren's suspected involvement with terrorist acts. He left a space for the video of Levi being tortured by Crane, and the video of Levi talking about the CALM program and magic. He exposed the amount of money Cole Industries funneled into political campaigns reducing mage rights.

As he sifted through official CALM research reports, he paid more attention than usual. Before, it had been a blur of data. Now every data point correlated to a living, hurting human being. One fact stuck out: most mages had levels of power so small they were likely incapable of causing harm with magic.

They were binding mages for no reason.

Had he looked over that detail before or willfully ignored it? Fresh guilt washed over him like ice water.

As Byron sifted through his task list, his chest felt like it was filled with mud. He tried, again and again, to do the deep-breathing things Levi did, but every breath rushed out of him. Freaking out became his new normal throughout the morning. He didn't even attempt to eat something, knowing his stomach would reject it immediately.

After noon, Warren sent him the details to board a private launch to the island. Warren, of course, would be arriving by helicopter. Having the specifics gave Byron something hopeful to focus on. On Tuesday, right after work, he'd take a small boat to the island. Within an hour of leaving the dock, he'd be in the Harvest facility, touring the grounds and making his way to Levi and the huge machines made to pull Levi's magic out of his body.

The constant awareness that Levi was already on the island being prepped for Harvest phase two fueled every word Byron wrote.

When he finished with the basics, the important information that would display directly on the Cole Industries homepage for as long as it took for the IT department to pull it down—hopefully long enough for a watchful internet to screen cap it and start sharing—he added one more section.

My name is Byron Cole.

I've only been working for my family's business for two years, but I've spent my whole life believing that magic was bad and needed to be controlled to keep people safe. I've told half truths and outright lies to make sure that you believed that too. My comfort and success in life hinged on the American government and the American people needing Cole Industries.

I'm here to tell you that CALM bands are unnecessary. Mages don't even need to be registered. We can regulate magic on a minimal basis by imposing restrictions on outright abuse of power. There's no reason to tear families apart. There's no reason to incarcerate and kill people for being born different.

A mage I care very much about explained magic like this: "We can do things you can't do."

He can make things float and fly. And he can create safety barriers out of magic. One of those barriers saved my life when a bomb exploded on the street less than fifty feet from where I was standing.

That bombing was orchestrated by my uncle, Warren Cole, in an effort to poison the American people against magic.

Magic saved dozens of lives that day.

Think of how many more lives could be saved if mages were given the freedom to use magic for good.

I know some of you reading this care about someone with magic, or have already lost someone with magic. I'm sorry it took me this long to see the truth. I'm sorry it took me loving a mage to understand the horror of what we're doing every day to good people—people who don't deserve to be tormented.

This is a lot to take in. Maybe you're afraid of change or afraid of what you don't understand. It's not easy to see the truth. Trust me, I know. But I'm asking you to do something revolutionary.

Byron smiled as he typed one last sentence. He'd played Levi's words over again and again in his head, until they echoed like a mantra.

Choose to be unafraid.

CHAPTER 30
SKY-HIGH

The hardest part wasn't the pain.

It was keeping his magic inside when all he wanted to do was shove the pain away.

Crane's breath bathed across Levi's cheek as he leaned over him to adjust a thick metal band restraining his head. The stale coffee smell brought back flashes of agony and white-laced terror, and Levi swallowed against an involuntary moan.

Levi wore nothing but a thin towel draped over his groin, and the metal slab under him was cold enough to send shivers through his whole body. The AC blasted down on him too, and he longed to find a blanket or anything to protect him from the endless chill.

"It's to prevent the system from overheating," Crane said absently, after a particularly violent wave of shivers ran through Levi's body, making his breath stutter. "You won't feel the cold once we're up and running. You won't feel anything ever again if I get the sedation formula right."

His thumb brushed at Levi's bare shoulder, drawing fond circles that made bile rise in Levi's throat.

"That's a big 'if,' though." Crane chuckled. "That's why we're trying with you first. No one will care if you scream yourself hoarse."

Crane added another set of clips that restrained Levi's arms. Levi was still wearing the fake CALM bands, and so far no one seemed to have noticed that they weren't working. It helped that he'd apparently spent the first day at the new Harvest place completely unconscious.

When he'd struggled back to awareness, he'd been in a small cell containing nothing but a rubberized floor and a single metal toilet.

For several hours, he'd alternated between shivering in the corner and retching into the toilet. He had never been so sick in his life, and hadn't been able to figure out what was making him so ill, until they came for him.

"Enjoying the system cleanse, I see," one of the scientists had said, laughing.

They'd dragged him from the cell to a huge, hangar-like laboratory that smelled plasticky and new. There, they'd hosed him down with clinical precision before beginning the slow process of getting him hooked up to Crane's massive machine.

He couldn't feel the catheter anymore, but the IV in his hand still ached—a dull throbbing that added to the symphony of hurt. His stomach muscles cramped from vomiting, and his shoulders and neck had gone from numb to prickling with pain from the angle his arms were spread at.

"I've made so many improvements since our little educational experience," Crane said. "Tweaks here and there. I'm more than prepared to handle the load of your magic now."

Levi didn't answer. He hadn't spoken a single word since leaving AMID, and no one seemed concerned about that. He was already nothing to Crane, no more than a source of magic and the butt of jokes. He tried to let his eyes drift closed, but every movement from Crane startled him—and he couldn't allow himself to be startled. He couldn't allow himself to lose his grip on his magic.

A silent tear ran down the side of his face. He didn't want to cry. He didn't want to feel. But every time his magic tried to swell up, his composure eroded. It would be so easy. He had intention to spare. All he had to do was give in and dash everything around him to pieces. Or at the very least dash Crane to pieces so he would never be able to hurt someone else like this again.

"Don't worry," Crane said, thumbing the tear away. "We're three hours to launch. Time flies when you're being integrated into a biotechnical system, right?"

Three hours.

Levi swallowed back a sob.

Three hours until Byron arrived and freed him and they could destroy this place, blowing it sky-high.

"This is going to sting," Crane said. He angled a metal tube toward Levi, and at the last minute Levi saw a massive needle at the tip of it. Flinching away, he felt his body tense up. Crane sank the long needle deep into the fleshy part of Levi's shoulder until it scraped against bone and anchored the tube there.

Crane patted his cheek as he tried to stop screaming between every shallow, choking breath. "Only five more."

But Levi latched on to only one number, even as Crane counted out each needle insertion before plunging them into Levi's hips and calves.

Three.

Three more hours. He only had to survive three more hours, and it would be over, one way or another.

Sea spray left a fine film of salt on Byron's skin as the small launch hired by Cole Industries crossed the East River toward North Brother Island. The wind kicked up choppy waves. Byron held on to a handrail as the hull slapped down against the waves. Each impact jarred up his legs and spine. It was just after five, and the sun cast a warm glow that made colors more vivid. Any other time, Byron would love a rare chance to speed across the water, passing all the sluggish ferries.

Now, he wanted to be there faster. The Harvest buildings gleamed in the distance, bright white and modern, and no higher than three or four stories. Only a small reception annex had windows. The surrounding area and small marina had been landscaped, but the rest of the island remained wild. He squinted, trying to spot a heron or egret, but he wasn't even sure what he was looking for. All he saw were gulls swooping and diving in the stiff wind.

The launch carried two other employees, young scientists who kept to themselves. One read a tablet and the other appeared to be snoozing despite the boat's movements. Byron checked his phone for the tenth time. No messages from Sam, Victoria, or Eleanor since the last message letting him know that they were secure in their room with a telescope trained on the island. If something happened to his phone, the chances of Byron being able to send a coherent signal to them were slim, but hopefully they'd be able to spot any disturbances from their viewpoint.

The skipper threw a line onto the dock and powered down the engine. It only took a minute or so to secure the launch. At the man's signal, Byron crossed the aluminum gangplank and stepped onto North Brother Island for the first time in his life.

As a child, he'd always thought it was haunted. The boarded-up windows and sagging eaves of the abandoned hospital invited ghosts and ghouls. He'd never been scared of it as much as intrigued. The monolithic white building that had replaced the demolished hospital wasn't creepy, but it scared him more.

Walking from the marina up to the building took less than five minutes at a slow, uphill pace. Byron would have jogged it had he not been walking with the scientists, who appeared unhurried and preoccupied by their phones.

"Have you spent much time here yet?" he asked the woman. She had long, thin braids that whipped in the wind despite her efforts to hold them in one hand.

"This is my first time over," she said, shaking his hand briefly as they walked. "I'm Donna, by the way. That's James. They're only taking observers in small batches right now. We won an office lottery to come over and see."

"Next month, when they're fully staffed, they'll accommodate much bigger groups," James said without glancing up from his phone.

Bright-purple flowers lined the path they followed on each side. It looked festive and clean, like a walkway through a theme park—not a path leading to a house of horrors.

"I'm Byron."

"Byron, as in Byron Cole?" Donna whistled out a breath. "You must be more excited than we are. I heard this Camden guy almost blew you to smithereens before our containment team got him."

"Yes, I'm anxious to get there." Byron gestured up at the building. He debated correcting her, but didn't want any extra attention. Not yet.

Warren met them in the lobby.

"Mr. Cole," Donna gushed, "it's an honor to meet you."

James elbowed her and hissed out, "We're not supposed to talk to him. Didn't you read the memo?"

Warren waved them off as if swatting a fly, and they rushed ahead, chattering like flustered squirrels. No one checked their identification at the automatic doors that took them into the main facility. Byron spotted an information and security desk, but it was unmanned.

"How was the trip over?" Warren asked. He carried his cane and wore a fine suit.

"Not bad. Quicker than I expected."

"Ah, good. Are you ready?"

"Absolutely."

"How was your interview with that . . . it was a bird person, correct?" Warren asked, taking Byron's arm. Byron led him through the automatic doors.

"Good. Very helpful," Byron said. "Which way are we going?"

"Corridor four. A right, a left, and then four doors down."

Byron could hear James and Donna ahead of them, a bright snap of laughter echoing down the corridor. He tried not to let his anger carry through him enough for Warren to feel the tension in his body.

How could they laugh when they were heading to watch a man be tormented? How could they not see it for what it was?

"The facility is beautiful," Byron said. That much was true. Cole Industries had clearly spared no expense. They walked on a polished stone floor that gleamed like a mirror. Along the wall, dozens of vintage photos of North Brother Island hung in oversized frames, reminding Byron of a museum's halls.

"I'll show you the plans sometime," Warren said. "We went three stories underground and four up. It was more than enough space for the Harvest reactor. And because we're dealing with the bleeding edge of this technology, we had a much easier time getting permits than we would have with a traditional power plant of any kind. It's a win-win for the entire city. I'm drafting plans for expansion. If we stay on schedule, we could have mages powering all of Manhattan within four years."

"Clean, safe energy," Byron parroted, his mouth dry. If it was true that most mages didn't have much magic, the Harvest Initiative would mean subjecting thousands to unspeakable torture.

Warren chuckled. "Precisely, my boy. Look for the observation deck. Should be quite soon."

Byron pushed the door open and led them into a small balcony at the edge of a cavernous room full of machines that stretched below them and up toward the concrete ceiling—an engine room on steroids. Gears hummed so loudly Byron had to speak up even with Warren right beside him.

"Wow," he said. "This is much bigger than it seems from the outside."

He counted at least eight more observation areas along the wall, each full of intricate monitoring equipment. Each cluster of equipment swarmed around narrow, metal slabs like morgue tables. There were hundreds of them—too many for Byron to count.

"You're only seeing a fraction of it." Warren smiled and opened his palm. "The floor above us holds containment cells for six hundred. Double that if we tighten quarters a bit. We'll be able to cycle mages in and out of active harvesting to give them time to recover to optimum levels. Truly sustainable."

"Amazing," Byron croaked.

"Go to the edge," Warren said. "I'm told you'll have a good view of Crane's work from there."

James and Donna stood at the rail. They moved over politely when Byron approached, and he was grateful for the clang and clatter of the machines when he spotted pale human skin through the tangle of pipes and wires and dials.

It was Levi, gray-faced and trembling. He was lying flat on one of the metal slabs, with gleaming restraints around his forehead, chin, arms, and legs. The machine held him down like he was trapped in a medieval torture device, and it took all of Byron's control to breathe through a wave of nausea. Six tubes protruded from Levi's body. Byron couldn't tell how they were attached, but even from thirty feet away, the lines of agony on Levi's face were clear.

A figure walked between the shiny steel pipes and thicker, insulated pipes that rose like a forest around Levi. Byron recognized him from the video: Kurt Crane.

Crane lifted a walkie-talkie, and his voice filled the small observation deck. "Good evening, visitors. In a few minutes, you'll witness history in the making."

"Dr. Crane has a flair for the dramatic," Warren said. "Would you like a closer look before we get started?"

"Yes." Byron wanted to get down to Levi so badly it made his hands cramp up. "Absolutely. I've never seen anything like this."

A scaffolding staircase similar to the one in Victoria's weapons-testing room ran along the wall from the observation deck. Byron carefully guided Warren down the precarious stairs, letting him take a firm grip of his arm for balance.

Above them, Donna and James peered over the railing, mouths hanging open in matching expressions of wonder.

It was louder down on the machinery floor. The floor vibrated faintly, like a purring cat. "Can you lower that racket?" Warren shouted.

Crane ducked from behind a wall of dials. His eyes lit up when he saw Warren. "Sir! Yes!" He dashed away somewhere, and a few seconds later, the noises dimmed to a more gentle whirr—nowhere near quiet, but not as cacophonous. "I only need to prime it for one minute before we flip the switch," Crane said, a manic grin stretching his mouth like a wound.

It was quiet enough for Byron to make out a soft, thready wheeze. He recognized it as Crane led them to the cramped area that contained Levi. Shallow, pained breathing. Levi's eyes were open, gazing at a fixed point where two gauges trembled like a moth's wings.

"The subject has an elevated heart rate and blood pressure, and an elevated temperature. All within working parameters," Crane said. "The body's systems will regulate once sedation is on board. I waited to start that process until you arrived, like you asked, sir."

He sounded like a little boy showing off his science project. Byron wanted to vomit.

"I was hoping Byron could see exactly what we're doing here," Warren said. "This is one of two hundred and fifty input bays, correct?"

"Yes. Until we come closer to a hundred active subjects, I won't be able to calculate the load on the grid, but I expect beautiful output." Crane stroked one of the pipes in a loving, near-lascivious way that made Byron's skin crawl.

"It was Byron here who suggested we use Levi for the Harvest," Warren said.

Levi's fingers twitched. He didn't move his head, but his gaze sluggishly tracked toward where Byron stood. Byron stared at him, willing him to meet his eye, but Levi's gaze remained empty, blank with torment.

Levi's muscles twitched. It had to be the tubes fastened to his body—piercing him, Byron realized with horror.

Byron went hot and shaky, sick with adrenaline and fear. Was it the right time? How could he free Levi from this mess? Could Levi use his magic now? Was he too weak?

"I'm sure it will give you satisfaction to hear that this rogue mage's last thoughts will be knowing that you put him here, where he belongs," Warren said to Byron. "I know it pleases our talented Dr. Crane to know that he's working on a perpetrator of heinous crimes."

"I'm sure it does," Byron said, hoarse.

Crane clasped his hands together and nodded, beatific. Byron didn't know who Warren meant to influence—him, or even Levi—but he was well beyond taking his uncle's words at face value. Not anymore. Never again.

"Are you all right, my boy?" Warren asked, patting Byron's hands. "You sound a bit woozy."

"Always had a weak stomach, I guess," Byron said, strained. He coughed, trying to clear his throat—and cover how fast he was breathing.

"Why don't we head upstairs? We'll get started and then get you home."

"Right," Byron said, dazed, letting Warren turn him away. When he looked up, Donna and James were watching them, rapturous. His phone felt like a brick in his pocket. He needed to text Sam and Victoria—he needed them to get started. He needed the whole world to know what was happening here.

The machines came back to life, rattling like a thousand cans full of marbles, until Byron felt the vibration in his bones. It was happening too quickly. He didn't know what to do.

Then Levi shouted. Byron turned back, struggling against Warren's surprisingly firm grip.

Levi's eyes were closed, his face twisted in a pained grimace, but he shouted something over and over—something Byron couldn't make out over the din. He focused on Levi's pale lips, the desperate movements of his mouth.

"It's Warren. Warren! Warren's—"

Warren leaned across Crane to the control console and slammed a metal switch. The lights in the room flickered and sparked, and Levi stopped shouting. His face contorted with a silent, convulsive scream.

"No!" Byron shouted. He looked back at Crane's face, the doughy folds of it lit a sickening green by the console's lights. The scientist smiled like a child on Christmas morning.

"Stop," Byron said, struggling for the switch. "Stop the machine!"

Warren yanked Byron's arm harder than an old man should have been able to. "Careful, boy," he hissed in Byron's ear.

The console was within reach. Byron had to stop the machines now, before the Harvest sucked Levi dry—before all was lost. He struggled desperately with Warren, unable to break free—

Then James landed on the controls with an ugly thud, blood pouring from a ragged head wound.

His mouth gaped. He didn't move.

Crane flinched up at the observation balcony, eyes wide with fear. Byron followed his frightened gaze. Someone was grappling with Donna.

"Is that the *bird expert*?" Crane shouted.

It was the opening Byron needed. He shoved James's body away and lunged for the button Warren had hit to start the machine. The ear-splitting rattling cut off. Donna screamed and went silent above them, and a familiar face leaned over the edge—a small firearm in one hand and the antimagic device Donna had been carrying in the other.

"Your uncle is a fucking mage," Penny yelled.

CHAPTER 31
FLASHING LIGHTS

The moment the machine released Levi, he unleashed his magic. It lashed out of him, full of rage and grief and pain.

Hulking metal sparked and screeched, twisting away from him. The cuffs bent from his head and face. He tried to shove the tubes, but agony seared through his muscles, and he cried out and froze with his hands clenched around them. Above him, great billows of steam poured out of a thick pipe like rolling storm clouds.

Penny appeared beside him, her lip split open and bleeding. She touched his face and yelled. His ears rang, and it took a few tries for him to understand her.

"I have to pull these out," she was saying. "I'm sorry!"

She climbed right onto him and grabbed one tube in both hands and yanked. He gasped—but it didn't hurt coming out as much as it had going in. She made quick work of the rest of the tubes. "One sec, honey."

He lay there shaking, cold, watching the sparks soar above him, beautiful next to the steam.

"Getting the catheter. Levi, I'm sorry. I'm sorry."

"I can't feel it." His voice rasped, bloody and broken.

Hadn't Byron been there? His thoughts scrambled together, and his magic hurt again, a soul-deep soreness he had no words for.

"Here," she said, helping him shove his bare legs into a pair of khakis. "They're too big, but I only had one dead guy to pick from."

"Dead guy." Dazed, he let her pull him up. The room spun. "Crane?"

"No, but let's go kill him."

"I don't want to kill anybody." Levi shook his head, trying to clear it—trying to shake away the ringing in his ears. "Where's Byron?"

"Warren grabbed him and took off. We have to go and find him. Can you walk?"

"Warren has magic!" Levi shouted hoarsely, remembering what had been so important right before his vision exploded and something awful started happening. "He's a mage. He's a goddamned mage."

"I know. I felt it too. That son of a bitch," Penny said. "Doing this to his own kind." She helped Levi down and struggled to catch him when his legs buckled. "Oh, you're a mess. Oh, Levi."

Thin rivulets of blood ran from his hips and shoulders. The pants didn't fit him and hung low on his hips. Blood stained the fabric at his calves.

"I *do* want to kill Crane," he said, not really meaning it as much as remembering why he was bleeding. "Wait. Warren has Byron? Right now?"

"Yeah, sweetie, we have to move. I don't think he's taking him to shelter, if you know what I mean."

Something clanged near them. Penny ducked and tugged him down. "We're being shot at. Levi. Someone is shooting at us."

He nodded, unsteady in a crouch.

"Levi! I can't stop bullets. *You* can. Can you shield us if we try to follow where I saw Warren take Byron?"

"I can stop bullets." Levi drew in a shuddering breath. "Okay."

"Intention," she said, taking his face in both hands.

"My intention is to not get shot."

"Right. Exactly. Now hang on to me."

She stood, and he held on to her shoulders and let her momentum drag him. He managed to move his feet, his face tucked against her back, and his magic focused on one thing—not getting shot.

"What if they have weapons like Victoria's?"

"They will. So we are hauling ass off this island as soon as we find your boyfriend."

Levi wondered if he should tell her that he could sense the bullets striking the shield around them. Each shot stung like being snapped with a rubber band.

"Hurry," he said, tired underneath all the urgency and adrenaline. Tired enough to sink to the floor and sleep.

It was like walking through a maze. None of the corridors of pipes and machinery led to a door, and whoever was shooting at them seemed to be aiming more carefully now, waiting for clearer shots instead of spraying bullets into the machines.

He looked back and gasped. "Wait!"

Crane stalked between the machines, sweaty and purple with rage, leveling a handgun at them.

Levi shuddered at the murder in his eyes.

"I don't have to kill him," he whispered. "But I can stop him."

Intention. He'd tipped a whole bulldozer over. He made things fly. He had to believe, had to want it.

He drew his breath in, and one of the pipes twisted apart from the rest of a machine. Crane came up short, staring at it, the rage on his face giving way to panic. Crane lifted his gun and fired at the pipe. The bullets sparked against the metal. Mouth pulling into an ugly grimace, he tossed the gun away and drew a small plastic device out. Levi didn't recognize it, but he knew what it must be and what it would do to him.

Intention.

A twisting, heavy pipe slammed against Crane and crushed him against one of his machines.

"You, uh, might have just killed him," Penny said.

The antimagic weapon dropped out of Crane's limp fingers.

"Maybe." Horror registered somewhere inside of Levi, but it was distant—strongly outweighed by his desire to not die in this hellhole of a factory.

"I'm not sticking around to check." Penny slung an arm around Levi's waist, and they kept picking their way through the machines.

"I need to break more of these. So they'll never work again."

"Then start button smashing," Penny said.

He coughed out a weak laugh and started flipping every single switch they passed.

The remaining machines began to groan and rattle, and the floor shook beneath them. Penny tugged him frantically. Chased by the growing roar, Levi found the strength to run.

Byron tried to shake himself out of Warren's crushing grip, but all it earned him was an obviously broken wrist that throbbed with white-hot agony. Warren dragged him down a long corridor.

"Are you even blind?" Byron panted, sick with pain.

"Of course I am." Warren showed Byron his milky-blue pupils. His glasses had fallen away in the struggle. "My magic is simply strength—a brute talent. Useless."

He stumbled and cried out when Warren yanked him to his feet.

Doesn't feel too useless to me.

"Where are we going?"

"To the surface."

That's what Byron needed to hear. He reached into his pocket, unlocked his phone with his thumbprint, and swiped a short pattern he'd practiced over and over.

The machine floor roared to life behind them, louder than it had been before. Byron's head jerked up, momentarily forgetting what he was doing.

Levi.

Warren's expression darkened. "What are they toying with?"

His confusion meant Levi was alive. Meant it wasn't Crane turning the machines back on to keep hurting him.

Warren started dragging him again. Ahead, a fiery orange light shone through the window in the door at the end of the corridor—the setting sun. They were almost outside.

"Why are you doing this?" Byron had read enough crime novels to know that you had to keep the bad guy talking.

At least until you had cell phone reception.

"Because it's a good story. Isn't that always what you're saying? Isn't that what you learned in school?" Warren laughed out an ugly sound. "People don't want facts or data. They want a compelling story."

"Harvesting magic from your own kind is a good story?"

"Byron Cole dying at the hands of Levi Camden is a good story. They'll make a movie about it. People will remember it forever. They'll talk about the first, botched attempt to run the Harvest machines, and the way Camden took revenge on you before we managed to kill him."

Byron shook his head to clear the fog of pain and focus on the plan he'd made with Sam and Eleanor. "He's not going to hurt me. He's half-dead! Your machines were killing him."

"He's not going to do it, because *I'm* going to do it." Warren wrenched Byron forward, squeezing Byron's fractured wrist until Byron cried out and stumbled hard. He tripped a few steps until he caught his balance again, and then they were pushing through the door.

Salty wind blasted against Byron's face. They were near the water, but still about fifty yards from the marina. Trees soared above them, the leaves rattling and whipping in the wind.

"It'll be a good story, and people will tell it instead of asking exactly what's powering their television sets and lights." Warren let him go and brushed at his suit, smoothing out wrinkles. "I'm sorry it has to be you, Byron. You've been surprisingly adept at your job, and you're inexpensive."

"Why do you hate your own kind?" Byron tucked his uninjured hand into his pocket, made sure his phone was still there.

"Don't be dramatic, son. I don't hate mages. I certainly don't hate myself. But I don't have a misguided sense of loyalty either. I saw a business opportunity, and I took it."

Byron needed to understand. He needed *everyone* to understand. "But you've killed so many people."

"So has the government." Warren scoffed. "I didn't pull the trigger. I just gave people the little pushes they needed to become bloodthirsty."

"What about the bombings? The terrorist attacks."

"Oh, those." Warren laughed. "Collateral damage. I needed to build a market for my brand."

Byron tried to sound shocked, like he was finally figuring it out. "Wait, you tried to kill me before. The day Levi saved me!"

"Of course I did. But this? This is so much better than my original plan. When the Coast Guard arrives, they'll find me hunched over your broken body, trying to feel a pulse, trying to make sense of your caved-in face. It'll be poetry." Warren wiped spittle from his mouth. "Maybe someone will win a Pulitzer by taking a photo of it."

Byron pulled his aching wrist closer to his chest, hunched over it wincing, and used the movement to cover his fingers dipping into his breast pocket to remove the lighter-sized device he'd hidden there.

Warren was still talking, saying something about becoming the only mage, the most powerful one of all, the most powerful man on the planet. That it wouldn't matter if he couldn't use his magic if he had power and money and influence.

When Byron pressed the button on the device, Warren choked and dropped like a puppet with its strings cut, landing in an awkward sprawl in the dark green grass.

"Oh." Byron stumbled back. "Yes! It worked!"

He dug into his pocket and grabbed his phone. The red light blinked in the corner of his screen, still counting the seconds being recorded—it was up to several minutes now. "Vic, it worked! The thing you gave me to stop Levi if he freaked out. It worked—on Warren. *Warren*. He's a mage!"

"We heard," Victoria said, a tinny voice on his speaker.

"Shit, how long will he stay down?"

"Not long," she responded. "Get CALM bands on him if you can. If not, the dampener has a few more pulses in it, but it'll take Levi and Penny out too if they're near you. You need to get away from there. We can see smoke from all the way over here. It's on TV already."

"Are you uploading the recording?"

"It's at eighty percent uploaded. It'll be up in a minute or so."

"Byron." Sam's voice cut through, frantic. "Where's Levi? Is he with you?"

The door they'd exited from was gaping open, exhaling smoke. Byron's stomach dropped in a free fall of dread. "No. He's with Penny. I'm going back for them now."

"Something's happening in that building, Byron." That was Eleanor, her voice sharp—scared. "It's coming on the news now. They're saying the building is giving weird readings. They're closing the airspace around it, and the river too. I think you need to hurry."

Byron was already running. "I won't get service down there," he yelled. "Keep going, send everything everywhere. Tell everyone what happened."

Her voice became staticky and distant. "God—it—ron."

The line went dead.

"You should stop button smashing now," Penny said, coughing.

Levi hung on to her shoulders where they'd stopped to catch their breath. The machine floor was hemorrhaging steam and smoke behind them. The building had started to shake, as if an earthquake was rumbling beneath them. "I think I broke them. Is everyone out? The other people? The people who work here?"

"Honey, that's not our problem right now. Which damn door is the exit?" Penny wiped her watering eyes.

Levi squinted, trying to see through the hazy air. His throat stung from the acrid smoke.

They both flinched when something exploded at the far end of the machine floor. A small fireball launched up toward the ceiling and ignited the insulation. Heat radiated from the flames like a crashing wave. It hurt.

"Shit," Levi said.

"I'm going with 'any door will do.'" Penny grabbed at the nearest handle, and a door opened about a hundred feet away.

"Levi! Penny!" Byron shouted, beckoning. Another explosion boomed, and Byron started sprinting for them, one arm held at an awkward angle against his body. He reached them, and Levi's heart squeezed so hard it hurt.

"Take him, he can barely move." Penny shoved Levi into Byron. Levi wanted to say that she was exaggerating, but his legs were heavy and useless.

With Penny's help, Byron hefted him up over his shoulder. "Wrist is out of commission," he explained with a wheeze before he began to run. "Try not to fall."

Levi swayed and clung to Byron, the blood rushing to his head. He wasn't going to complain. They were moving much faster now. "I think I set the Harvest stuff on fire. It's Penny's fault. She said to hit all the buttons."

"Every single one," she panted.

They reached the door Byron had come in from, and he locked it behind them, as if that was going to discourage fire and destruction from entering the long corridor.

Byron's so weird.

"It isn't far to the surface and the marina," Byron said, breathing raggedly. "I don't know if the boat took off though. We may end up in the river."

"Better wet than blown up," Levi said.

"Where's Warren?" Penny asked.

"I knocked him out with one of Victoria's devices."

The door behind them shuddered in a really awful, not-good way after another series of loud rumbles.

"So. Warren," Levi said, trying not to think about the building potentially crashing down around them. "I did not see that coming."

"I've always done a little magic check," Penny said. "It's a habit. Sweeping the room, seeing if anyone bounces magic back at me. He bounced back like a car crash. I think that's why Levi felt it too."

"His magic felt slimy." Levi's head hurt. He wanted so much to close his eyes. "Bad."

"It did. I've never felt anything like it," she said. "You know that feeling you get when you find a spider or a snake? It was like that, but ten times worse."

"That's exactly it," Levi murmured. He could almost feel it again—a deep prickling sensation that screamed danger, tensed his muscles up, told him to run. Run away.

They were running away from the fire, but right toward the bad feeling.

It's real. I can feel it.

"Wait." Levi tried to shout, but his voice was so raw and weak. "Wait!"

A door opened, and they were outside in gray twilight. Sirens sounded distantly, whipped away by the wind, and Penny didn't make a sound—not a single sound—when Warren punched a hole right through her middle.

Byron startled back, losing his grip on Levi.

Who fell to the ground in a heap. Fluffy grass cradled him, and Penny, who was already gone, gone. Her eyes empty and open, her blood bright like spilled paint.

Warren Cole's weathered face was cold and expressionless, but his cloudy eyes held malice. He wiped his gore-covered hand on his pants, and only then did his mouth curl with distaste. "It's messy work, this uncommon strength. Magic. I would have preferred a more refined talent."

Warren faced Byron, and his lips hooked into a sharp gash of a smile. Levi lifted his hand, scrambling for intention, but his mind raced—scattered and panicked. Death hadn't been real until now, until Penny. His magic wanted to scream, and if he let it, he feared it would overcome Byron too.

Stupid, brave Byron—who was lunging at his uncle as if he had a chance.

Warren chuckled and grabbed Byron by his purpling wrist, driving him to his knees beside Penny's body as if it took no effort whatsoever. Byron let out a hitched cry.

"Stop!" Levi's voice was strained, hoarse from screaming. He wobbled up onto his hands and knees and stretched his hand out, fingers trembling. "Don't hurt him."

"I'm not going to hurt him." Warren spoke softly, calmly—as if the facility weren't burning behind him. "I'm going to kill him."

"Why? It's over." Levi's vision wobbled, gray with exhaustion. "The machines are ruined."

"The destruction of the Harvest facility is only a roadblock," Warren said.

Of course. Warren had the means—the ludicrous wealth—to start over, to hurt more mages, to bend the world to his whim. Levi's chest went cold.

He'll kill Byron without a second thought.

Byron struggled in Warren's iron grip, punching and kicking him.

Warren didn't flinch. He coughed delicately as a wave of smoke washed over them. "Such a waste of resources. Perhaps I will hurt him." His knuckles whitened, grip tightening, and Byron gave a ragged scream.

The truth gripped Levi's heart: *He'll never stop hurting people to get what he wants.*

His magic snapped Warren's neck with a brutal twist before the intention caught up with him.

Warren fell on top of Penny's body, as if trying to cover the gaping horror of what he'd done to her.

Levi started shaking.

Byron untangled himself from Warren's dead grip. "Come on." He stumbled to his feet and took Levi's hand with his good arm.

The air was hot and shimmery.

"Levi, come on. Come on, babe." He dragged him through the thick grass. "You have to move—we have to go."

"Byron." Levi choked on a sob. Penny and Warren were still and waxy, like mannequins. But they were real. They were real dead bodies. "She's gone."

"I know. I know. We have to go. Please, Levi." Byron's voice broke, raw with emotion. "We have to go."

Levi let Byron lead him. Warren's death replayed in his mind like an aftershock. It had been the kind of whip-crack burst of magic he'd always feared, but this time he didn't feel anything. Not regret. Nothing but the physical pain that made it harder and harder to stay on his feet.

I'm tired, Byron.

The way to the water sloped, and the grass was smooth like a slide. They alternated between running and slipping, approaching the dark, churning water that seemed inviting compared to the radiant, awful heat behind them.

Byron angled them toward a dock, and Levi's breath caught on a frustrated sob when he saw a group of people huddled there—where no boat waited.

Several of them had guns and antimagic weapons trained on Levi and Byron.

"I'm Byron Cole," Byron shouted. "Hold your fire."

He shouted it again and again, but no one dropped their weapons.

Levi wanted to stop. He just wanted to sit down and close his eyes. "Byron," he said, digging his heels in.

His magic flickered weakly, spent and hurting. How could he stop more bullets when he was so tired?

An ear-shattering *crack* caught everyone's attention. A few of the men and women with weapons lowered them, turning to the black smoke pouring out of the Harvest building.

The air trembled and buzzed.

"It's going to explode," someone said, jerky with fear. "The whole thing is going to blow."

"We have to swim for it," Byron said. "We have to get in the water. Under the water, maybe. There's no other way."

A shout rang out. "There's a boat coming!"

"Stay back," a woman yelled at Byron and Levi. Her clothes and hair were singed, and her eyes held the wide-eyed, hysterical terror of an animal in a thunderstorm. The barrel of her little handgun wavered like she was trying to write her name with it. "He's a mage! He's that terrorist!"

Levi didn't have the energy to argue. Their lives were in danger now because of him. He'd broken too much, all at once.

Flashing lights raced across the water, but the Coast Guard boat wasn't moving quickly enough.

It'll never get to us before the building goes up.

There was only one thing left to do.

"Byron, help me sit down." Levi struggled to make the words. It hurt to breathe. He'd need all of his energy for this.

Ignoring the guns, Byron eased Levi down where the dock met the grass.

"We can't give up now," Byron said. He had Penny's blood on him. It smeared wetly against Levi's face when he touched Levi's cheeks with trembling fingers. "Please."

Levi offered him a tired grin. "Listen. Everybody needs to stay behind me. Nobody in front. Everybody behind." His words slurred, and he hoped Byron could understand. "If someone can talk to that boat, tell it to keep coming. They'll be safe."

Realization dawned on Byron's face, draining the last of the color there until he looked scared and young. And very, very sad.

"I love you." Byron kissed him once, softly. "Is that weird?"

Levi smiled. Byron's words warmed him, gentle breath on the weak embers his magic had been reduced to. He didn't mind crying in front of Byron this time. "No, it's not."

He wanted to tell Byron not to get excited about this whole thing just yet. Chances were pretty high that they were all about to get spectacularly torched right off the face of the Earth. Instead, he said, "You too. The love part. Hurry up."

Byron stood up and shouted instructions, explaining that Levi was their only hope for survival—that he'd stopped fire once before. Maybe because they didn't have any better options, people listened. Even the lady with the gun stopped yelling at them and gathered in close like Byron told her to.

There were only a dozen of them, and they huddled behind Levi, cramped on the small dock. Waves struck beneath him, slapping the underside of the wood and wetting his legs with frigid seawater. People had once believed tides were magic, and maybe they were. He needed that magic, right now: the magic of the tide, the pull of the moon, even the deadly alchemy of the fire.

He needed Penny's magic: her stubborn bravery and her relentless belief in him.

He needed Byron's magic too: the stupid, sweet, happy way that Byron made him feel. The wonderful way that Byron loved him.

When the building went up, it caved in first, as if someone had reached out and crumpled it like paper. It made a deep *boom*, and then the air went empty and silent.

Byron wrapped his arms around him, pressing one warm palm against Levi's bare chest. "Levi," he whispered.

And then the shockwave came like before, like the day on the street, a brief magnetic pull before a violent reverse, and that was when Levi put his hands out.

The force of it pushed them all back a few inches, but the barrier held. There was no time for relief. Heat and flames followed the initial boom—towering waves of fire and heat. Trees started to go up. Benches along the path. Everything was burning.

Levi could tell, in a detached, tired sort of way, that it was killing him. But it wasn't burning him. None of them were burning. Not yet.

"How close is that boat?" he gasped each word out weakly.

An unfamiliar hand braced one of his outstretched arms, clammy fingers grasping his skin. It was that woman, the one with the gun. But her gun was gone now, and she was mumbling a prayer. He didn't mind. He needed all the magic he could get to hold off the fire until the boat arrived.

He pressed his forehead against the inside of his arm, struggling against the recoil. His magic wasn't steady anymore; it wobbled and crackled. It hurt.

Someone else braced his other arm. Another hand rested against his shoulder.

"Byron!" His vision began to darken at the edges. "It's slipping."

"The boat's close. A minute. No more than a minute," Byron said, voice warm and close, right at Levi's ear. "We're moving back. We're moving to the edge of the dock. I've got you."

Levi held the shield, his arms trembling and sore, propped up by others now. For all he knew, he didn't need to have his damn hands out at all, but it seemed to help.

The fire danced around them, licking and nipping his magic. Pain seared him, like touching a hot pan. But his magic kept them tucked away from the inferno.

A voice on a loudspeaker called out behind him, but he couldn't make sense of it. The flames were only starting to recede—they were still so high, so hot.

"Byron," he said, his mouth numb. The sound didn't come out, and he was too tired to keep trying. Too tired.

His shield fizzled, his magic wisping away with it, gone, as if it had never been there. The air went smoky and dark. He fell back into Byron's arms, and kept falling and falling and falling.

The Coast Guard boat bobbed, its inflatable hull making sucking, slapping noises against the water. It was the most beautiful thing Byron had ever heard. He held on to Levi as the evacuees helped each other on board, hurrying in a patient way that reminded Byron of when they'd climbed out of the subway car. The flames were hot, but the dock wasn't on fire yet. They'd be underway in a matter of seconds. They were safe.

"Levi," he said. "Our turn." He hefted him up, ignoring the way his wrist protested. One of the uniformed men from the boat reached for Levi, and for a moment, Byron hesitated.

"I've got him," the man shouted over the engine's thrum. "Come on!"

As Byron transferred Levi's weight to the man's arms, he caught sight of Levi's face, and his legs went weak. Something wasn't right.

Strong hands pulled him onto the boat. It was already moving, reversing with a high whine from the engine. Everyone huddled, grasping emergency handles—faces lit by the orange glow of the flames. The Guardsman who had taken Levi still held him.

Byron stared.

Ice cold water crashed over them, but Levi didn't flinch. The spray left a soft sheen on his face, in his curls, on his lashes.

Byron struggled to find his voice. His throat felt tight. He didn't want to say it, but he had to. And that would make it real.

"He's not breathing." He grabbed the sleeve of the man holding Levi. "He's not breathing!"

His shouting caught the attention of several of the drenched, frightened evacuees clinging for safety as the boat hurtled through the rough chop. The Guardsman holding Levi stripped one glove off and pressed his fingers to Levi's throat.

"Slow down!" the man yelled. People moved out of the way as best they could, clearing a space to lay Levi down. Water pooled around him on the rubber. They'd been so close to burning, yet now he looked cold, pale and lifeless.

CPR didn't go like it did on TV. It was violent and awful. Levi's face remained slack as the Coast Guard paramedic performed compressions on his bare chest.

Nothing happened.

The boat slowed alongside the hull of a massive Coast Guard clipper Byron hadn't even seen coming. Its crew were tossing ropes and ladders down, but no one moved. Everyone was watching Levi.

Someone put an arm around Byron. He pressed his hands to his mouth, silencing the wrenching grief that threatened to pour out of him.

"Levi, please," he whispered, his breath hot against his cold fingers. "Please. Please. Please."

"Let me through," an elderly woman said. She wore a bird sanctuary volunteer badge, and her palms and elbows were scraped and bleeding. A young scientist in a soaked lab coat helped her get closer and wobble to her knees. She reached out and placed her hand on Levi's ankle.

The old woman met Byron's questioning gaze. "I've been waiting my whole life to do this," she said quietly, just for him.

The ship's horn sounded, piercing and startling. Everyone looked up but Byron and the woman.

She shuddered, and Levi's fingers twitched. He took a hoarse, gasping breath.

In the chaos, no one else seemed to have noticed what she'd done. Byron reeled, watching for the next ragged breath. But he lost sight of Levi as more Coast Guardsmen flooded the boat and swarmed him.

Byron saw Levi again, and he wasn't moving or awake. They had him on a stretcher attached to a winch and lifted him up to the deck of the bigger boat, the paramedic riding on top of him, squeezing a bag against his face.

When Byron couldn't see him anymore, he stared down at his lap, his ears ringing.

It began to rain—cold, pelting rain that stung the back of his neck.

His wrist was on fire, more agonizing than he'd ever felt, but it was eclipsed by the hollow terror of seeing Levi there, so still.

"I'm waiting for my chariot." The old woman gestured at the winch that was already lowering another empty stretcher. One of the Coast Guardsman tucked a metallic blanket around her shoulders. "These old bones won't be scaling any ladders, no sir."

She took Byron's hand and patted it, and some of the torment in his broken wrist subsided. He remained rooted to the spot though, kneeling in a puddle that had gone pink as Penny's blood washed out of his clothes.

"He's alive, dear," the old woman said.

He glanced up at her, dizzy with hope.

She winked. "I can feel it."

A paramedic eased her frail body onto the stretcher. "Don't be afraid," she called out.

"Sir." Another paramedic began examining Byron's wrist, rolling back his wet sleeve to expose purpling, swollen flesh. "Sir, can you tell me your name?"

He pressed, and everything went white.

EPILOGUE

Four months later

Byron hated fire.

Even the smell of cigarette smoke took him back to that night.

He always walked home from work these days, needing to move his body after too many hours in front of a computer and sitting through long, tedious meetings, but the walk to his apartment was a minefield. Dust from construction, a passing smoker, acrid exhaust—all of it made him think of Levi on the boat. Sometimes he had to sit down, struck to the core with helpless grief.

Sometimes, like today, he made it through his entire commute without a hiccup, and the future seemed doable. Promising. Bright.

That was what the others called it: A bright future. A chance. Each of them had found purpose in the days since the charges were dropped against them and Cole Industries crumbled without its leader. Sam busy with Summons, now a meeting place for mages and their allies. Eleanor teaching at a new charter school welcoming mages. Victoria continuing her work at AMID with new funding—benefactors with a common vision of protecting the innocent from wars waged with magic.

Byron had purpose now, but he struggled to find their optimism, to catch his breath.

The incident at North Brother Island had kicked off a nationwide outcry fueled by social media. Within days, online petitions had cropped up demanding that legislators overturn everything from Charlotte's Law to mandatory registration and CALM bands. A pop star came out as a mage, galvanizing the MTV crowd. Even a beloved actor in his late sixties admitted to hiding his mage status for his entire career—drawing sympathy from generations of fans. But as huge as these wins seemed, they were nothing in the face of decades of hatred. Hate crimes continued—even surging as if fueled by the momentum toward mage rights.

The hard part would take years—the tremendous shift in perception and momentum, and the intricacies of changing . . . everything. Byron knew with complete certainty that this was his true calling, but it was so much—so important—that he often wondered if he deserved the honor of helping to shepherd a more peaceful future for mages.

And he never knew when his vision would gray over with memories of North Brother Island.

Byron's therapist said his difficulties were caused by post-traumatic stress, and he didn't disagree. But he hated feeling weak, struggling with everyday tasks.

Especially when he was still alive. And free.

He didn't have time for the flashbacks: Penny lifeless and left to burn beside Warren, dead before she could see the world made new for her kind. Levi limp in his arms. Levi empty and still, his body too taxed and his magic sucked dry.

The images always overtook Byron without warning, tearing the breath out of him, sending him to his knees. Tonight he pushed them away, rubbing his eyes until he saw sparks.

He tiptoed through his room, undressing with each step and leaving his clothes in the hamper by the door. Daisy nudged her pudgy body against his leg and let out a chirping meow. He ducked to pet her, but she snaked away, her tail flicking.

His long evening shower was Byron's favorite time of day, and he lingered in the hot water, washing his hair twice and rinsing off the stubborn smells of the city. The heat soothed the ache in his wrist where the scars from reconstructive surgery gleamed.

He hesitated to get dressed half an hour later, considering slipping into the sheets naked instead. His antique bureau had a tendency to creak like a stubborn floorboard, and he wanted to be careful not to wake the bundled lump of mage sleeping in the middle of his bed, wrapped in a massive cocoon of winter duvet.

Sure enough, the wooden creak resulted in Levi parting the soft covers enough to peek out at him, his curls sticking every which way. "Good morning, Mr. Very Important Magic Reform Coordinator."

"Try again." Byron grinned, still unused to his new government job title. He pointed to the drapes. It was already dark. "It's after seven."

"You say evening, I say morning." Levi stretched, the covers falling away to expose his pale skin. "Come to bed."

"How was your infusion?" Byron sat on the edge of the bed and leaned down to kiss Levi's sleep-warm lips.

"Good. They think I can start practicing in two more weeks."

Byron lingered, kissing Levi slowly. The hours he spent away from him still ached, despite knowing that Levi was safe now, recuperating in their apartment and pestering Eleanor and Victoria when he wasn't sleeping. Victoria held Byron personally responsible for the way Levi blew her phone up with texts, but he knew she didn't mind. And she never complained to Levi's face when she and Eleanor came over for take-out picnics and binge-watching TV on Byron's bed.

All he wanted to do was stay at Levi's side, but the world was changing at a faster pace than he could have ever imagined—work kept him busy when he wanted to be kissing Levi, finding the places that made him cry out, listening to every story Levi would tell him.

Levi still slept for most of the day, but when he woke up he wanted to talk, wanted to know all about Byron's childhood and his parents and his favorite foods. He wanted to know how work had gone and wanted to hear the stories mages shared with Byron when they came forward and offered to help the newly christened Magic Reform Committee gather knowledge to present to lawmakers and outreach groups.

Byron took it one day at a time—and lived for every night in Levi's arms.

Uncovering the rest of Levi was like unwrapping a gift. Levi did little to help, but Byron didn't blame him. Infusions of magic left him blissed-out and uncoordinated, but every visit from mages willing to share their magic helped him heal a little more, brought him closer to being able to use his own magic again.

Beneath all the covers, Levi wore nothing but a loose pair of boxers.

Byron made a happy sound and nosed at Levi's stomach. He started kissing the soft skin there.

"Tickling . . . not nice," Levi said, laughing. He squirmed away, sat up, and worked himself onto Byron's lap in a warm straddle, kissing him slowly and deeply. Levi was under orders not to exert himself too much, but that didn't stop him from rolling his hips.

"Jesus, Levi." Byron reached into Levi's boxers and gripped the rigid heat of his dick.

"I told you it was morning." Levi's laughter became a gasp when Byron began to stroke him. He bent his head forward and pressed his mouth to Byron's shoulder, gnawing gently there as his breath grew uneven and shallow. "Yeah. Yeah. Byron!"

Byron cupped Levi's ass. Now that his wrist had healed, it was a lot more fun to tease pleasure out of Levi's body. "Show me, babe," he murmured.

Levi's head snapped back and he cried out, coming on Byron's fingers.

He flopped from Byron's lap and shimmied out of his boxers, more beached dolphin than sex kitten. Byron laughed. "Tempting."

"Laugh all you want." Levi smirked back at Byron, wiggling his ass obscenely. He showed off, pushing one finger into his hole in a slow slide that made his lashes flutter.

"Oh." Byron shuddered. Levi had clearly gotten into the expensive silicone lube Byron kept in the nightstand.

"Never a Boy Scout, but always prepared."

Byron made quick work of his pajamas and sank down against Levi's back. He didn't consider himself a sex expert yet, not by any means. But Levi made it easy. Levi made it so good: pushing up against him, letting out guileless, joyful gasps with each thrust. Byron lifted up on one arm to guide himself and entered Levi slowly, letting the tightness and heat pull him out of his head.

Like this, it was only them. Only Levi's breathing and babbling encouragement, and the pounding of his heart against Byron's chest.

"Fuck." Byron tried to take it easy, but there was no use. He sank his fingers into Levi's hair, gently angled his head to the side, and placed a broken kiss against the corner of Levi's mouth. "Love. Love."

Afterward, they didn't move much. They caught their breaths together, kissing lazily, sated and tired.

"Missed you today," Byron said between long, tender kisses.

Levi kissed him harder, worked his hands up into his hair, holding him close. Then his fingers dragged down Byron's back, and for the first time since Levi had bled dry in Byron's arms, ripples of warm magic trailed behind his fingertips.

He wasn't afraid. Not anymore.

Dear Reader,

Thank you for reading Kit Brisby's *Rogue Magic*!

We know your time is precious and you have many, many entertainment options, so it means a lot that you've chosen to spend your time reading. We really hope you enjoyed it.

We'd be honored if you'd consider posting a review—good or bad—on sites like **Amazon, Barnes & Noble, Kobo, Goodreads, Twitter, Facebook, Tumblr,** and your blog or website. We'd also be honored if you told your friends and family about this book. Word of mouth is a book's lifeblood!

For more information on upcoming releases, author interviews, blog tours, contests, giveaways, and more, please sign up for our weekly, spam-free newsletter and visit us around the web:

Newsletter: tinyurl.com/RiptideSignup
Twitter: twitter.com/RiptideBooks
Facebook: facebook.com/RiptidePublishing
Goodreads: tinyurl.com/RiptideOnGoodreads
Tumblr: riptidepublishing.tumblr.com

Thank you so much for Reading the Rainbow!

RiptidePublishing.com

ACKNOWLEDGMENTS

I wrote this book to the sounds of Belle & Sebastian, Cold War Kids, and The Shins.

But I needed more than a playlist on repeat to bring Levi and Byron to life, and their loyal, loving friends were inspired by the support I am beyond fortunate to have.

Indra: Thank you for getting shit done—and inspiring me to do the same. I miss you every day. There's always a kombucha waiting for you here.

Julie: Thank you for picking up the phone for my meltdowns twice a week without fail. (And not blocking my number.) I love you.

Diane: I am in awe of your unrelenting patience for my texts. Sadly, that does not inspire me to text you less. Sorry. (Thank you.)

Mackenzie: Thank you for falling in love with Byron in all his awkward glory. You believed in this book when I needed it most.

Sarah: Thank you for everything you do—and for sharing your courage and grace. I'm honored to be part of this family.

And finally, my editor, Carole Ann: Thank you for wrangling my words, putting up with my em-dash obsession, and making it clear where the boners were pointing at all times.

ABOUT THE AUTHOR

Kit Brisby believes in magic. She was born in Florida and spends as much time as she can in NYC catching shows and eating all the sushi. She shares a media career with Byron and a yoga hobby with Levi—and she wishes she had an ounce of Victoria's poise.

Kit can often be found frolicking with her rescue mutts and longing for a cat like Daisy. Sadly, she's horribly allergic. Connect with Kit on Twitter at twitter.com/KitBrisby or at her website kitbrisby.com.